Palermo Story

GABRIELLE
MARKS

Palermo
Story

THOMAS DUNNE BOOKS

ST. MARTIN'S PRESS

NEW YORK

THOMAS DUNNE BOOKS.
An imprint of St. Martin's Press.

PALERMO STORY. Copyright © 2002 by Gabrielle Marks. All
rights reserved. Printed in the United States of America. No
part of this book may be used or reproduced in any manner
whatsoever without written permission except in the case of
brief quotations embodied in critical articles or reviews. For in-
formation, address St. Martin's Press, 175 Fifth Avenue, New
York, N.Y. 10010.

www.stmartins.com

Designed by Kathryn Parise

LIBRARY OF CONGRESS CATALOGING-IN-PUBLICATION DATA
Marks, Gabrielle.
    Palermo story / Gabrielle Marks.
        p. cm.
    ISBN 0-312-27864-0
        Title.

PS3613.A368 P35 2002
813'.6—dc21

2001055323

First Edition: April 2002

10 9 8 7 6 5 4 3 2 1

For Duncan

Palermo
Story

1

The number 101 glided smoothly along the boulevard, the pleated rubber join between its two coaches shivering gently. Inside, the the newly designed ergonomic seats of smooth gray metal were inlaid with sky-blue fabric, and the still unscuffed leather thongs hanging from the overhead bars ensured that passengers would not be hurled forward should a car suddenly shoot obliquely across the bus lane. Instead of the tinny bell of the old vehicles, bright yellow buttons produced a decorous muted *ping* and an illuminated sign informing travelers that their request had been noted and processed. From up front the driver was able to activate the four sets of remotely controlled doors with the help of small screens set into the dashboard, and relatively few incidents of people being trapped in their rubber-lipped jaws had so far been recorded.

In spite of these improvements, a foreigner riding the new buses would still have felt they had been designed for the Latin way of life (which, according to Mayor Orlando, should now with no further prevarication *whatsoever* be brought into line with no-nonsense European standards). To start with, there were fewer seats than there was standing room, indicating a belief that Palermo's citizens had no objection to being on their feet for the entire journey. This wasn't true, of course, but then no Sicilian ever expected his personal comfort to be a concern of the powers that be. It had been quite a shock, for instance, to passengers on the AMAT bus company's new Belgian-designed fleet of vehicles to be confronted for the very first time with efficient suspension and soft upholstery. Used to being jolted about on bare metal, they now sat uneasily on the padded blue seats, eyeing the gently sighing automatic doors with suspicion, as though such luxury would soon be taken away from them.

No designer, however—Belgian or otherwise—had been able to reduce the risk of pickpockets on inner city buses. Thieves were notoriously successful on the number 101, especially in the busy central area lying between the old Via Roma and the graciously laid out Via Libertà. They preferred working these crammed north-going lunchtime buses because they contained a good sprinkling of the city's more well-to-do citizens. Women were the easiest prey, laden with plastic carrier bags or briefcases and tense with worry about children to be picked up from school. Their concern made them less vigilant, and thieves never ceased to be amazed at how easy it was to relieve them of cash.

The metropolitan police knew what went on and had statistics showing how many passengers were robbed on average per bus per day. Both they and the *carabinieri* noted fluctuations in victims' reports and the various factors that determined them. A decrease in activity might follow a crackdown on petty crime, for instance, and more robberies took place in autumn and winter— especially round about Christmas. Everybody, though, from the *Questore* or the *Maresciallo dei carabinieri* down to the hysterical housewife traveling on the number 101 bus knew that no attempt would ever be made to catch the thief, and consequently, no money would be recovered.

Of the two buses making their way along the plane tree–lined Via Libertà that November lunchtime, only the first was full to the bursting point. The second, having taken the overflow, had several empty seats, which meant that passengers were able to sit comfortably, gazing out of the windows or glancing briefly at one another in mild curiosity before returning to their thoughts.

From his seat halfway down the second bus Nick shifted the briefcase between his ankles and watched the circular platform between the two coaches swing slowly back in an anticlockwise direction as they came onto the straight. It reminded him of the shifting piece of floor between the old English railway carriages, which he used to cross with such delicious fear as a small boy. It would clank and shake, and you could see the rails rushing along through the gaps underneath. He had always enjoyed traveling— by car, ship, plane, and especially by train. That's why he liked these long articulated buses where, if you were lucky enough to get a window seat, you could sit and dream.

He watched the old villas and pastel-colored apartment blocks disappearing and reappearing between the tree trunks and thought how spacious and pleasing they were. A scattering of curled, brown-edged leaves blew over the broad pavements, one of the few signs that the year was coming to an end. Autumn was underplayed in the Mediterranean, a slow cooling down and sliding into winter rather than a season in itself, with none of the flamboyance of northern colors. And, like the bowing out of summer, the transformation of Via Libertà from exclusively upper-middle-class boulevard to thoroughfare-for-all had been both gradual and inevitable. Nick always thought the surviving villas had a vaguely stoical air about them, as if appearances were to be kept up at all costs despite such regrettable changes. It was here during the *belle époque* that the slavishly fashionable lapped the excruciatingly bored in their respective landaus before a gawping proletariat. He had seen photographs of them as they clattered back and forth from the Piazza Castelnuovo to the Giardino Inglese, and while the residents would probably have had no objection to being admired, he felt they would have regretted the coming of the *nouveau riche* as neighbors. But it was not until the mid-nineteen-fifties that the monied merchants moved into Via Libertà in a big way, and anyway, by then, Palermo's days as the *salon* of Europe were well and truly over.

Nick watched a young girl muffled up in wine-red scarf, dark jacket, and narrow black trousers hurrying along the pavement. How old would she be, nineteen or twenty perhaps? She reminded him of Giulia—the independent thrust of the chin, the way she looked straight ahead of her and kept the books she was carrying close to her body. The last time his daughter had come home she'd been wearing the same kind of scarf as that—a sort of cluster of chenillelike lambs' tails. It suited her.

Nick missed her—far more than he thought he would. She had left for Bologna right after school, as though she couldn't wait to get away. That had hurt him a bit. He wondered what had determined her decision: Palermo, the South in general, or the family. When he had asked her, she said she didn't really know, and did it matter? Didn't he *want* her to be independent? the English always wanted their children to be independent. She'd been accepted by an excellent university and thought it would please her parents. Well, they *were* pleased—especially Paola, and yet it had been a wrench seeing her off at the airport. He thought of her a lot, wondering what she was doing and who she was with, and was sometimes frightened by thoughts of what might happen to her and how he was powerless to intervene.

"I can't think why you're so upset about it," Paola said at the time. "You should be proud of your daughter. Instead of wasting time here, she's got herself a place at the most prestigious university in Italy. She knows exactly what she wants."

Nick wasn't at all sure about this and even less so about Paola's suggestion that the two of them should go up and visit their daughter this year at Easter. In fact, he thought it a very bad idea indeed.

From where he was sitting Nick wasn't able to see the crowded bus in front as, dark with swaying bodies, it made its way up the reserved lane some fifty yards ahead. He was still watching the girl in the wine-red scarf, who had now reached the curb. After a moment's hesitation she stepped into the road and disappeared from view. The driver of the first bus braked violently and swore with tight lips as she shot across his path.

"*Cazzo di Giuda, maledetto.*"

Just behind his seat, Paola clutched instinctively at the overhead thongs as she was thrown forward with the rest of the passengers. In the cry of protest and alarm and the crackling tail end of the driver's oath, she checked that the carrier bag of shopping was still at her feet. She had been worrying about the meeting with her boss that afternoon, and now, on top of that, her tooth had started aching again. As if that weren't enough, a male body was pressing into her from behind, and she closed her eyes and gave an irritable sigh. At her age she didn't expect to be groped anymore on public transport, but she disliked coming into contact with unknown flesh, feeling it an almost unbearable invasion of her privacy. She tried to shift nearer the window, putting a few inches between herself and the unseen body, and to her relief, as the bus slowed down and came to a halt, she was aware that the hot presence had gone.

The man behind her, whose name was Vito and who had no intention or need of getting his thrills from pressing up against female buttocks, had in fact moved down the bus. He was twenty-eight years old, unemployed, and a highly skillful pick-pocket. With Paola's wallet concealed in the folded jacket over his arm, he alighted with three other passengers and made off rapidly toward the port. The doors whooshed behind him, and with a clear path ahead of it the bus picked up speed and passed through the lights an instant before they changed to red.

Paola was wondering whether Nick would already be home and what time it would be best to phone Giulia. Round about seven probably, before her daughter went out for the evening. There was a sickening smell in the bus, ripe cheese or something. Nick said it was madness to take the car into town these days, but it just wasn't civilized traveling like this. She grimaced as her tooth gave another stab of pain.

The pastel-colored facades of Via Libertà fell away as the bus entered the translucent green grotto of the Giardino Inglese.

Twenty-seven thousand species of trees and shrubs had once graced these public gardens, some (like Palermo's newest buses) being imported from Belgium. But a century and a half later only a few of the original plants survived, among them three tall palms, a cluster of umbrella pines, and a giant ficus tree whose junglelike aerial roots hung to within inches of the well-kept paths. The artificial hillocks and gazebos intended to imitate English landscape gardening had long since gone, but the twelve-foot-high jets of water in the circular fountain still rose and fell with the change in pressure as they did every lunchtime.

On the opposite side of the road, unnoticed by every passenger except an American tourist, stood an equestrian statue of Giuseppe Garibaldi. The tourist, whose name was Stella, recognized him at once: she thought him an intensely exciting and powerful figure sitting up there above the ornamental flower beds in the parterre—no, *more* than that, he was *sensual* as great patriots and statesmen on horseback often are. It was something to do with their commanding presence and height, the way their thighs clamped the animal to them and held it still. With his left hand loosely holding the reins of his steed and his right arm outstretched at shoulder level, Garibaldi gazed proudly out over what would soon be his domain: "Bixio, tomorrow we go to Palermo!"

The gesture reminded her a bit of Charles V, whose statue she had seen that morning in the Piazza Bologni. Only in this case—according to generations of disenchanted citizens—what the Angevin monarch was saying with *his* outstretched arm and downturned palm was not "I swear allegiance to the Constitution of the Kingdom of Sicily" but "In Palermo the shit comes up this high." Stella would have laughed heartily at that because her father had been Sicilian and had been disenchanted himself. He wouldn't have emigrated otherwise. And if he hadn't she probably wouldn't be in Palermo now searching for her own identity. She turned away from the window, forgetting instantly about Garibaldi and the king, and gave her attention to Paola, struggling along the aisle toward the exit.

Stella saw that the woman was younger than herself—probably in her late forties—and had a drawn, anxious face and an unhealthy sallow complexion. Tufts of lusterless hair of indefinable color stood up over her head, each parting company with its neighbor to reveal gray roots and a pale scalp underneath. Tinted too often, Stella thought, who was fashionable and cared about her appearance. She took in the unsmart olive green wool jacket and slightly uneven hang of the skirt, the scuffed small-heeled shoes and bulging shoulder bag. It certainly wasn't true then that all Italian women were chic and well-groomed. Yet, in spite of the defeatist slope of the shoulders and neglected appearance, the woman must once have been pretty—and maybe could be again: the small straight nose and large eyes and (Stella moved her head to get a better look) the delicately shaped ankles. A stressed-out teacher, perhaps, taking home her bagful of exercise books to mark. Or maybe a disillusioned civil servant.

As they came up to the large white Banco di Sicilia building on the corner, Paola reached for the yellow bell. Bending down to retrieve her carrier bag, she knocked clumsily against Stella's seated figure. *"Mi scusi,"* she mumbled, half turning round.

The bus came to a stop, folded back its doors like a pair of wings, and let Paola out. For a few seconds Stella watched the worried figure hurrying along the pavement before shifting her gaze to two taxi drivers locked in gesticulating combat on the curbside.

The distance between the two vehicles had widened at the lights, and by the time Nick let himself into the flat Paola had been home a good fifteen minutes. She told him her wallet had been stolen. "Everything's gone: money, driving license, credit cards, bus pass . . ."

He asked where she had lost it.

"I didn't lose it, it was stolen, *stolen!*" she shouted at him. "On the bloody bus. I told you I hate going on them. Now what am I going to do?"

"Calm down, Paola. There's nothing you *can* do about it now. We'll have to report it to the police."

"But that's not going to bring all my papers and cards back, is it?" Her mouth sagged open and her thin chest heaved. "I *know* when it happened. When the bus braked suddenly, I *felt* there was someone behind me, I felt it. That *man.*"

"Do you mind if I come in?" Nick was still on the landing holding his briefcase. He closed the front door behind him with deliberate calm. "How much did you have with you?"

"I don't know, I don't know. About sixty thousand. But it's not that. I don't care about the money, it's all the rest. I've got the meeting at the office this afternoon, the dentist tomorrow, then Christmas is coming . . ."

They went to report the theft at the local *carabiniere* station, and by that time it was too late for lunch. Nick drove his wife to the dentist. She said she was too ill to go to the wretched meeting.

"Are you *sure* you're sure?" his father had asked softly when Nick told him he was getting married. Nick wouldn't have taken that from anyone except his father. He nodded. The older man nodded too. "Mmm . . . well then." And both of them laughed. That was *that* out of the way.

"Like it, do you?" he asked his son about Palermo. "Don't know Sicily at all. Mum and I went to the Dolomites years ago, do you remember? But never down south. Fred was there in the war, of course—always said it was the most beautiful place he'd ever seen." His brother's description of snow-capped Mount Etna, the piercing scent of dry soil under pines and incredibly dark blue sea had sounded almost unbearably romantic to him in dreary fifties London. It still did.

Nick missed his father terribly. Looking down at him on his deathbed, he had felt that this was a completely different person from the one he had known in childhood. It was almost impossible to imagine the thin sunken face and crumpled body walking briskly home from work, grabbing hold of his children, squeezing his wife in an embrace. His father had known it too. "This strange, eventful history, eh?" he had said, smiling ruefully one evening as he tried and failed to get out of his armchair. That had been just four months before he died.

Despite his father's misgivings, Nick realized that things hadn't worked out at all badly for him in Sicily—against all odds too in a place with such dismal employment prospects. Ironically, being a foreigner had helped, and his four years working in the commercial section of the British consulate in Palermo had enabled him to land a job in a shipping office when the consulate closed down. Then (with almost unbelievable ease, it now seemed to him) he got into university as an English language *lettore*. It didn't bother him that this was the lowest rung of the academic ladder with no hope of promotion; it brought in a regular salary and was something he was good at and—surprisingly—quite enjoyed. On its own the job could have palled, but there were spin-offs: talks he was asked to give (usually on British writers he knew next to nothing about), the occasional interview, voice-overs for travelogues, lucrative translations, and any number of private lessons.

It always amused him how being part of the university conferred such prestige on its professors, automatically transforming them into undisputed authorities on practically everything—in his case, everything British. Very nice too, although as Professor Griffo, with whom he worked, condescendingly informed him, Nick was not really entitled to be called *professore* at all. Language assistants like himself were simply *dottori*—a far less exalted category. Griffo, like the majority of the Italian staff, defended his place in the academic hierarchy with single-minded tenacity, giving as little leeway as possible to enterprising assistants lest they should outdo him in efficiency and scholarship. Any new ideas on teaching methods or show of initiative on their part would be first democratically discussed and more often than not, incorporated into his own curriculum. Articles would then appear in scholarly journals under his own byline and he himself would be ready to take the next step up the career ladder. Griffo very much wanted to be dean, but the way was long and strewn with obstacles. Clever English L.A.s were some of the most insidious.

Nick, who despite these machinations didn't dislike his professor, was popular—especially among his female students. Physically, he was probably in better shape now at forty-seven than when he was younger—and didn't have to do much to maintain it either. Tall and broad-shouldered, *il professore* Stirling was known to have the most gorgeous sleepy gray eyes that would look right into you. His hair was always falling disarmingly over his forehead, and he had that lovely accent. His classes were well attended.

Had his father come back to life and asked him whether he was happy, Nick would have replied that he was probably as happy as could be expected. He didn't miss England and had no wish to live there ever again. Its cold, dismal weather, tasteless food, and uniformity struck despair into his heart. He had become convinced over the years that the country was losing its identity; that by trying so hard to be something else—American, Mediterranean, whatever—it was turning into some grotesque theme park, and it alarmed him that the English couldn't see this for themselves. Maybe this uncertainty about who they really were lay behind the young people's drinking. It was as if they were driven by a mixture of doubt, fear of the future, and some kind of deep unhappiness. He used to love London. Now it seemed merely a place of vomit-covered pavements, suffocating tube trains, and seething masses of slouching, unlovely people. Life out here was different—not necessarily better, simply more to his liking. There was the sun, of course, which always helped, and people weren't trying so hard, weren't striving. The color, the wholesome and affectionate Italians—the *beauty*—suited him well.

What was not good, though, was his marriage. He had tried to be a good father (after giving up on trying to be a good husband), yet when he looked at the results, they weren't all that brilliant. Giulia had gone her own way, and Sandro seemed to exist on an entirely different plane. Nick kept telling himself this was natural; that his son hadn't dropped out of school and wasn't on drugs (at least he hoped not); it was just that he didn't seem to be aware of his father at all. There were times when Nick felt himself a shade drifting almost unseen from room to room.

Giulia had been easier and had spent more time at home, but Nick hadn't wanted a docile, accommodating daughter, he'd wanted an independent, happy one. He hoped she'd had a life of her own in her school years and, much as he missed her now, knew she had done the right thing in going off to Bologna.

"Neek!"

He went into the bedroom.

Paola was raised up on one elbow, the skin on her neck twisted like a wrung-out floor cloth. "We've got to phone Giulia tonight. No later than seven, otherwise she'll be out. What are you doing out there? What about supper?"

"What do you want?"

She closed her eyes briefly and fell back onto the pillow. "For Christ's sake, you don't think I could *eat* with this pain, do you? These pills make me feel dreadful, it's unbearable. Just bring me a chamomile tea."

Nick went over to the window, leaned out, and started pulling the shutters to.

"No, no!" Paola protested. "I feel I'm suffocating in here as it is. At least let me see some lights outside." She laid four fingers against her forehead. "I've got a temperature too. God, that's all I needed: first the tooth, then my wallet . . ."

"It's not that bad," Nick began. "You'll be going back to the dentist the day after tomorrow and—"

"Nothing's ever bad for you, is it?" she burst out. "I've never known anybody as calm as you. The house could be falling down round your ears and you'd still say"—she mimicked him—" 'It's not that bad.' "

"Look, I don't feel like having a row."

"You never do, you never do. It's all that English reserve."

Nick turned to go.

"No, wait, wait, it's just that everything seems to happen to *me*. It's one thing after another." She scrabbled about under the pillow for a handkerchief. Her nose was a chapped raw red when she'd finished with it. With weary resignation she fell back onto the pillows.

"Hand me over my mobile, I'll try Giulia now." She started jabbing at the keys.

After a second or two he heard her voice rising and falling on the phone. Every so often words reached him like pebbles thrown up out of the unending stream of complaint: "Wallet—your father—molar—buses—meeting—*terrible*."

He stood at the stove in the kitchen, slowly stirring the watery soup he had made from a stock cube and bits of broken-up spaghetti, and wondering whether it was worth getting anything ready for his son.

"Neek!"

He *had* been in love at the beginning, but things had started going wrong after Giulia was born. While he was still basking in the wonder of becoming a father, Paola, full of the *unimaginable* suffering undergone in labor, had declared herself totally unable to cope. It was such a shocking reaction to the world-shaking marvel of birth that he couldn't take it in.

"You've no idea what I've been through," she began as soon

as he arrived to visit her and the baby in the clinic. "The nurses are totally useless, you can lie here and call and call and *call* and nobody comes. I'm exhausted. And it's no good their saying I must feed the baby because I can't. I've got no milk, and that's that."

He wondered in alarm how much was his fault and what he had unwittingly done to provoke such distress. Maybe he had been a bad husband and lover without realizing it. She became possessive (although it had never occurred to him to be unfaithful), narrowing her eyes and lips and saying God only knew what Nick was doing all that time he was away from her. As the months went by, his reaction to this strange, rather frightening state became a mixture of exasperation and compassion, a longing both to shake and comfort her. Sandro had obviously been conceived in the second instance, and to his relief Paola seemed genuinely happy to be having another baby. During the pregancy she grew rounder and pretty again, and gradually he began to forget about what they had been through before.

At about the same time he got the job at the university, Paola had finally been moved to a department in the large regional government offices situated in the center of Palermo, which meant she didn't have the long daily trek out to the eastern suburbs anymore. Every year during the holidays they took the children to England so that their paternal grandparents could see them grow. Sandro said he wanted to live forever in his grandpa's shed and invent things like he did.

It wasn't until Giulia was eighteen and waiting for her final exam results to come through that Paola began to change. With a sinking feeling Nick recognized the symptoms. Now when she spoke of her colleagues she narrowed her eyes, tightened her lips, and lowered her voice to a bitter hiss. Everything was a chore, a terrible burden, especially taking that godawful *bus* twice a day. It was all right for Nick: he went quite happily about, with no idea what she was going through. The house was just too much; why on earth they had to have such a huge place she couldn't imagine, and the Tamil who did the cleaning had to be shown everything over and over again, otherwise he'd never do a bloody thing. She was *almost* sure he was stealing too. This was almost certainly untrue, for the Tamils, Singhalese, and Mauritians who had flooded into Palermo at the end of the nineteen-eighties took care to stay on the right side of the law rather than put their hard-won jobs in jeopardy and face repatriation. Industrious, unassuming, and cliquey, they did domestic work or, failing that, cleaned car windscreens at the traffic lights.

Apart from harboring suspicious thoughts, Paola was plagued by headaches and so tense that she couldn't digest anything. She wanted Giulia near her all the time and, when her daughter left for Bologna, started pestering her with telephone calls. Nick finally came to the conclusion that his wife's condition was chronic: what his mother would have described in an undertone as "neurotic."

He still couldn't explain to himself why he hadn't left. Inertia perhaps or the unrealistic hope that things would get better. Supposing he were to go now? Giulia was twenty-one and leading her own life; Sandro was seventeen and probably wouldn't even notice if his father wasn't around anymore.

"Neek! How much *longer* are you going to be? I can't stand this pain!"

· · ·

Two days later the telephone rang as Nick was halfway out of the flat. He grabbed the receiver, keeping the front door open with his left foot. A man's voice, gruff with authority: "Genovese speaking. Does Paola Lentini live there?"

"My wife. I'm afraid she's out. Can I take a message?"

"Is that the husband? I've found your wife's wallet. Perhaps you'd like to come and pick it up this afternoon?" He repeated his name and gave the address. It was along the 101 bus route.

For lunch Nick had a beer and a ham and mozzarella–filled calzone in the bar opposite the university, then went back to mark some papers. At half past three he picked up his now comfortingly lighter briefcase and left the building. He knew the street, which ran in a dead straight line from Via Libertà down to the waterfront. It was lined by unremarkable solid gray stone buildings put up in the nineteen-twenties and thirties. Most rose through four or five stories to tiled roofs where every April the swifts would return to make their nests and spend the summer evenings screaming overhead. The large rectangular windows were heavily shuttered, and the railings around some of the balconies bore window boxes or sheltered standing pots, which at this time of the year drooped with untended greenery. The unexpected sight of ships' funnels rearing up at the far end of the street gave one the impression of moving about in a Dali-like landscape where things were disturbingly not quite where or how they should be.

The money, of course, will have gone, thought Nick, as he stepped into the road around an overflowing communal dustbin with KEEP PALERMO TIDY written on a gaily colored poster peeling from its flank. They'll have taken the money and chucked the wallet into the gutter. Not all that easy to spot, though, in all that filth, where spindly trees fought for survival among empty cardboard boxes, broken glass, and toppled cones of dried dog turds. The cracked paving stones were smeared with grease and dotted with blackened chewing gum stains, and a loop of graffiti adorned the ashlar veneer of one of the houses. As Nick stepped up onto the pavement again, a wafer-thin cat turned a terrified gaze on him before slithering to safety beneath a parked car.

The massive wooden entrance door of number 18 stood closed and hostile. Set into the wall at eyebrow height was a plaque bearing a double-columned list of residents. Nick had to search it twice before finding the names Genovese—Maselli at the top of the left-hand column. He pressed the button.

"*Si?*" A woman's voice.

He put his mouth close to the entry phone grille. "*Il dottor Genovese?*" (Better to give him a title; he'd sounded educated on the phone.)

"I'm afraid he's out. Who is that?"

"My name's Nick Stirling. Doctor Genovese telephoned this morning saying he'd found my wife's wallet."

There was a short silence while the woman took this in. "Wallet? I'm afraid I don't know anything . . . You'd better come up."

The entry phone clicked into silence before Nick could ask what floor she was on. "Fifth," the voice told him when he rang again, and this time the ten-foot-high door gave a loud crack as the lock was released. It swung open six inches.

It was almost dark inside the marble lobby, the porter's desk empty save for two business letters lying waiting for their recipients on the counter. An elegant flight of steps rose to the left of the central stairwell and disappeared tantalizingly behind it. Swags of electric cables festooned the damp upper reaches of the lobby walls, and he could hear the familiar hoarse grinding of a motorized water pump somewhere deep in the bowels of the building. Palermo's eccentric and antiquated mains system provided houses in the old center with water only every other day, so residents were forced to install their own emergency tanks as well as activating pumps to hoist the water to the upper floors.

When he opened the cagelike lift, the wrought iron gate squeaked, then clanged shut, making him wince at the thought of his fingers being trapped in its jaws. Slowly and with considerable gravitas it began wheezing upward, while Nick stared equally gravely at himself in the full-length mirror. At each floor it gave a muted double click as though reminding its passenger of the various alighting points available. Gradually the gloom fell away, until with a jolt and a politely suppressed belch the lift stopped under a circular skylight. Sunshine flooded the white-washed walls.

There were two front doors on the landing, only one of which bore a name plate. Going closer, Nick read the name Ricci set in gothic lettering on a discreetly crafted and well-polished brass oval. Not that one then. He rang the bell on the opposite door: no answer. Ten seconds went by before he felt he could ring again, and this time footsteps could be heard coming rapidly nearer.

"I'm so sorry. I was out on the terrace. Do come in."

She seemed taller than him, with her hair pulled off her face and a soft rainbow-colored scarf wound round and round her neck as though she were suffering from a cold. The ends of the scarf hung down in front over the rest of her clothing—dark trousers and a long-sleeved sweater.

Nick had to stoop to get though the doorway and into the

narrow book-lined corridor. Light streamed in from an opening ahead, illuminating a plaster bust and some grinning African-looking masks hanging from the wall.

The woman closed the front door behind him. "I'll lead the way."

Following behind, Nick saw she wasn't as tall as she'd seemed at first, that her hair was tied loosely back in a knot that was coming undone, and that she wore thick ankle socks under back-less mules. It was only when they turned into the light-drenched room that he saw her face properly.

"I'm sorry," she said again, pushing strands of hair behind one ear. "I didn't quite understand. What is it exactly about your wallet? Did you say Dante found it?"

"My wife's wallet. She lost it—well, it was stolen—on the bus. Doctor Genovese phoned me this morning and said he'd found it. That's all I know, I'm afraid."

She had one of the most intensely expressive faces he'd ever seen, with full lips, a rather large straight nose, and heavy-lidded dark eyes. It didn't occur to him to think "not young anymore," but rather "my age," perhaps unconsciously seeing her as a suitable mate. He didn't register anything else about her except that he liked what he saw and that being in the same room as her gave him a nice warm feeling.

"He had to go out to the paper—well, they called him after lunch—and he obviously forgot to tell me anything about it," the woman was saying. "We can look around and see whether he left it out anywhere."

"I'm so sorry to give you all this trouble," he began. All this apologizing to each other.

"It's no trouble. It's his fault for not telling me." The woman was frowning, moving glass paperweights and figurines about on a small round table, picking them up and putting them down again, even looking behind the cushions piled along the back of the old gold sofa.

It was a grossly overburdened room—bookshelves, occasional tables, their heavy fabric covers brushing the oriental carpets and dotted with small silver objects; antique prints and maps of Palermo sharing wall space with lowering sylvan landscapes on canvas as cracked and lined as ancient skin; magazines stacked up in the corners, display cabinets holding delicately turned glass goblets and chipped ceramic plates from Caltagirone. The sunlight streaming in from the open French windows fell onto what looked like the previous night's ashes in the fireplace and glinted on the brass handles of a huge pair of bellows propped up against the grate. A vigorous broad-leafed plant rose a good four feet from a dull green and eggshell blue pottery vase, threatening to take over the entire room. Everything, he felt, was well used and of good quality and lineage.

Nick had seen plenty of rooms like this; they belonged to well-read professors from old Sicilian families and sometimes contained a grand piano or a collection of silver-framed family photographs, neither of which was in evidence here. Very different anyway from his own place, which Paola had furnished so anonymously that he couldn't say which item of furniture stood where.

"What was it like?" the woman said. "The wallet?"

Nick couldn't remember.

"Mm . . . I just *might* know where he put it." She went through the French windows, the colored scarf trailing in her wake. "Come on out," she called back. "You can give me a hand."

The terrace, which was no more than fifteen foot square, had tubular iron uprights fixed between the outside wall and the waist-high balustrade. Up and over these had been trained a variety of climbing plants, which obviously had the function of providing shade in the boiling summer months. Now the few remaining heart-shaped leaves hung limply from black stems as though praying to be allowed to break free like their brothers and whirl away forever into the sky.

Every spare bit of the pale blue–tiled floor space was crammed with garden furniture and odd-looking objects, so that Nick was forced to squeeze past what appeared to be the fossilized skull of a giant mammoth and a sagging basket chair to get to the small rattan table where the woman was standing.

"Ah!" she said triumphantly, holding up what Nick recognized vaguely as Paola's wallet. "I thought it'd be out here."

A typewritten manuscript half folded back lay on the table between a cradlelike cordless telephone and an overflowing ashtray. The page had been heavily scored in red, the pen then having been thrown—or having fallen—onto the ground. A delicate porcelain coffee cup had a leaf from the overhead creeper adhering to its rim like a shred of spinach on a beautiful lower lip.

"He was working here after lunch," she said unnecessarily, handing the wallet to Nick. "I'm glad we found it. Did you say it had been stolen? You'd better take a look inside."

He did. The credit cards were there, as was the driving license and bus pass. A small holy picture fell out, which he quickly stuffed back. He found his wife's belief in the miraculous powers of saints embarrassing and an insult to human intelligence. There was no money.

"Everything there?" the woman asked, smiling at him.

"Everything except the money," Nick said, smiling back, then immediately feeling he had made a gaffe, said, "No, I mean, well, of course you don't expect to find that, do you? I really am grateful to you for giving it back." That sounded wrong too, but the woman didn't seem to notice.

"Did Dante say where he picked it up?"

Nick had an absurd picture of the cowled and laurel-wreathed poet bending gravely and gracefully earthward to recover the wallet. "Just in the road, he said."

She crossed her arms over her breast and clutched herself. "Not very warm out here, is it?" she said. "Forgive me, I can't remember your name."

He told her.

"Mine's Lea" (she gave it the Italian pronunciation, lay-er) Maselli." She shook his hand.

There was a pause, and the woman glanced at her watch. Realizing he had stayed long enough, he said, "Thanks so much again. I really must be going."

"Come over here and have a look at our view before you do."

Nick almost overturned a massive pewter jug full of shoulder-high dried grasses. It teetered dangerously back and forth, threatening to spill its contents over a heap of seashells and smooth rounded stones piled against the side wall of the terrace. He managed to grab hold of it just in time. Lea laughed.

"There's far too much stuff everywhere. I keep meaning to throw it all out but never get round to it." She wound the ends of her scarf round her forearms, resting them on the low balustrade. "There."

Immediately below them the roofs of the Borgo slums lay wedged up against each other, mercifully screening the filthy decaying streets beneath and forming a single uneven orange-ochre surface that you felt could be easily and lightly run across. Farther to his left rose the bell towers, steeples, and ponderous domes of the old city, where slender palms reached for the sky above unseen cloistered courtyards. Beyond lay the gantries of the shipyard and next to that the port with the yellow-funneled ship Nick had glimpsed at the end of the road. It wasn't old-fashioned—rather like the *Titantic*—as he had imagined it, but modern and, seen from up here, quite unremarkable. Nearby he made out the luxurious Palermo-Genoa ferry standing at one of the quays like a wedge of sparkling wedding cake, and opposite her the smaller, no-nonsense overnight roll-on roll-off to Naples, which was already loading up. A gray warship anchored out in the bay looked as though it had been assembled with a child's construction kit, its guns as thin and brittle as matchsticks.

He made the right sounds of approval and turned back to the flat, watching this time where he put his feet and wondering whether shells, bones, amphorae, fossilized eggs, and grasses were in their permanent places out there or awaiting arrangement somewhere else.

"I'm glad it's all ended well. It's a horrible experience being robbed," Lea said as she led him to the front door. "As though you'd been defiled." She stood on the landing with the ends of her rainbow scarf still wound round her upper arms and waited until he had incarcerated himself inside the lift with a desolate clang of the door. He found he was sorry to be leaving her.

While Nick had been upstairs, the porter had officially come on duty in the lobby, opening the great double entrance doors and taking up his position behind the desk. He regarded Nick with suspicion and dislike, having missed his arrival and having no means of knowing which of the residents he had been visiting. The only way he could find out was by pulling him up over the incorrect closure of the lift. Unfortunately for him, Nick had carried out this operation faultlessly. The porter watched his retreating back and returned to his newspaper.

"Hmm. Just as well it turned up," Paola said grudgingly that evening. "Where was it?"

Nick told her. "Everything's there," he went on, "except the money, of course. I've checked."

"I'm sure you won't mind if I check again." She took the wallet gingerly from him, opened it out, and slipped her fingers inside. "It is mine, after all." She flicked through the contents one by one, muttering, "Bus pass, credit card, driving license" as she went, finishing off by gently running the pads of her fingers over the colored picture of Saint Anthony of Padua as though caressing him. Then she looked up.

"*Who* did you say found it?"

"A guy called Genovese. Lives down by the port."

"Never heard of him. What exactly did he say to you? Where did he find it?"

"He wasn't there. A woman—I suppose it was his wife—gave it to me. I imagine he found it in the street where the thief had chucked it. That's what they do—take the money and—"

"I know very well what they do. I just don't like to think of people touching my things, that's all. Whether they're thieves or . . . whatever. It makes me feel quite sick."

"You've got everything back," Nick said. "Surely that's the main thing?"

"No, it is not," Paola said, "and it certainly *does* matter. I don't think I can bear to keep this any longer." She brought the wallet to her nose, immediately pulling back with a grimace. "It even smells different. You know very well I can't stand *contamination*."

"Do as you like," Nick said wearily. Then, seeing her face: "For Christ's sake, Paola, instead of being pleased you've got it back, all you can do is moan."

"Just a minute," she said slowly as he turned to go. "Is that woman—*Genovese* or whatever her name is—an opera lover by any chance?"

He turned round. "How the hell do I know?"

"Well you see, my opera season ticket's missing. It's not here." She put her head on one side and smiled at him sweetly. "Rather odd, don't you think, that everything else is here except that? I can't imagine the thief would have taken it, can you? A musical mugger? And don't say, 'It was probably in another bag,' " she went on as Nick opened his mouth. "Because it wasn't. I always keep it here." She hit the leather three times with her fingers: *"In this wallet."*

She flung the offending object on the floor and pushed past him out of the room.

2

Just over a week later, Giulia was sitting on the train halfway between Bologna and Rome. She had spent the previous night tangled up in the sheets in her minute bedroom with a colleague from the faculty of engineering, had turned him out at half past ten and spent the rest of the morning packing her rucksack. At half past twelve she had made herself a sandwich using up everything that was left in the fridge and washing it down with the remains of some slightly sour milk, which she drank straight from the carton.

The intercity train was warm and soothing, the winter sun pouring into the carriage as it sped through the ordered Umbrian countryside. She rested her head on the back of the seat and watched the hillsides and woodlands pass in the golden afternoon. Every so often the man on the opposite side of the aisle glanced furtively at her over the top of his newspaper, but she hardly saw him. Dressed entirely in black with a dark red scarf wound round her neck and three silver studs set into the upper part of one ear, she picked absently at the colorless nail varnish on her beautifully shaped hands and shook back her heavy dark hair.

It was this movement that so unsettled the man with the newspaper and made him keep looking at her. Each time she did it, her breasts shivered imperceptibly. He took a deep breath and shifted in his seat, and almost simultaneously the girl stood up, reached for her rucksack, and took out a Walkman. Fitting on the headset, she lay back once more and closed her eyes.

She wished she didn't have to go back to college and could go off to Madeira instead. Or Brazil or Mexico perhaps—somewhere hot anyway. She felt she was wasting her life studying things she had no interest in and would never use in a career. She had no idea yet what she wanted to do, but knew it would be something she herself had chosen freely. Opening her eyes as the music came to an end she found the man opposite staring her full in the face. He colored when she met his gaze and hid himself behind his paper. *Coglione,* she thought; how could you *be* like that at that age? It was pathetic.

She felt like a smoke, but that meant getting up and going into another carriage, and she couldn't be bothered to move from the warm seat. She removed the headset and gazed out of the window. It was no good ringing Serena yet, she'd still be at work. Now *she'd* done the right thing, leaving her family for good—telling them she was through with studying. Her parents had to give in. She'd found a job and a place of her own and was now completely independent.

"Why don't you do the same and come with me?" she had asked Giulia after they finished school. "You don't really want to go on studying for another four years at university, do you?"

"It's my parents," Giulia told her.

"For heaven's sake, Giulia, your father's English. You come from an 'enlightened' family, not one from the dark ages like mine."

Enlightened? Is that what it was? Giulia had a mental picture of her mother's anxiety-ridden face, her mouth in that drooping shape as she complained about her job, her ill health, her bad luck. "Palermo's a useless place," she told her daughter. "You've done the right thing choosing Bologna. If I were your age again I'd be off like a flash. You'll never get anywhere staying down here." Then she'd gone around telling everybody how brilliant her daughter was and what a future she had ahead of her. Once—my God!—she told Giulia how she had prayed to Saint Anthony for her.

Her father wouldn't have minded where she went as long as she was happy and doing what she really wanted. But it had never been easy talking to him, partly because neither of them could refer to what Paola had become. It was unthinkable, for instance, that she should tell Nick how her mother drove her mad and how she longed to shriek at her sometimes to shut up. "I do know," she had often wanted to say to Nick. "I do know what you're going through, but I can't do anything about it. It's your problem, not mine, and you must solve it yourself." She couldn't make up her mind whether she loved and respected him for sticking with Paola or despised him for not breaking away.

Of course her parents had no idea what she was like—that she'd smoked since she was fifteen, experimented with drugs, and slept with whoever she liked. What they saw was Giulia at home—very different. She was lucky because she could handle this kind of double life, but Sandro couldn't deal with the situation at all and stayed out of the house most of the time. Hardly ever spoke to his parents. She worried about him.

The train had crossed the border into the wilder landscapes of Upper Latium and was running parallel to a swollen river tumbling and rushing its way through a gorge. The sheer drop on the far side was lush with long grass and dotted with little trees that leaned over the abyss as though to get a better view. They peered into the depths, their spindly but resistant trunks waving slowly to and fro in the wind. Giulia saw how the hurtling rush of water parted on either side of huge boulders lying in its path and how the thick white foam was sent spraying up into the air. She put her face closer to the window, resting her forehead on the glass to get a better view, but at that moment the train roared into a tunnel and the river was gone.

As they emerged at the other end, her mobile phone bleeped into life. For an awful moment she thought it was her mother, although Paola hardly ever used it, knowing how her lengthy calls sent the cost soaring. The phone had been a present from her parents last summer.

"Giulia, it's me. Where are you?"

"Serena! I'm on the train. Quite near now, I think. I thought you were still at work."

"I am. I just wanted to see whether you were actually coming or not."

"Mm. You thought I'd rather stay up in that freezing place doing bugger all. Get the drinks ready for when I get there."

"We're going to have a terrific time. How's Massimo?"

"Don't mention his name." She shivered.

"Listen, I must tell you . . ."

The man opposite watched the muscles moving in the girl's face as she listened, registering delight, incredulity, disgust. How she threw back her head and laughed, running her open fingers through her long hair. He folded his newspaper and put it on the empty seat beside him, aware that the dreaming and looking had been pleasant but that now they were approaching Rome and it was over. In fact, the sooner he was out of the train the better. He was on his feet and out onto Termini platform before she had got her things together, merging into the crowds surging toward the ticket barrier. Giulia too immediately forgot his existence and after shrugging herself into her padded jacket hooked her rucksack over one shoulder and left the train.

Outside, the clear primrose sky was filled with the cacophanous screeching of starlings going through their evening ritual, taking off from the trees in their thousands, lifting themselves into the air and resettling. The upper reaches of dark green leaves boiled with frenzied black wings as though being peppered by bullets, and so loud was the din that people were having to raise their voices to be heard. Unlike the tourists, who found the sight extraordinary and unforgettable, Rome's municipal authorities were becoming increasingly rattled by the damage being done to the capital's artistic heritage. Already the pavements under the trees were lined with a thick slimy layer of compacted droppings, and these were now threatening the survival of the hallowed ancient buildings clustered around the station.

One of the solutions dreamed up to frighten the birds off was the bansheelike siren now wailing eerily on the far side of the square like some unearthly animal in distress. But to Giulia, emerging into Piazza Cinquecento, it was barely audible. Lifting her eyes she saw a dark mass like an elongated balloon sweep smoothly across the sky from left to right. As she watched, the thing mutated into a perfect sphere, and as it did so its color flashed from silver to black and back again as if it were a blinking eye. She saw another curved mass coming toward it, then another, until it seemed the air was full of the swirling diaphanous shapes. Foreigners in Rome for the first time watched awestruck as the flocks of starlings flung themselves diagonally across the sky in their strange dance, changing direction as one, coming low over the treetops, then shooting straight upward and disappearing beyond the roofs of Via Nazionale.

One of the people watching was Stella, who had left Palermo two days after the incident on the 101 bus to come to Rome. She planned to spend a fortnight there before going up to Florence and Siena. People might have wondered why her Italian trip had started in the South rather than vice versa, but she would have told them it was Sicily that was most important to her and it was there she wanted to begin. Besides, Goethe had claimed that the island held the key to understanding the rest of Italy, and she wanted to see if it was true. She stood watching the changing formations in the sky a few moments longer before making her away toward Piazza della Repubblica and her hotel.

The afternoon was fading, and the first lights were coming on in the shops under the arcades. Giulia caught a bus outside the station and three-quarters of an hour later was ringing the bell at Serena's flat. That evening the two of them went out to the Quo Vadis trattoria round the corner, where Serena insisted on paying.

"You next time," she said. "You're still a penniless student."

"And you're a woman of means," Giulia said. "I wish I'd chosen lobster."

They both had a brimming plateful of chunky pasta mixed with haricot beans, followed by a large mixed salad, and finished off a bottle of the red house wine. As Livio, the owner, brought them each a tiny glass of grappa at the end of the meal, Giulia told Serena she had to visit Hadrian's Villa out at Tivoli while she was in Rome as part of her studies. Livio placed the glasses before them with pursed lips and a brief lowering of heavy Roman eyelids. *"Bevete, signorine, che è buona."*

As they were sipping the burning liquid, Giulia's phone rang.

"Where on earth are you? I've been trying the house all evening."

Oh no, she thought, not now. Not now. Serena raised questioning eyebrows, but Giulia just shook her head. "I was out," she told her mother. She hadn't said anything about leaving Bologna. There was a short muttering sound as Paola digested this. "Mm. Well. I was a bit worried."

"Well, don't be. I'm fine. How are you both?"

There was a histrionic sigh, and Giulia's heart sank. "I'm terribly tired, Mum," she began before her mother could launch into her moaning. "Was it anything special? Don't forget this is the mobile."

"I haven't forgotten. What's it like up there with you?"

Might as well tell her: "I'm in Rome."

"Rome! What on earth are you doing there? What's happened?"

"Nothing's happened. I'm just spending a couple of days here with Serena."

"Serena? What for? What about your lectures? You'll be missing—"

"I'm not missing anything, Mum."

Livio pushed lightly by their table with two steaming dishes balanced on his palms at shoulder height. *"Ah, la mamma, la mamma!"* he crooned as he passed.

"Shut up, Livio," Serena told him, draining her grappa.

"What was that noise?" Paola's voice came down the phone. "Where exactly *are* you?"

"I'm in a trattoria, I told you."

"You didn't, you said—"

"Look, I'll ring you tomorrow. It's far too noisy here."

The glass-fronted door suddenly opened to admit a North African with a piano accordian strapped to his chest. He immediately began to play, as though afraid of being ejected, his long dark fingers flying over the keys, the notes spilling and cascading out. Smiling and nodding, his body bending forward from the waist in time to the rhythm, he played faster and faster, stretching and compressing the pleated bellows on his left, so that the bass sounds were drawn out into the love calls of cats, the lowing of animals in heat. The trattoria fell silent, several of the diners staring transfixed at the swaying figure, the food lying unchewed in their mouths. Then, as abruptly as he had begun, the young man stopped, took his hands from the accordion, and inclined his head. He began moving from table to table, arm outstretched, pale pink palm upward. *"Grazie, grazie."*

But the spell was broken and the offerings meager. Serena gave him a five hundred lire coin, which was the only change she had, and from the counter Livio pushed a tumbler of red wine toward him, indicating with a jerk of his head that he was to take it. The Algerian stretched his lips over beautiful even teeth and shook his head.

"Please yourself, mate. Some of your lot like it." He opened the till and pushed two thousand lire toward him, which the man pocketed with alacrity.

"Poor sods have to work," Livio said as the door closed behind the Arab. "Better than those bloody gypsies—never do a stroke of work. Won't let them near the place." These opinions were addressed to anybody who happened to be listening; in this case, a balding man seated on his own near the till, who nodded sagely without taking his eyes off his soup.

"Life's hard for everyone nowadays," Livio went on, drawing in his stomach to squeeze between the table and the bar counter.

"More bread, please," the balding man said between mouthfuls.

At half past nine the next morning she was driving along between the white gashes of open marble quarries, which had eaten their way deep into the once tranquil countryside. A flock of sheep grazed on a patch of coarse grass, the young shepherd leaning on his staff and gazing longingly toward the unbroken line of cars and heavy vehicles thundering by on the Tiburtina trunk road.

She was a skillful driver with an instinctive sense of direction and had only needed to hear Serena's instructions once. The Renault had taken her through the northern outskirts of Rome to this ravaged landscape in which it seemed nothing of beauty or interest could possibly exist. Ahead of her, the Tivoli hills rose above a smut-filled haze as though gasping for breath.

"Vittorio says to look out for the sign to Hadrian's Villa,"

Serena had said. "On the left." And there it was. Giulia had to slow down to let a bright blue bus ahead of her disgorge a passenger. It was a woman who glanced up at the road sign and set off in the direction of the villa, her drooping knapsack adhering to her back like an empty scrotum. Giulia took the same turning, soon leaving the plodding Teutonic figure far behind on the grass verge. At the entrance to the villa she parked the car and went in.

If it hadn't been for the glory of the morning, her dismay at the vastness and emptiness around her would have sent her back to Rome. But the winter sun shining from a cloudless sky set the grass sparkling and winking as though strewn with millions of diamonds and made her feel it might be worth staying after all.

She had no map and no idea of where she should begin or what she should be looking at. Trying to remember what her professor had told her, she passed through an opening in a soaring ochre-colored wall and found herself before a long, still lake. Cypress trees rose at its four corners, their solemn reflections in the motionless water like fingers admonishing her for her ignorance.

As one gaping ruin followed another, she began to wonder why it was called a villa at all, what the vast concave walls and broken columns were part of and why they were scattered around and so far apart from each other. If it was the emperor's country house, what did it all mean?

She was quite alone. A bird sang lustily from the bare branches of a tree, and two more hopped business-like across the black-and-white mosaic floor of what might once have been a temple but was now, like everything else, open to the sky. It was as though the birds had taken over every building, as though the whole place belonged exclusively to them. She picked her way through the dew-soaked grass and across cold little pockets of shade where the groundsel leaves were still covered in a soft furring of frost and the earth crunched underfoot. Every so often she would stop dutifully to gaze at a fragment of masonry or an arched ceiling, and after ten minutes or so found herself on the edge of a spit of high ground where the land fell away at her feet in a rush of stones and soil. Below was a scattering of trees, their leaves a mixture of rich wine red and glinting gold. She stood still for a few minutes listening to the deep silence.

The first thing she saw when she turned back was a woman sitting on a low wall some ten yards ahead of her. Her legs, in narrow black trousers tucked into ankle boots, were crossed, and she wore a padded dark gray jacket with fur-lined hood. Her hands, in gray gloves, were laid together in her lap, and she was looking straight ahead of her as though in contemplation. Just then she swiveled her head and saw Giulia.

"*Buongiorno,*" she said as Giulia came up.

"*Buongiorno.*"

"*Molto bello,*" the woman said slowly in a thick foreign accent.

"Mm," Giulia offered and then, in spite of herself, "English?"

"American. How nice to be able to speak English!" She was quite old, with short, well-cut hair and a lovely smile. "I was just admiring all this," she went on. "An amazing man, wasn't he?"

"Who?"

"Hadrian! What a place it must have been!"

"I don't know much about him—well, nothing really," Giulia said. Without knowing why, she sat down on the wall next to the woman. It was just the right height for her and was cushioned with soft springy lichen.

"Well, I can tell you he filled the place with philosophers and intellectuals and spent the days and nights discussing life with them," the woman said. "What could be more wonderful than that? And in this setting too. I suppose you could say he had everything he wished for: wealth, leisure, intelligent conversation, beautiful surroundings. . . ."

"What about happiness?" Giulia asked, again surprising herself.

"That I couldn't say," the woman replied, turning toward her. She paused. "You don't look as if you've been enjoying yourself very much here."

"It's so sad and so empty."

"Well, I suppose it's not a way of life we can relate to nowadays—on such a grand scale, I mean. Their pleasures were so different then as well—*time* was different, wasn't it? What we're seeing now doesn't really give an idea at all of what it must have been like. Maybe that's why you feel sad." The woman clapped her gloved hands together gently several times as if to warm them. "Ruins distort, give quite the wrong idea. Try and imagine the buildings with roofs on them, painted inside and outside, full of people having Turkish baths, sweating, laughing, talking, playing, eating. People'd be walking along the paths here, going into the libraries, waiting to have an audience with the emperor. In a way," she went on, "it's as if we're spying on them, don't you think?"

"Or on their memories."

"But without malice, I hope," the woman said. She uncrossed her legs and began to stand up. "I was just about to go to the canopus. Have you been there yet?"

Giulia shook her head. She didn't even know what a canopus was.

"Well, come with me then," the woman said, smiling and putting a hand under Giulia's elbow to encourage her.

As they walked, the woman told her that some of the buildings had been inspired by those Hadrian had seen and admired on his travels throughout the Roman Empire—in Greece, Egypt, and Persia. That the elaborate bathhouses for men and for women contained hot, cool, and cold chambers, that there were banqueting halls, libraries for his collections of Latin and Greek books, temples and theaters—a real self-contained city. She said he began building it in 118 A.D., the year after he became emperor. "And he was only sixty-two when he died," the woman said. "Far too young, don't you think?"

Giulia, who had never contemplated being sixty-two, wondered what one could possibly expect from life at that age.

"Of course, you're so young yourself, I suppose you can't imagine being that old, can you?" the woman said smiling. They were picking their way over an uneven stretch of rough ground, avoiding the deep puddles that had formed from the melting ice. "But I can assure you there is still a great deal left to be lived," she went on in the same gentle voice. "Remember that, won't you?" She took another look at the leaflet in her hand. "You know, I think this must be it."

Giulia saw the white duck before anything else; it was on a flat stone plinth sticking out of the water, fussily cleaning its plumage. First it thrust its beak under the soft white feathers, pulling and straightening the quills, then, with its webbed feet sturdily apart on the stone, ruffled its rear and straightened up.

It gave a further shiver before stretching its neck skyward and quacking noisily. When she thought in years to come of Hadrian's Canopus, it was the duck she remembered.

The long, narrow pool was set low in what looked to Giulia like a man-made valley, with a steep grass-covered escarpment on one side rather like half a railway cutting. The opposite side was thickly wooded and flanked by a series of draped female statues, some of them headless. A delicate colonnade ran down the other side, its arches interspersed with more figures whose every detail was reflected in the motionless surface of the water. Giulia realized the woman was no longer beside her and had walked round to the other side of the pool some twenty yards away. Her voice floated quietly over the water: "What do you think of this? Isn't it beautiful?"

When Giulia joined her the woman said the female figures were called caryatids and had been copied from ones in Athens. "The building at the end there was some kind of banqueting hall, I *think,* but it doesn't seem to matter very much what it was, does it?"

She then said she was afraid she was talking too much and didn't mean to bore Giulia. "I'm in love with Italy," she said. "And there's nothing I can do about it." She asked Giulia if she was from Rome.

"No, Palermo."

"Do you know, I've just come from there," the woman said, stopping in her tracks and turning toward her. "And you're from there? You speak such good English."

"But you realized I wasn't."

"Well, you don't really look it," the woman went on. "That's why." She pointed to some wooden steps cut into the steep slope.

"I'm going to walk up there. Will you come with me?"

As they climbed she told Giulia her name. "My father was Sicilian. From just outside Palermo. He left Sicily when he was a young man and never went back. I used to think that so very strange. I used to ask him why, and he said that Italy was dead for him, that it no longer had anything to do with him. I know now that he meant he would die of hunger there because there was no work for him, but at the time I thought it a terrible thing to say about his own country. I decided to come out one day to see it and try and understand for myself. And here I am."

Giulia told the woman her name, that she was only in Rome for a few days, was studying in Bologna, and that her father was English.

"And does he want to go back, I wonder?" the woman asked, smiling. "I mean to England."

"I don't know . . . not for good, I would imagine." What had made her say that?

They had reached the top of the embankment. The path they had been following disappeared into some overgrown bushes, then petered out into muddy cart ruts. They stood looking down over the pool.

"Would you have lunch with me, Giulia?" the woman asked. "I see they've got some snacks in the bar here."

They made their way back, passing through a silent pinewood where trees soared upward into infinity on crooked coal-black trunks. Giulia realized that nearly three hours had gone by.

In the tiny bar, which had steamed-up windows, they had beer and hot medaglioni rolls oozing mozzarella cheese. Afterward Giulia offered to give her a lift back to Rome, but Stella said she wanted to have a last look round because she was anxious to find the little temple of Venus before she left. "It's such a lovely name," she said, as though that were reason enough.

Driving back, Giulia found herself thinking about her father. The wintry day was fading, the sky growing dark, and necklaces of lights beginning to twinkle from the distant hills. She felt suddenly homesick, her life totally useless and without any sort of pattern to it. What was she going to do, just drift, or what? Did she really want to go off to Mexico, or should she stay on in Bologna and finish her studies? That woman Stella had seemed so *tranquil,* so contented with her life. Perhaps you had to wait till you were old like that before you knew what you wanted. Giulia reached forward for the headlight switch and realized she didn't know where it was. As she fumbled about on the dashboard the car gave a tiny sideways leap, and a frightened, angry shout came a few inches from the window: "Hey, what the hell are you doing?"

Dusk always made her sad, especially when she was away from home and among melancholy streets, shuttered windows, or cold empty fields stretching away like these into infinity. She found she was crying.

"She's in Rome," Paola said coming into the study, "staying with that friend of hers, Serena." She turned the corners of her mouth down and spat the name out. "You remember her, don't you? That large girl—at Giulia's school. I said she might have let us know before she left Bologna, I was getting worried. I said to her 'What about your classes?' but apparently she isn't missing anything important, so I suppose that's all right. Still, it does seem a bit odd, don't you think?"

Nick turned back to the computer screen. "What's odd about wanting to take a few days off?"

"I think she could have let us know."

"Why should she? For God's sake, Paola, can't you leave her alone? Can't you see you're driving her *insane* with all these phone calls? People have to live their own lives. Why d'you think she went to Bologna?"

"Oh it's all right for you. You never worry about anything, do you? Everything's wonderful for you, just as long as you've got your computer and your translations."

Nick sighed and sat back in the chair. "Giulia's twenty-one now," he said patiently. "She's a woman and able to look after herself. We've got to let her get on with her life. I'm far more worried about Sandro."

"Why, what's happened to him?"

"Nothing's happened. It's just that he's unhappy."

"Well, you're the father, you should talk to him."

"I will. I *will* talk to him. But perhaps you could spare him a bit of time as well."

He made a show of angling the desk lamp and peering closely at the manuscript beside him to show Paola the conversation was at an end. She stood there breathing deeply and noisily, as though trying to control herself. Then she opened her mouth: "You just couldn't care less, could you?" she began in a low voice. "Never interested in what your daughter's doing. Never asking her how she is, whether she's—"

"Oh shut up! Just shut up!" Nick shouted in English. "I'm sick to death of listening to your bloody rubbish. Just leave me alone and let me get on!"

Shocked into silence, her chest heaving, she stood her ground a second or so longer, then turned and left the room.

Nick sat a full five minutes, head in hands, before going back to his work. The half-empty glass of whisky at his right elbow lay illuminated inside the pool of light thrown by the Anglepoise like a gallery exhibit—casually but deliberately positioned for effect. On his other side lay the copy of the magazine. It was only after he had read the article on Palermo right through the day before that he'd noticed the byline, and then it took him a few moments to remember where he had come across the name before. He picked it up again.

The article was about how the children of Mafia bosses were treated at school and in their local communities. Practically everyone interviewed thought the kids were not answerable for their fathers' crimes and shouldn't be ostracized. The journalist, however, concluded the article by remarking that innocent as the children may be, they were also indirectly enjoying the benefits of ill-gotten gains such as large, comfortable houses to live in, exotic holidays, and more and that this should not be condoned or tolerated in a democratic society. The children should be made aware, the writer went on, that what their fathers (and in some cases, mothers) had done was wrong and not something to gloat over—that it was simply not acceptable. It was their teachers' job to do this and that of the other children. This was the crux of the whole issue, for when such a Sicilian loses—his *honor*—and is no longer someone to look up to, he is finished.

Nick had never been particularly interested in the phenomenon of the Mafia but found the argument persuasive. The journalist, Dante Genovese—whom he now remembered as the man who had found Paola's wallet (as well as being Lea Maselli's partner, whose name he *hadn't* forgotten)—had constructed a good case. Nick remembered the smirking, arrogant faces of arrested bosses on television as they were frog-marched from their homes and bundled into police cars, the way they raised an arm in salute. "I'm one up on all of you shits, and I'll be back."

A quarter past ten; he turned back to his translation. It didn't have to be finished by tomorrow, but he worked better in the evenings when he was on his own. He heard the front door click open.

"Sandro?"

"Yeah."

Nick got up and went out into the hall. "Hi. You're late" (the first mistake). "Where've you been?"

"Out."

"Had anything to eat yet?"

Sandro shook his head.

"Want something? I was just going to get myself a roll."

"Okay."

"Right, I'll get something together."

Sandro grunted, head down, and went toward his room. Nick found his retreating back in the brown jacket unbearably tender. The collar was turned up so that just a bit of hair showed over the top, and Nick had an overwhelming desire to put his arms around his son and hug him hard.

Nick's own father had loved Sandro and used to miss him terribly when the family returned to Sicily after the holidays. They used to talk together, Sandro in his not very good English and Dad bending gravely toward his grandson, listening, nodding, and saying "Mmm" and "Right-oh" and "I certainly will." They'd go for walks, which his father said were exclusively for men. No women admitted. "But I'm a man," Nick would complain, laughing. "Ah yes, but I know all about you already. I've got to make up time with Sandro here."

Dad took the little boy to fly a kite they had made together. It was an old-fashioned triangular one with a smiling face and long wavy tail made up of colored pieces of paper. "I made it," Sandro said, bursting with pride, to his mother. "And it flew right up into the sky for miles until we couldn't see it anymore."

Nick's parents were still living in the gloomy, damp house in Twickenham where he had grown up. It had a strip of back garden—more like a shrubbery really—with just a bit of coarse grass down the middle. Dad's shed was in the far corner under the fence, overshadowed by a sycamore, which over the years had grown to gigantic proportions. Nick's children loved to stand beneath its protecting branches during summer storms with him while the rain thundered on the leaves above their heads. "Now, we're all dry like in Palermo," Dad would shout as it pelted down. "Doesn't rain like this with you, does it?"

So they called the tree the Sicilian sycamore.

Inside the shed were dad's inventions.

"A very clever man, your father," a former colleague of his had said to Nick at the funeral. "What a pity he never tried to market all his ideas."

Too late now anyway.

Paola never learned to pronounce the name Twickenham properly, and this made Nick and the children laugh.

"It's easy, Mamma," Giulia said. "Listen: *Twee*-ken-um."

"Too-eek-ing-hum."

"No! *You* tell her, Daddy."

The good days.

Nick got two rolls out of the bread bin, cut them in half

lengthways, and placed a layer of salami and two cheese slices inside each of them. He opened a bottle of beer and put it on the table with two glasses, then went to knock on his son's bedroom door. "Sandro? It's ready."

Two doors farther down the passage Paola stood in her underclothes before the heavy wardrobe mirror, hands hanging loosely by her sides. Her reflection in the glass appalled her. I hate the sight of you, she told herself. I hate it. Half-listening to the low voices coming from the kitchen, she turned away and saw the wallet lying on the floor next to the double bed—*il letto matrimoniale*. Gingerly picking it up and holding it at arm's length, she took it toward the wastepaper basket and dropped it in.

"Hey. Over there."

"Who?"

"Over *there*. Look."

Jeans, dark gray sweater, a jacket over his arm, eyes creased up in the sun. Looking for somewhere to sit.

"Wait, I know him . . . just a minute, that's right, he came to the flat about the wallet—must be about ten days ago now. I knew I recognized him."

"Who is he? What wallet?"

The man glanced in their direction. When Lea lifted her chin and smiled, he half-raised his arm in recognition and came over, weaving his way between the crowded tables.

"Hi, I wasn't sure it was you."

"It was," Lea said.

He saw she had done her hair a different way and that she wore a chocolate brown sweater with a deep V cut into it, which left her neck and collarbones bare. Her jacket was draped over her shoulders, and when she tugged at it gently he noticed her hands were ringless. She'd had a whole lot of rings before. There was something else missing about her person too, which he couldn't place—something she'd had on that last time.

The woman with her was muffled up to the throat in a fur coat despite the temperature and was leaning back in her chair, legs crossed, unashamedly sizing him up. Both women had glasses of white wine in front of them. He thought of the cool liquid and of the warmth of the air and suddenly remembered it was the rainbow scarf that was missing from Lea—the one she had been wearing in the flat.

"How are you?" was all he was able to manage. "Wonderful day."

"Beautiful. Why don't you join us?" She leaned forward and removed a large camera bag from the chair beside her, putting it carefully on the ground under the hedge. "Flora, this is—"

He supplied his name before she could stumble, and lowered himself onto the vacated chair.

"And what do you do, Mr. Stirling?"

"I work at the university."

"Ah, so it's *Professor* Stirling then," the woman called Flora went on. "American?"

"English."

"Aha."

"Professor Stirling's wife had her wallet stolen on the bus," Lea began.

Nick listened to her explaining and thought how he liked the way her hands accompanied the words and how she put her head on one side to emphasize a point. He wondered what she was doing here at lunchtime when she lived just round the corner.

"...and Dante said it was just lying there on the pavement outside the house," Lea was saying now. "Not even in the gutter."

"My dear," Flora said, "what they sometimes do is to *post* the thing. You know, take the cash, then just slip the rest into a pillar box. I suppose that's something."

When the waiter stopped at their table, Nick ordered a steak for himself. "With or without chips?" The waiter's face was shiny with sweat, and he was jigging up and down with impatience.

"Without. And bring me a beer too."

People strolled by beyond the tubs of evergreens circling the restaurant, glancing over the top as though envious of the fun taking place on the other side. The street had been declared an experimental pedestrian precinct some years before, which now, with the dwarf palms and mimosa trees in its centrally planted beds at full maturity, had become a permanent fixture. In the beginning, shopkeepers had grumbled they would be ruined by lack of through traffic, but in fact they had probably gained by it. Palermo's citizens enjoyed strolling up and down and sitting in the pavement cafés as much as the tourists did, and were in a more relaxed mood as a result. This meant that they were more willing to look in the shop windows and buy. A kind of symbiosis between retailers and café owners thus grew up, the one depending quite heavily on the other for its well-being and livelihood.

"What on earth are you doing in a place like Palermo?" Flora asked Nick as the waiter scurried away, stuffing notepad and pencil into the back pocket of his tight trousers.

"I like it," he said. "Of course it's got its pros and cons like anywhere else."

"Tell me one of the pros," Flora said, uncrossing her legs and leaning forward to take a drink of wine.

He smiled. "Life's never boring here."

"You can say that again," she said. She reached under the table and eased one foot in its shiny black high-heeled shoe. "My God, you're right there."

"Flora's got a ceramics shop just nearby," Lea said, as though that explained things.

"Never a dull moment," Flora went on. "Which is fine in your line of business."

"Mine?" Nick asked.

"No, Lea's—but maybe yours as well, I don't know. Variety is the spice of life, eh, Lea?"

"You're a photographer?" Nick asked.

Flora raised her eyebrows and snuggled further into her fur. "I thought you two knew each other."

Lea nodded. "I'm a photographer, yes."

Flora said, "Wish I'd had the sense to do that instead of getting involved in effing commerce; I'd be a far happier person. Worst thing you can possibly have, professor, a shop."

Nick wondered whether she was referring to lack of business or something darker only open to those in the know, but he wasn't sufficiently interested to ask. She was artfully and expertly made up, and it was difficult to tell her age, probably mid-forties. Hard-featured anyway and with those blond streaks all over her jaw-length hair. Not his type.

"You must come and have a look at it," she went on. "Is the university near here?"

He said it was.

"Well then. Might find something you like. For your wife perhaps."

Their food arrived almost simultaneously: Nick's steak flattened, black-barred, and faintly steaming from the griddle, and the women's salads. He took his beer and asked whether either wanted any more wine. Both shook their heads.

"Wouldn't get any more work done if I did," Lea said, picking up her fork. "Thanks anyway."

"Plays havoc with the complexion," Flora added. "Unless you like old parchment."

As they ate Nick asked what kind of photos Lea took. "Our delightful city," Flora said between mouthfuls. "Eh, Lea? The filthier and more decayed the better. Disgusting little boys, stray cats, places falling to bits."

Lea smiled. "I'm just finishing off a series on Palermo at the moment," she said. "By the way, Flora, you didn't manage to find out about that book, did you?"

"Oh darling, I'm so sorry, I quite forgot. I knew there was something I had to ask Piero. I really will get on to him today. What was the title again?"

"*Immagini palermitane della mia morte*. It shouldn't be all that difficult to find. It's just that I never have the time to traipse round the bookshops looking for it."

"Hang on, I'll write it down this time. Then I won't forget." She leaned down and started rummaging about in her handbag.

Nick mentally translated it into *Palermo Images of My Death*. "Odd title," he said. "What's it about?"

"They're pictures taken by, well, practically an *amateur* photographer—in the forties or fifties. Just after the war. He—"

"*Immagine palermitane della . . .* what was it?" Flora interrupted. She had started writing on the back of a letter she had found.

"*Della mia morte,*" Lea supplied. "By Francesco Martinucci." She turned to Nick again. "He was a doctor by profession who used to go round visiting patients in the Danisini and was so shocked and horrified by what he saw—by the conditions the people were living in—that he decided to take a series of photographs and send them to the then Home Secretary. Whether he did or not—send them, I mean—I don't know. But things haven't changed all that much since then, so it obviously didn't have the impact he'd hoped for."

Nick had heard of the Danisini slums near Piazza Independenza right in the center of the old city but had never remotely thought of visiting them.

"I'm afraid it won't be for at least another week," Flora was saying, zipping up her handbag, "because I know Piero's in Florence at the moment. Hope that's all right."

"Yes. I'm not in any desperate hurry for it," Lea said. "I don't know what he meant by the title," she went on to Nick. "I think it was the way people were forced to live there that he found so dreadful—worse than death, if you like. But I suppose you can read whatever meaning you like into it."

"So you're working on that—on the same sort of thing," he said. "I mean the poor parts of Palermo and so on?"

"Do use the *tu* form," she told him, "and call me Lea."

"Fine. My name's Nick."

Flora followed this exchange with a crooked smile.

"It's not only the slums," Lea said. "There are other . . . aspects of the place too. It'll be a book with . . . well, words, I suppose you'd say."

"All in black and white?" he asked, imagining the stark images, one to a page, staring brutally up at the reader.

"No, not necessarily. It's often the color that gives impact." She started telling him of some of the places she found most satisfying to work on.

"My dears, I shall have to interrupt," Flora said, standing up and brushing down her skirt. "Awful having to leave you here, but duty calls." Her arms disappeared one after the other down the gray silk tunnels of her coat sleeves. "Lea, I'm counting on you to bring the professor to the shop."

"I shall have to go too," Lea said, standing up. "It was really nice seeing you, Nick." He felt absurdly pleased she had used his name.

The next morning he woke suddenly at ten past three, his eyes springing open to stare up at the dark ceiling. Paola was turned away from him snoring softly and giving off that slightly sour odor he had once found so sensual. He found he was thinking of Lea, that he could see her quite clearly sitting across from him in the soft brown sweater with the deeply cut neck; the way she frowned as she spoke and moved her hands. And he thought how nice it would be to see her again. How would he manage it? Go back to Longhi's in the hope she'd be there; walk up and down outside her building. Or else he could ring her. . . . Ring? And what would he say? I'd like to see you again, I was wondering whether you'd like to come and have lunch with me? Don't talk crap. Anyway she had this guy living with her—the unseen journalist, Dante.

Paola stirred and muttered something. She turned toward him so that the bedsprings heaved and twanged. The movement obviously calmed her sinuses because she stopped snoring. Perhaps he could call Lea's publishers. What publishers? She hadn't said who or where they were. Or he could go to that woman Flora's shop. The ceramics place. She'd said it was nearby. Yes, and then what, make an excuse like "I have to get in touch with Lea but I've lost her address"? For Christ's sake.

A gust of wind rattled the heavy shutters, which hadn't fastened properly for years now. They were the old-fashioned kind that folded back against the outside wall and had shards of brown-painted wood flaking off. The whole flat was old now, dingy and cold, with floors of marble chip. Its long corridor served no purpose other than having frightened the children when they were small. Giulia had once told him how she and Sandro used to lie terrified in bed when he and Paola were out, imagining footsteps getting closer and closer. Poor kids! He thought of Lea's place with the sunlight pouring into the sitting room and all those books. The book! That was what he'd do: find that book she was looking for. What was it called? *Immagini di Palermo della Morte?* No, *Immagini palermitani dalla mia morte,* or *della mia morte—della* or *dalla?* And the author . . . Francesco Martellucci, no Martini . . . Martinelli . . . Martinuzzi? He'd get hold of the book, then ring her. And what if her guy answered? Well, he'd get round that. But it would have to be quickly, before that other woman found a copy.

The next day, Saturday, he told Paola he had to see a colleague. She looked at him sourly: "I thought we could have done the shopping together. There's masses to do with Mum coming over tomorrow."

His mother-in-law was eighty-six and getting too frail now to be on her own. Nick was fond of her and hated the idea of having to put her into a home, but she'd had two falls already, and there seemed no alternative.

"I'll do the shopping this afternoon."

"That won't be much good, will it," Paola said, "when I've got to spend the morning cooking?" She sighed. "It's a pity you're never available when I need your help. Not even on a Saturday."

"I told you, I'll—"

But she had left the room.

Nick took the 101 bus as far as Piazza Pretoria, where a group of Japanese tourists were regarding the marble figures round the great circular fountain in nonplussed silence. The naked statues stared back almost insolently. As if to put an end to the matter, one of the tourists lifted his camera and the others followed suit. Over on the far side of the square a small untidy knot of protesters hung dispiritedly around Palazzo delle Aquile, the Town Hall, chatting to the the two policemen on duty. Their banners drooped at half-mast, and some of them were sitting smoking on the fountain steps. Orlando was evidently out of town.

The bookshops along Corso Vittorio Emanuele, Palermo's most ancient and historic street, served students and scholars from the faculties of political science in Piazza Bologni (where Stella had admired the statue of Charles I) and occasionally those who couldn't find what they wanted in the regional public library further along on the opposite side. Ill-lit and smelling of mold, the shops also held a supply of illustrated guides to the city in various languages, which tourists would occasionally peruse and buy. Only occasionally, though, for non-Palermitans were not made welcome and would scurry out with their purchases feeling as if they had unwittingly committed some social blunder. The bulk of the stock was secondhand and intended to be unloaded on unworldy first-year students, while the better-quality merchandise was kept for the more discerning customers. Woe betide the newcomer, however, who showed a spark of interest in some forgotten volume on the back shelves, for his zeal would instantly arouse the bookseller's suspicion and the volume be declared either not for sale or of exorbitant price. Curved old professors peering shortsightedly at musty tomes were tolerated, as were those self-styled experts on Palermo's hallowed and often bloody past, yet neither were accorded any particular respect. The booksellers weren't in the business for that.

It took the owner of the first shop three seconds flat to classify Nick as an academic. Not just his clothes (thick-soled shoes, unpressed trousers, and roomy jacket with upturned collar) but the longish hair, hands in pockets, the way he glanced around. Not the ambitious or the cutthroat, nor the head-in-the-clouds; more the modern sort. On a par with his students. Streetwise possibly. Have to be careful. Not a browser either, the owner realized, watching Nick's eyes dart round the shelves. Wants something in particular.

"I'm looking for *Immagini palermitane della mia morte,*" Nick announced now. "The author is Martelucci or Martinucci, I'm not quite sure."

If he had said "I can't remember" instead of "I'm not sure," things would have taken a quite different direction; people who couldn't remember could be ripped off.

"Photographs, are they?" the bookseller asked, disguising his interest. "No, I haven't got it. You won't find it anywhere in Palermo."

"Won't I? Why not?"

The owner turned up his palms. "Because you won't."

He watched Nick's back as he stepped though the door up to pavement level and disappeared. Then he went to the shelves at the back of the shop and reached up to the top. This Martinucci guy's book wasn't there, in fact. He'd have to remember to ask Totò about him. The prof might well have had some project in mind: copies for his students and so on. Be worth looking into.

The next shop didn't have the book, but the third one did. "You can have a look over there," the young man at the counter said. He had the sports page of the *Giornale di Sicilia* open in front of him on the counter and was munching an *arancina*, a ham-filled rice ball, held in a square of white absorbent paper. "That's where the old photographs are." He wasn't at all sure about this, but it seemed to satisfy the guy anyway. The young man was standing in for his cousin, who'd had to go to the registry office that morning to collect a certificate of residence. Shouldn't be long now either, he thought, glancing at his watch.

Meanwhile, Nick had found the book. It was smaller and less conspicuous than he had somehow imagined it—not much bigger than his hand—with a grainy picture of what looked like a bomb site on its soft cover. The title was in black italics and the author's name in no-nonsense capitals underneath. Inside was a short preface with Martinucci's name and the date September 1952 below it. Nick flicked through the pages, stopping at one showing two naked children staring into the camera in front of a filthy hovel. The shadowy figure of a woman in the dark doorway could just be seen, looking as though she had wanted to escape from the lens. Hens pecked in the running gutter, and a dog lay in a patch of sunlight against the crumbling wall.

Another photo showed a man within the shafts of a cart, holding them high in his armpits as though he were the horse. The cart was piled with what Nick was almost sure were chunks of animal carcasses and bones. Once again there were dogs—two this time—sniffing around, and a barefoot child. The man wore a flat cap, an undershirt, and a pair of trousers held up with a twist of wire. A rag was tied round his neck, and he was scowling at the photographer.

There was no price on the book.

"I'll take this," Nick said at the counter. "How much is it?"

The young man looked up from his newspaper and took the book. He turned it over and looked inside the cover.

"*Trentamila.*"

Nick handed over the money so readily that the young man was sorry he hadn't doubled the price. "You've got a bargain there," he said, but the customer had already gone.

With the book in his jacket pocket Nick felt quietly triumphant. Suddenly hungry, he decided to walk to the open air café in Piazza Independenza where he could sit outside in the sun and think about Lea. He passed the cathedral, rising like one of those wonderfully intricate sand castles they used to build on English beaches. Then came Villa Bonanno on his left—more a plantation really than a park, its massed palms like phalanxed soldiers. Nick always expected to see turbaned caliphs wandering in the dappled shade or hear the strains of oriental stringed instruments whining among its trunks. After years in Palermo he still marveled at its mysterious beauty without knowing exactly where the magic came from.

Sitting at a table with the warmth of two jam-filled croissants and a cappuccino inside him, he watched children shouting and running about in the sunshine. He'd ring Lea on Monday. "I've found the book you were looking for," he'd say. "If we meet I can give it to you." Or: "Just by chance I was looking in this bookshop, and I came across that book you wanted. Perhaps we could meet and . . ." He wondered whether it would it be best to phone her at lunchtime or in the evening.

An Alsatian came purposefully toward him, nose to the ground. It stopped by his chair and seemed about to lift its leg when a shrill, commanding whistle from its owner sent it bounding away. There'd been an Alsatian like that next door to his parents' place. His mother hadn't liked it, said it had the mange. Nick had had a Christmas card from his mother yesterday: "I know this is early," she had written, "but I thought it might not get to you in time. Love and a very happy Christmas to both of you and the children." It had a picture of Santa Claus with a wreath of holly set jauntily on his head.

Monday: five minutes to one. Nick crossed the road, inserted a card in the public telephone next to the bus stop, and dialed the number he had found in the phone book. He was too tall to fit under the Perspex half-dome and had to stuff a finger into his free ear to shut out the roar of passing traffic. After five rings the receiver was lifted at the other end.

"Hallo. I'm afraid we're out at the moment. If you want to leave a message, please speak after the tone and we'll get back to you later: *ble-e-e-p.*"

Her voice.

He tried again after lunch, shutting himself in the sitting room while Paola was resting.

"Hallo. I'm afraid we're out at the moment. If you want to leave a message, please speak after the . . ."

At seven o'clock that evening he offered to go to the bakers and do any other shopping. He asked Paola how much bread she wanted for the next day.

"How much *I* want? How much *you* all want, you mean. I've no idea whether Sandro'll be in or not, he never tells me anything. Oh, just decide for yourself."

Halfway down the quiet backstreet he got his mobile out of his pocket and dialed Lea's number again.

"Yes?" A man's impatient voice.

"Er, hallo, this is Nick Stirling. I don't know if you remember me."

"*Who?*"

"Nick Stirling. You found my . . ." Oh for Christ's sake. "Is Lea there?"

"Hang on."

He heard irritable shouting: "Lea! Phone!" and after a couple of seconds, her voice.

"Hallo?"

"Lea, this is Nick. Nick Stirling. How are you?"

"Nick?" There was a brief pause. "Oh . . . *Nick*. I didn't recognize your voice. How are you? I was all wrapped up in this awful . . . awful thing. What time is it?"

"Just after seven. How's work?"

"Bloody. I've been up to Corleone today, then had to rush back and get these prints done, and they wouldn't work out and . . . Anyway, that's it for today, I swear."

He heard Genovese's muffled calling in the background.

"What?" Lea called back.

The voice came again, angrier this time.

"It's on the shelf over the computer," Lea called back, then to him: "Sorry, Nick, Dante can't find the . . ." She called again, "Well then it must be in the drawer."

"Perhaps I should phone later," Nick began.

"No, no, please don't, What's your news? University OK?"

All his carefully planned strategies suddenly seemed useless. "Lea, I've found that book you were looking for."

"What book?"

"The one with the photographs. By Francesco Martinucci."

"Really, where?"

He told her.

"Wonderful! D'you think they've still got a copy?"

"No, no . . . I've bought it for you."

"You *haven't*, have you? You shouldn't have done that. How much do I owe you?"

"Nothing. When can I give it to you?"

There was another pause. "Well, whenever you . . . I mean, you mustn't come here specially. I'll get to you somehow."

"What about tomorrow . . . at Longhi's? I'll be there at lunchtime."

"Mm, no. No, I can't, not tomorrow. Unless . . . unless . . . I might be able to manage a bit earlier, though—about elevenish. That's if you're free. What about that place opposite, what's it called? The one with sunshades outside. I'll buy you a coffee."

He'd finish his lecture early. "Yes, I can manage that. La Rosa, then."

Lea put the phone down, turned round, and almost collided with Dante. His glasses were pushed up on his forehead, and he had a cigar butt clamped between his teeth. "I still can't find it," he said. "Are you *sure* we brought it back?"

"Quite sure. Look, don't bother about it at the moment. You don't have to write the article tonight. I'll have a look for it."

Dante removed the cigar with finger and thumb and squeezed his eyes shut. "Lea, Lea. Too much bloody work, too many useless people who don't know whether they're fucking alive or dead. How can you possibly *hope* to get anything done?"

"Do you have to smoke that thing?" Lea said, wrinkling her nose. "It makes the most filthy smell."

"The news," he said, looking at his watch and switching on the television. "Bring me a whisky, will you? Here"—he handed her the cigar butt—"and take this too."

"Dante . . ."

"My sweet darling . . . a whisky." He slumped down in the armchair, pulling a tooled leather hassock toward him and putting his feet up with a grunt of satisfaction.

Lea came back with his drink, sat on the arm of his chair, and let her head fall onto his shoulder.

"What's—?" she began.

He took the glass from her. "Shhhh, let me listen."

She noticed he had got slightly heavier, the folds of his maroon sweater raised into sausages by the thickening midriff. Specks of ash lay over the soft wool, which already bore a stain like a miniature Ireland on the front. She had bought the sweater for his fifty-fifth birthday last September; very expensive it had been too.

She hardly ever thought of the age difference, and she only remembered Dante referring to it once in a moment of deep depression, saying she'd still be youthful and beautiful when he was a clapped-out old codger ready for the scrap heap, and she'd be wise to bugger off while she had the chance. That was the only time, almost as if—she had sometimes felt—he was trying to tell her to take their relationship at its face value. It suited her well that way because nothing ought to be considered permanent, especially when both had a broken marriage behind them.

She ran her fingers tenderly though his hair, lifting his reading glasses off with her other hand and twisting round to put them on the table. His right hand came up behind her shoulders and began stroking her own hair, then suddenly stopped. "Bloody idiot," he burst out at the screen. "You don't know what you're talking about. What does he mean. 'The Communists knew nothing about it?' How in fuck's name does he think they were able to keep the party going at all? *Charity*?"

"Dante . . ."

He jerked away from her grasp. "It's no good, I can't watch this shit, I just can't watch it. *Povera Italia, povera Italia.*"

Lea let a few seconds go by before asking what he wanted for supper. "What? Oh anything, anything. Or don't bother, I'm not really hungry. Bring me another of these, will you?" He held out his glass. "And pass me the paper. Hoping," he added as she put the *Corriere della Sera* into his hand, "that it'll be less sick-making than what the RAI serves up."

He caught hold of her as she was turning away. "Forgive me, my love, it's just that I can't stand stupidity—anything but that. I'll see to the supper. Just let me read the end of this. Then I'll make some sandwiches for us. Or soup." He began kneading her bottom through the black trousers. "And I haven't even asked you how your day went."

"Later," Lea said, breaking away gently. "I want to have a bath first—really relax. We'll talk later."

It was after one when he came to bed. Trying to undress in the dark he banged his shin against the chair leg and swore with the searing pain.

"What is it?" Lea mumbled.

"Nothing, *nothing*. Go back to sleep." He started furiously massaging his leg, easing out of his underpants as he did so. Lea was lying diagonally across the bed, and he climbed gently into the narrow space beside her, trying not to make the springs groan. The warmth and smell of her skin and her woman's juices under the duvet was overpowering, and he instantly forgot the pain in his leg and felt himself stirring with desire. He drew her toward him.

"Dante," she protested.

A police siren ee-awed by in the distance, then another. He started kissing her and caressing her breasts, feeling himself growing harder and harder until it became unbearable. Putting his hands on either side of her face, he pressed her head gently but firmly downward. *"Mettilo in bocca,"* he growled.

And she did.

He fell asleep almost at once, turning his back on her and breathing deeply and regularly. She lay quite still for a few minutes listening, not wanting to admit to herself how little it had meant.

"I've got a bloody awful character," Dante used to tell her in their early days together. "I don't know how you put up with me." He didn't say that anymore. It was more or less assumed that she knew, and accepted his outbursts. Which, she supposed, she did.

· · ·

She was woken by the rain at a quarter to seven the next morning. Rain meant she'd have to change her plans and think all over again about what to wear. Boots and a skirt or the black lace-ups under trousers? The best way to get to work would be for Dante to drop her off. Or she could go by bus, of course. Dante had never been known to take a bus in his life and would drive round the traffic-choked streets until he found a parking place, swearing and cursing Palermo and its politicos as he went. It became a matter of principle to him, and she had given up asking why he did it. Then she remembered Nick's phone call and that they were seeing each other.

The gray light was creeping gradually through the shutters, showing up the blades of the ceiling fan one after the other, the top of the wardrobe, the door jamb. Pitpatter *pit*, pitpatter *pit* was the rain dripping from the eaves onto the outside windowsill. She was aware of the empty space beside her in the bed, the smell of coffee, and the murmur of the radio through the closed door.

Nick saw her coming toward him under an umbrella. She almost collided with him at the entrance to the café.

"Nick!"

They sat at a corner table. "Now this is on me," she said, taking off her dripping jacket. "What are you going to have?" She hung it over the back of a chair and shook out her hair. "I'm not moving from here until it stops. They'll just have to wait."

When the coffee was in front of them Nick brought out the little book. He watched her while she leafed through it.

"Have you had a look at this yet?" she asked.

"Bits of it. It's very depressing."

"Mm. And yet the terrible thing is, you know, that it hasn't changed all that much, not really." She looked up. "I wish you'd let me pay for this. I feel awful."

"Let's say it's to thank you for returning the wallet," Nick said.

"You know I had nothing to do with that."

"Indirectly you did, and anyway it makes no difference. Why are you interested in the book—is it for your own?"

"No, no, that's all finished now—well, the important part anyway. No, it's just that I think these things—certain things—shouldn't be forgotten."

She told him that the text of her book was by the distinguished Italian writer Giorgio Fontanini (whom Nick had heard of). "I met him when I was working in Rome. He knew I was Sicilian and told me he'd been in Palermo not long before for a conference and had spent three whole days walking round the city and then come back, shut himself up in his study, and written this essay—account, *impression,* I don't know what you'd call it. He was so moved by his experience, by what he saw, that he's never been able to get it out of his system and said it would be with him for the rest of his life. When I read it I said I'd like to put photographs to it, and we decided to combine them in a book, but we didn't actually get down to doing anything right away. The hard part was deciding how to set it out, of course. You're bored out of your mind."

Nick shook his head. "No, go on."

"Well, we didn't want it to be just an illustration of his text or for the words to describe the images—the one had to complement the other. I mean, you couldn't have a photograph on the right-hand page and a piece of text on the other, and yet there had to be some kind of connection between the two. So we ended up by having perhaps two or three pages of the text followed by three or four photographs, and so on throughout the book."

"And do your photos match his words—I mean does he actually describe places in Palermo?"

"Sometimes he does—he *did* go to the Danisini, for instance." She tapped Martinucci's book. "That's one of the reasons I wanted this. Mostly, though, it's his impressions: people, markets, expressions on children's faces, statues . . ."

"And so your photos are . . ."

"Varied, things that struck me—still do. You'll see," she said smiling, "when it's out."

"When will that be?"

"Well it should be for Christmas, but things aren't going too well at the moment. Big launch, of course, thanks to him."

"Down here?"

"Mm. We both decided it was to be published in Sicily. With his name it could have been done by his own publishers in Milan—they wanted to, of course—or by Mondadori or *any* of the giants, but I'm glad we decided to do it here. It's right that way."

"So he'll be down?"

Lea nodded. "And you'll come? Force you to listen to all my drivel." She twisted round and looked out into the street. "Is it easing up or not? I don't really want to go to this thing."

"What?"

"I've got to see someone at the gallery at Porte Felice. But I'd rather not."

"Don't then."

"All right, I won't." She slowly and carefully spooned up the silted sugar in the bottom of her coffee cup and put it in her mouth, licking her top lip as the spoon came out.

"What about you?"

"What about me? I'm glad you're here. I'm glad you came."

She smiled. "Yes, but what about you?"

"I have to take a bloke from Channel Four up to Monreale."

"Today?"

"When I leave you." He looked at his watch. "At twelve."

"Channel Four, the television company? A program about what—the cathedral?"

He shook his head. "The Mafia."

She smiled ruefully. "Things don't change, do they?"

He thought vaguely of telling her that the only way a British television company would agree to finance a program on Sicily was if it mentioned the Mafia. Said it was what audiences "expected," Cathedrals, Mediterranean cooking, or holiday villages were all fine, but the whole lot could go by the board unless corruption (or better still, violent death) was brought in in one form or another. Instead, though, he asked her: "And you?"

"I'll be at the printers after lunch. Then I'm meant to be going to a concert tonight."

"I could come with you."

"To the concert? Do you like music?"

He shook his head. "No."

She laughed. "Well, then."

"Can I ring you later in the week?"

She didn't say anything at first, just scraped round the bottom of her cup again, frowning slightly. Then she picked up the book holding it vertically and tapping it gently three or four times on the tabletop. "I don't know."

"I'll give you my number. Then you can phone *me*." He took out his card, turned it over, and wrote the number of his mobile on the back. Then he handed it to her. She took it and glanced toward the window again. "Yes, I think it's stopped."

Nick said, "I like that sweater, and I like your hair like that."

"Thank you very much," Lea said, formally inclining her head. "And I like the way you pronounced the word *hair*. How do you say it in English?"

He told her.

"Hay-er," she said.

4

It was after six and Giulia still hadn't found a Christmas present for her mother. Nick was so much easier and was always delighted with whatever you gave him. Or said he was, anyway. She had bought him that years's Booker Prize in an English bookshop in Bologna and just hoped it was the kind of thing he read. It looked mind-numbing to her.

The only thing Paola liked was opera. She had an ancient collection of phonograph records—a great dusty pile from the late sixties and seventies, which she kept at the back of her wardrobe. For her last birthday they'd given her a CD player and some discs to go with it, so at least she could actually listen to something. But you couldn't keep giving her CDs—besides, she never seemed to play them, as far as Giulia could tell. What else? Books she hardly ever read—said she had no time. Clothes? Out of the question; her mother was totally disinterested in fashion. Chocolates she couldn't eat (Giulia didn't really believe this and hated herself for thinking it was just her mother's way of inviting pity). A plant was no good because Paola wasn't fond of flowers; their balcony at home had nothing on it except a grotesque cactus in rock-hard soil which nobody thought of throwing away. It suddenly shocked Giulia how little her mother seemed to enjoy life.

She'd been round all the obvious places, making her way through the crowds in Via Ruggero Settimo under the Christmas lights and gazing into one gleaming shop window after another with mounting despair. The assistants were short-tempered and disinterested or else offered inane advice. And there were only four days left, for Christ's sake. Nick said the Sicilians always left things to the very last moment, paying their road tax and bills, getting to the theater, doing their Christmas shopping, and so on. He was probably right.

Then she saw the bowl. It was in the window of a place selling Sicilian ceramics and pottery in one of the roads off Via Libertà. It was quieter here, the shops smaller and more exclusive, selling antiques, oriental rugs, and so on. A pair of dove-gray suede boots shared the window of a minute shoe shop with a pair of glittering high heels, both tastefully mounted on cream-painted blocks in their own spotlight. They looked as though they were just about to perform a little dance for the passersby. Rather an underplayed, dignified one. A gavotte, maybe.

The window of the ceramics shop contained the usual dishes, oil jars, vases, and statuettes but had some nice stuff as well. As part of its Christmas decorations, cherubs and angels made of ruched gold and silver paper had been placed at strategic points in the display, and candles glowed in the grottolike interior. The bowl Giulia had seen was no more than four inches across, with a wide powdery-blue band on a burnt orange background. It somehow reminded her of the colors in the still lake she had seen at Hadrian's Villa at Tivoli—sky and bare winter trees. It was something her mother couldn't take offense at and might even like. She could keep her earrings there. Paola had small, delicate ears.

The woman in the shop slipped the fur coat from her shoulders, draped it over the back of a chair, and brought down an identical bowl from one of the shelves. "Lovely isn't it?"

"Mm. How much is it?"

"Fifty-five thousand. It's hand-painted."

It had been an excellent day for Flora, and looked as though it was going to continue that way until Christmas. Must have taken in over a million since yesterday. Made up for all the lean weeks anyway. She seemed to be doing better than anyone in the street; poor Olimpia was having a bad time with the shoes— said business was worse than last year. And of course there was Maurizio. God knows what was going to happen there.

Giulia took the little bowl and held it in her palm, smoothing the sides with the tips of her fingers. It felt nice and friendly. Unthreatening.

"It's from Caltagirone," the woman said. "Or there's this one here, look—a little bigger with a *slightly* different design."

Giulia was aware of the overflowing ashtray on the cramped table and of the woman's nauseating flowery scent. "No, I like the small one best."

"Yes, so do I," Flora said confidentially, as though they shared a secret. "Is it for a present?"

"My mother."

"She'll love it," Flora said. "It's so feminine."

Giulia watched the woman making a big thing of wrapping the bowl in black and gold paper, tying it with an elaborate bow, and finally slipping one of her cards under the shiny string. How did she know her mother would *"love"* it? Silly cow.

After Flora had closed the door she sat down behind the table and gathered her fur about her. Five to seven. She'd give it another half hour, then lock up.

Retailing Sicilian pottery wasn't her livelihood. In fact, she didn't need to work at all. It was something she did—as her husband told their friends—"to pass the time." Well, it was true; sitting at home all day would drive anyone insane. She used to spend the mornings shopping and the afternoons playing canasta, then take in a film or go for a meal with friends in the evening. The usual thing. Then it palled. That was the trouble when you didn't have children, *couldn't* have them, there was nothing to fill the blank days. A few years ago her husband had suggested she open the shop.

"I don't know the first thing about pottery," she told him.

"That doesn't matter. You're good with people. Anyway," he added, "there's no need to kill yourself. Just start with mornings and see how you go."

Kill yourself. God, that was good.

He had seen to renting the place—knew the previous tenant—and to the supply of local pottery from a well-established firm. Later he had suggested she add a few pieces from further afield ("just to see how they go"). To her surprise, Flora found she rather liked the business of buying and selling. She never became really knowledgeable about her stock, believing people weren't really interested anyway and only bought things they liked the look of. Of course, she knew the basics: what was hand-painted, where and how a bowl or vase or plate should be displayed in a house, how it should be cleaned, and so on. She had got the shop really pretty—everybody remarked on it, and if it hadn't been for the bloody *pizzo* . . .

"We'll pay up like everybody else," her husband told her. "And forget about it. Anyway, it's a guarantee."

"A guarantee against what?"

"For heaven's sake, Flora, you weren't born yesterday. You're a *palermitana*, aren't you? We'll only get into trouble—real trouble—if you start questioning things, you know that as well as I do, and I'm not having you involved in any way. Besides," he added, "it's me who pays, so I don't know what you're worrying about."

It had started one morning four months after she'd opened the shop. A young man came in, nicely dressed, and had started looking round. He seemed very interested in a tall umbrella stand—the highly varnished yellow and purple one she'd had for ages—had wanted to know how much it was. She had told him and shown him another different one, which he seemed to prefer. Then he'd wanted to know the prices of the large *spaghettiere*— the bowls for serving pasta. After they had been talking for about ten minutes, he gave a great sigh and shook his head.

"Lovely, very nice indeed. It's for a friend of mine—well, his wife. He, poor guy's inside."

"Inside?"

"In prison, *signora*. Bad business, wife and four kids without a penny, really having to struggle: school, food, clothes. We all do what we can for them, but . . . that's the Italian state for you, *signora*, put a man away and forget all about his family. Can't even pay the rent." He shook his head and clicked his tongue sadly.

Still she didn't catch on. "Terrible," she agreed, slightly alarmed at the way the transaction was going. "Well, I'm sure she'll like this *spaghettiera* here."

The man slowly reached two fingers inside his jacket and brought out a packet of cigarettes. With raised eyebrows he offered it to Flora, who shook her head. "What would be nice would be if I could count on you to make a small contribution to the man's family," he went on. "Just a small monthly sum." He looked around the shop. "You're doing nicely here, I can see, and you won't miss a couple of hundred thousand a month. You're a real lady, I can tell that. It would make such a difference to his wife and children."

Flora had opened the till with trembling hands and handed over the money, heart pounding, mouth dry. It disappeared into the same inside jacket pocket.

"And I'll take this bowl for her too. I know she'll appreciate it." He lit his cigarette with a click of the lighter. "*Arrivederci, signora,* and my compliments on your delightful shop."

And that was what her husband said she wasn't to question. After that first visit the man came back every two or sometimes three months, always polite, well dressed, and always willing to chat. She hated and feared the sight of him. Olimpia at the shoe shop paid up. So did the gay guy selling the silk flowers on the other side. But Maurizio, two doors up from her, didn't. She was scared for him. They all were. But he wouldn't listen.

"You know what I think about it, Flora. I've built up this business from scratch, entirely on my own. Nobody's helped me. I've worked extremely hard, and I've worked honestly, and I'm not letting anybody threaten me, it's as simple as that. The first time I went to Tunisia and saw their carpets and decided I was going to import and sell them here, that was that. I've got to know the makers and producers one by one, built up a relationship of trust with them—and that's needed years of patience because they're not easy people. From there I went on to Persian and oriental, and the result you can see for yourself: the finest collection of carpets in the city—probably in the South. People have been coming to me for years, and now I've opened this second place, I don't intend to let any stinking little mafioso come round for his cut. They'll have to drag it out of me.

"I'm not asking you or Olimpia or any of the others to do what I'm doing, Flora, because everyone must decide for themselves, but just think: if nobody paid up—*nobody*—extortion would come to an end. It's as simple as that."

"I'm scared out of my life, Maurizio."

"Of course you are, we all are, but that's no excuse. It's the *injustice* of it, Flora, surely you can see that? For Christ's sake, we live in a democracy where everybody is free to decide and has the right to live in safety."

"But what about Grassi and the others who have been murdered?"

Maurizio sighed. "What do you want me to say—that they were brave people? They were people with a belief in what's right and"—he raised his eyebrows and closed his eyes in the gesture Sicilians use to show weary resignation—"faith in our government. For what that's worth," he added bitterly.

"That's exactly what I'm getting at," Flora said. "The police aren't going to do anything, you know they're not. If I *knew* we were protected, I'd . . . well I'd think of doing . . . doing what you are," she finished lamely.

He didn't expect her to understand, her sort didn't—or couldn't. He'd met her husband: look after number one and bugger the others, that was him. The very worst kind. He condemned them bitterly but knew they would never change. Olimpia, on the other hand, who had the little shoe shop, might just possibly be persuaded to join him. He had tried talking to her, too.

"I know you're right, I *know* you are," she said. "And I really wish I had the guts not to pay up. But then I start thinking of all the work I've put into the business, all the effort and all the money. I don't want to see it all destroyed, because that's what they'll do, Maurizio, you know very well. And I've got the family. First it'll be a smashed window or the car set on fire and then . . ."

"Olimpia, I'm not asking you to do anything, just try and understand that."

"But you make me feel like a shit. And you're right."

Maurizio had had unequal success with the other shop and restaurant owners in the vicinity; nobody wanted to know, none of them were willing to risk their livelihood and their lives. All preferred to pay up rather than live in constant fear of reprisals. And it was a very real and justified fear too, because the Mafia would continue to operate along well-tried lines against its enemies—it had already done so. One of Maurizio's shops had been ransacked and set alight—everything burned to a cinder, billions of lire worth of stock. But he'd got the business going again, and this new place here was a small triumph of determination. *Small* perhaps wasn't the right word, and people were always amazed when he took them down the spiral staircase into the basement and showed them the huge stock he kept. He'd had the whole two hundred and seventy-five square yards damp-proofed, white-washed, and set at a constant temperature, and it made a perfect warehouse. His customers had returned, word had got around, and business was good.

Then that filthy little bastard had appeared and demanded an exhorbitant sum. Maurizio had kicked him out, and it was a full month and a half before he had received a second visit. Again Maurizio had kicked him out. That night his car tires had been slashed, and two weeks later a bomb had exploded at midnight in the little courtyard behind the shop. Nobody had been hurt, and there was only superficial damage, but the incident had been reported in the press.

He knew that until owners of businesses organized themselves into a syndicate, things would never change. Never. So that no matter how progressive and open-minded southern Italy professed to becoming, it would always be a parody of a civilized society. The police wouldn't act (had their "hands tied," as he was sick to the teeth of hearing), and individuals were always going to be afraid for themselves and their families. Maurizio had a wife and a son, both of whom knew what was happening. They had never tried to dissuade him, and he respected and loved them deeply for it. If he died, well, so be it. He couldn't ignore the fact that none of the people who, like him, had refused to pay up were alive today. He had provided for his wife and son in his will and left a letter telling them—if the worst came to the worst—not to let the press make a hero or a martyr of him. "What counts," he wrote, "is that justice is done and that we never forfeit our freedom or lose faith in God."

· · ·

Nick had been trying to find a present for Paola as well, only now it was Christmas Eve, and he knew he was going to end up with a book. He imagined her opening the wrapping and not saying anything for the first few moments, then thanking him politely and putting it aside. It was common knowledge in the family that she didn't read very much—hardly at all—so Nick's choice would be seen as a sign he didn't care.

Whatever I gave her would be wrong, though, he thought. He remembered getting her a little silver photograph frame for her last birthday. "What am I going to put in this?" she asked him with a stiff little laugh. "A portrait of us two?" He never saw it again.

But then you couldn't win. Not with Paola. Getting her nothing at all would be far worse. He edged his way sideways into the packed bookshop between the two detecting security bars. Perhaps something on music—opera, composers, or something like that. She just *might* find it interesting. Where would it be? Upstairs probably with the art books. Or maybe not.

He stopped a distracted-looking girl with an armful of books and a card ("Stefania") pinned crookedly to her sweater.

"Eh?"

"Books on music," he repeated. "Where can I find them?"

He was having to shout above the noise and Vivaldi's piped *Four Seasons*. The girl ignored him, stretched up on tiptoe, and called out to somebody over his shoulder. "I've got three of them here! Can you get the others? The customer's over at the cash desk."

Nick tried again, but she had disappeared.

It took him another quarter of an hour to find something called *Musica all'aria aperta, Music in the Open Air,* a beautifully produced volume of photographs of musicians against ravishing Italian landscapes. Some played in medieval squares or on a long-boat floating down the Arno, others against the backdrop of floodlit castles and in an art *nouveau* bandstand overlooking Lake Maggiore. A grand piano stood on a deserted moonlit beach. A lone trumpeter played on the lip of a crater on Mount Etna. Surely Paola couldn't object to that?

Walking back along Via Ruggero Settimo with his purchase, Nick saw Lea coming toward him. "More books?" she said smiling when they had shaken hands. She had on a long gray coat with the rainbow scarf wound round and round the upturned collar. Her hair spilled out over the top.

"Presents," Nick said. "Last-minute ones."

She nodded and held up a carrier bag. "Me too."

"You didn't ring."

She shook her head. "I know. I kept meaning to, really, but never got round to it."

Nick put out his hand and touched her coat lightly as though testing that it was real. "What happened about the book presentation? I never got your invitation."

"Nobody has. We've had to put the whole thing off. Giorgio—Fontanini—was in a car crash. He's been in plaster for two weeks now, so it's going to have to be next month." She made a face of comic hopelessness. "And who's going to buy books in January?"

"I will," Nick said, gently twisting her coat button, secretely pleased that the illustrious man's misfortune had prolonged the chance of seeing her. "Have the presentation just for me."

She smiled and asked him how his visit to Monreale had gone with the journalist and when the program on the Mafia would be out. He said he didn't know, and it would probably be better anyway if it never saw the light of day, because that sort of thing did Sicily no good. She nodded her agreement. "As long as you get paid for the work you put into it," she said.

They were being jostled quite painfully now by passersby, some of whom pulled bags and parcels angrily out of the way and clicked their tongues in irritation at being obstructed in this their last-minute rush.

"We're in everybody's way here," Lea said, "and you are about to pull that button off my coat." She put her hand over his and removed it with a smile of exaggerated politeness.

A traditional bagpipe player, the *zampognaro,* dressed in fleecy jerkin and cross-laced trousers, brushed past them, the inflated goatskin under his arm giving out a hideous two-tone whine. Mouth lewdly stuffed with the pipe, eyes bulging, he looked Lea up and down appraisingly. Nick drew her into a shop doorway to let him pass.

"That's the only thing I've ever heard them play here," he shouted, meaning the Italian carol *"Tu scendi dalle stelle"* issuing dirgelike from the pipes. "Don't they know anything else?"

Lea laughed and cupped her gloved hand round his ear. " *'Ave Maria'?"*

The player passed, and Lea held out her hand to Nick. "I'll have to get on now," she said. "Happy Christmas if I don't see you again."

"Before January," he added.

"Yes, before January."

• • •

"Squisito," *signora* Lentini said, sitting back and wiping her mouth on her napkin. *"Sei stato bravissimo."* Despite her eighty-six and three-quarters years, Nick's mother-in-law still had a prodigious appetite, devouring the traditional turkey and trimmings with more relish than anybody else. But then, Nick supposed, there wasn't much to look forward to when you got to her age, so why not enjoy your food? He watched her bring her face close to the plate, soak up the gravy with chunks of crusty wholemeal bread, and thrust them one after the other into her mouth: *uno, due, tre....* Interesting how her hands never trembled when she ate.

"You should learn to cook like that," she said now, turning to Paola.

"Why should I bother," her daughter replied, "when he does it all?"

Nick picked up the ruby red wine and raised his eyebrows.

"No, no," *signora* Lentini protested. "I don't want to fall asleep before the pudding." She gave her plate a tiny shove forward, giving tacit permission for it to be removed, and touched her lips again with the napkin. "You've hardly eaten anything," she told her daughter accusingly, looking at the untouched slices of white meat, little heaps of carrots, sprouts, and roast potatoes.

"I'm not hungry, Mamma, and Nick knows I don't eat sprouts." She pushed one of the tightly furled globes to the edge of her plate with her fork. "They make me ill just to look at them."

"Well, I eat them," Giulia said. "Look. And I can't stand them either." She popped one into her mouth and made a face. "I do it for Daddy, you see," she explained to her grandmother. "Otherwise he gets all upset."

"I certainly don't," Nick said, noticing how his daughter's cheeks were flushed from the wine. "I don't care what you do—leave them, throw them away. You're the loser if you can't appreciate one of the world's greatest vegetables."

"Of course," Giulia went on, picking up a sprout between thumb and finger, "instead of eating them I could always throw them back at the cook." The bright green ball landed on her father's plate, splashing gravy over his pullover.

"Oh God, I'm sorry, I didn't mean to." She tipped back her chair, rocking with laughter. Sandro joined in while Paola looked on stonily.

"What's going on, what's happening?" *signora* Lentini inquired, turning her head first one way then the other.

"Nothing, Mamma, nothing."

After the Christmas pudding, which Paola left untouched on her plate and her mother put away in two huge dessertspoonfuls, the children disappeared.

"And now, *lo sherry*," *signora* Lentini said to Nick. "To finish off the meal properly." She twisted round in her seat trying to locate the bottle.

"You shouldn't, you know," Paola said. "It's bad for your blood pressure."

"Nonsense. Once a year won't hurt. Isn't that right, Neek?"

"Of course it's all right," he said, pouring her out a generous glassful. "Oh come on, for heaven's sake, Paola. At least for *Christmas*." But she had already covered her glass as though to protect its virginity.

He poured one for himself, lifted it, and clinked glasses with the old lady.

"*Salute!*"

"*Cin cin!*" she replied and pursed her lips over the sweet golden liquid. "Wonderful!"

"I don't know why you go on so about it," Paola said, watching them with distaste. "There's nothing special about it at all."

"Ah, but there is, isn't there, Neek?"

"Of course. This is the real English sherry. Can't beat it."

Paola gave a snort and pushed back her chair. "Where are you going to have your rest, Mamma—on Giulia's bed or in the sitting room? Come on now, I'll help you."

"I'm not tired yet. Where have the children got to, Neek?"

Five minutes later she was snoring gently in the armchair, crimson paper hat askew over one eye.

"It's too much for her," Paola told Nick. "She's absolutely exhausted. And you shouldn't let her eat all that."

"I don't *let* her, she enjoys it."

The idea of having to put *signora* Lentini into a home was still deeply repugnant to Nick, but he knew she wouldn't be able to cope for much longer on her own. He remembered with a shiver of horror the house he and Paola had visited the week before— Villa della Serenità or something, it was called—a shuttered two-story building set back from a divided highway on the outskirts of town where traffic thundered past in an unending stream. On one side of the road (known as an "avenue" because of a line of stunted horse chestnuts down the median strip) stood the luxurious homes of Palermo's professional classes, whose considerable wealth had quite possibly been accumulated by decades of skillful tax evasions. Here, in their emerald-lawned gardens, the families of heart surgeons liked to barbecue juicy steaks and splash about in their swimming pools, protected (as they liked to think) by ten-foot-high walls topped by shards of glass. No names appeared on the bells next to the massive wrought iron gates against which hairless dogs would fling themselves, curling back their lips and breaking into hysterical barking at the rare passerby.

Although the hastily erected old people's homes opposite were in a different class architecturally, Nick felt they were still pervaded by the same undercurrents of the rather underhand dealings that characterized the billionaires' residences. He had never given much thought to the matter before, but care of the elderly, he now realized, was obviously a highly profitable business, requiring little provision for the comfort and sustenance of its "guests" and bringing considerable rewards to its owners. He was right: like Palermo's funeral directors, with whom they operated very closely, the owners and directors of the homes were doing very nicely indeed. Kindness and respect for human dignity didn't really concern them.

When nobody answered the bell at Villa della Serenità, Nick pushed open the front door. A vase of puce and lemon yellow plastic flowers stood on a dresser that was as richly brown and highly varnished as a chocolate lake. Above, ornaments crowded flimsy shelves. A musty smell clung to the crimson striped wallpaper. When still nobody appeared, they peered round what might have been the sitting room door and saw seven or eight silent figures in a semicircle of armchairs around a flickering television screen. All were fully and formally dressed, although it was only half-past nine in the morning. Nick nodded to the room.

"Buongiorno."

Heads slowly turned, but nobody answered his greeting. It was as if they were drugged. One heavily made up woman held her hand protectively on a large leather handbag beside her on the floor as though waiting any minute to be collected.

"Let's get out of here," Nick said.

The next home was even worse, with plywood partitions cutting the rooms into hospital-like cubicles. They got glimpses of pulley-assisted ablutions in slimy-floored bathrooms and overheard impatiently raised voices and the hopeless drag and scrape of walking frames.

"We could never leave anyone anywhere like this," Nick said softly. "Never."

At last Paola had been told about a place run by nuns not far from where she worked. "They say it's clean," she told Nick, "and that she'll share a room with just one other person. It's near me too, so I'll be able to go and see her most days."

A tiny white-veiled nun opened the heavy front door and let them into a vast atrium where a woman inside a glass cubicle sat running a rosary through her fingers and watching a portable television screen. Upstairs, another nun led them along a bright, airy corridor, punctuated at regular intervals by pots of trailing ivy. At the end of the corridor stood a life-size statue of the Virgin Mary, as though, Nick mused, to reward visitors for having persevered thus far. The doors of the bedrooms on either side stood open, and Nick got glimpses of frail little women propped up against mountains of pillows.

"This is the refectory," the nun said, opening a glass door. "A three-course lunch every day." Pale blue cloths covered geometrically positioned tables with places laid for supper. She closed the door and turned briskly to the right. "And these are the bathrooms." Shining basins and bidets, lavatories with their seats closed, towels neatly folded on the rails. Where was the catch, Nick wondered.

"This is the room your mother will occupy," the nun went on. She turned to them testily. "Whose mother is it?"

"Mine," Paola said.

The nun grunted and opened the door. Nick saw two immaculately made beds covered by white counterpanes. Curtains of cool white net hung at the window. "Each room has its own balcony," the nun went on. "The telephones are outside. *Prego.*" She stood back and motioned them to exit ahead of her, then closed the door with chilling precision.

A recess at the end of the corridor contained two rows of easy chairs facing each other. Three of them were occupied by women doing nothing. Copies of the Catholic magazine *Famiglia Cristiana* were neatly arranged on a low coffee table.

"This is the area for relaxation," the nun said. She turned snappily to one of the women. "Have you had your medicine, Maria?"

"Yes, sister."

The nun grunted again. "The television room's down the other end," she said to Paola. "I'll take you downstairs now."

Signora Lentini moved in at the end of the week. "It's a lovely place, Mamma," Paola had told her. "You'll have your own room."

"To myself?"

"No, you'll share, but it's much better that way, you won't be lonely."

"I'm never lonely," *signora* Lentini said. "How long am I staying there—just while you're away?"

They had decided to tell her they were going to Bologna for a week to visit Giulia. Nick felt a terrible sense of betrayal toward the old lady.

"We'll see," Paola countered. "I'm sure you'll like it there, Mamma. The nuns are really nice."

"Nuns are never nice," her mother replied. "They're money-grabbing, mean people. What about all my things?"

As soon as the week was up, Nick went to visit her. He found her sitting in the "relaxation area" staring straight ahead.

"Ida."

She didn't move or reply.

"Ida? It's me, Nick."

She turned her head: "Neek," she said slowly. There had been a dramatic and rather frightening change in her, although it wasn't easy to define; something about her gaze and the set of her mouth. It was as though, Nick suddenly realized, the joy had gone out of her. He leaned over and put an arm gently round her, but she stayed rigid under his touch.

"They won't let me keep the light on at nights," she said, "so I can't read my magazines. They turn the lights out at nine o'clock. They won't let us rest after lunch because they don't want the bedclothes disturbed during the daytime."

"You hate having a nap after lunch," Nick tried to chide her. "You always say you're not sleepy."

Not the flicker of a smile. "Where's Paola? Why hasn't she come to see me?" She turned to look at him. "When am I coming home?"

There was a shuffling sound from the corridor, and a woman came limping very slowly into the rest area. "Hallo Ida," she said. "Is this your son?" Her hand trembled on the handle of the walking stick.

Signora Lentini ignored her. "Are you taking me home today?" she repeated to Nick. It was an entreaty.

"She doesn't eat anything," the limping woman told Nick. "She doesn't like lentils."

His mother-in-law started to rise from the armchair. "I'll get my things together now," she said. "It won't take a minute."

Slightly alarmed, he helped her up. "Let's walk along the corridor," he suggested. "Get a bit of exercise."

He wanted to say he hated her being here, that he could see how she was suffering and that if only he had . . . well, *what*? If only they—he and Paola—had room in the flat (well, they *did* have room, didn't they? Plenty of it), Ida could come and live with them. "She doesn't want to," Paola had repeatedly told him. "She likes to be independent. I know my mother, she'd never want to be with us." Well, maybe not, but she doesn't want to be here either.

A nun bustled up to them. It was the same one who had shown them round the first day. She nodded curtly to Nick. "Your mother-in-law isn't eating," she said. "If this goes on we'll have to get the doctor to give her something." She turned a cruel gaze on the old lady. "You'll have to start eating, Ida. You don't want to get ill, do you?"

When she had gone, Nick asked what the food was like. Wasn't it nice, was that why she wasn't eating? With his arm under her elbow he steered the old lady slowly along the corridor. A door banged somewhere ahead and he heard the nun's angry raised voice.

"They give us lentils every day with the pasta," *signora* Lentini said now. "Every day. And just one roll, which is always stale. We only get an apple for fruit. I said I wanted a bit of chicken, but they wouldn't give it to me. They gave us meatballs once, and they were all gristle." She stopped, and he realized they were standing outside her room. "I'll pack my case now."

Nick suddenly hated Paola for not being there, for not fulfilling her duty as a daughter. Duty? It was his duty too, he couldn't get out of it that easily. He put a hand gently on his mother-in-law's arm. "Paola'll be here to see you this afternoon, Ida. Wait until she comes." The cowardly way out.

She gave him a funny look. "You don't want me to come home, do you? You want to leave me here. If you leave me here, I'll die."

It hit him in the belly. "Don't say that, Ida. You mustn't say that."

"Never put me in a home," his father had told him once. "Just finish me off." Said jocularly enough but deadly serious underneath. "When I'm old and useless just throw me away." Nick's mother had laughed, given him a playful push, and told him not to say things like that. Nick must have been about fifteen at the time, so that made his father only forty-five—far too young to think about dying.

"We're worried about you being at home on your own, that's all," he told his mother-in-law truthfully now. "What would happen if you fell? Who would there be to help you?" They were still standing on the threshold to her room. "Paola and I wanted you to be here so you could be looked after. We thought it a nice place for you." But had *he*? Not really.

She was looking down at the floor and trembling slightly with the strain of standing still. "If you won't let me come back with you, I'll go and sit down again." And with that she turned and started back down the corridor. Halfway along, the nun appeared out of one of the rooms and began propelling her forward. "Come on now, Ida, it's nearly lunchtime. You don't want to miss your lunch, do you?"

Dante lay in the bath, a cigar clamped between his teeth, a glass of whisky cradled in his left hand draped over the rim. With his head resting on the broad curve of enamel at the top of the tub he idly watched the milky water rising and falling with his breathing. A swirl of scum drifted over the dark hairs on his chest, and he rubbed at them rythmically with his free hand so that they sprang up again. Just beneath the surface, his navel was a dark cave large enough to insert a finger into but too small to clean properly. Sometimes—especially in summer—it got clogged up with an odorous cheesy substance which he gouged out slowly and lovingly with a cotton bud.

All his secretions pleased him, from the soft toffee-textured wax in his ears, which he removed with a fingernail, to the crusty fragments of mucous that collected in his nostrils. He enjoyed sloughing off the body's dead cells: levering the hardened pads of dandruff from his scalp, which sometimes, much to his satisfaction, came away with one or two hairs embedded in them. There was the dry skin on the inside of his ankles, which after a softening in the bath yielded to vigorous circular rubbing, and there were the oily layers of accumulated sweat in the small of his back, which he scraped off and watched floating away like black sickle moons over the surface.

After his soak he liked to sit on the closed lavatory seat, balance one bare foot after the other on the edge of the bidet, and produce toenail clippings, which would skitter across the floor to unseen corners, never to be found again. He would run one of Lea's thin wooden orange sticks round the base of each nail, collect the damp gray skin between thumb and forefinger, and roll it into tiny balls. Then he would pare the bottom of his heels with a metal scoop. It annoyed him that he wouldn't have time for any of that this evening.

With a sigh, he placed his glass on the tiled floor, stuck the cigar stub in an ashtray, and heaved himself into a sitting position, causing a tidal wave to rush down from his chest toward the taps at the far end. Then he let his knees fall apart, brought both hands to his penis, and gently peeled back the foreskin. After removing the ring of smegma that clung to the sides of the shaft and under the rim, he ran the pad of his thumb over the tip, gently squeezing and pinching, finishing off the operation by opening and closing the organ once or twice like a telescope until it was quite clean.

It had been a mistake to have a bath at this time of the evening, when all he wanted was to collapse into an armchair with a fresh whisky and the paper, which he hadn't opened all day. The thought of having to get dressed, get the car out, and drive across town dragged a groan from him. Entirely his own fault— he should have refused the invitation. They were all Lea's people, after all—the ones involved in the book, a few of whom he had already met and had no wish to get to know better. But she had given up parts of her life and time for him, so it was right he should do the same for her. It was the unwritten part of their arrangement. He remembered their meeting in Rome when they had both been working on the same paper. He was living in that tiny place near Piazza Barberini, which he had been thinking of giving up for some time. It seemed absurd to keep it on when he had the vast flat down in Sicily, and anyway, there was nothing he was doing in Rome that he couldn't do in Palermo. It made even better sense when he got to know Lea. After they'd been together five—or was it six?—months, he couldn't remember, he told her of his plans and asked if she felt like coming with him. Think it over before you decide, he told her, you may hate the place.

"Why should I?" she said. "Don't forget, I'm Sicilian."

"How long have you been away, though?"

"Since I was five."

"You may hate it," he said again. "And you may get to hate me."

She said that yes, that was a possibility.

That had been three years ago, and they were still together. Levering himself up, Dante yanked at the plug and reached for the bronze-colored bath towel behind his head. Palermo wasn't as bad as he remembered it—in fact, it was pleasanter in many ways than Rome. Distances weren't so great, and he hadn't realized just how much he'd missed the presence of the sea while he was in the capital. Here it was never more than minutes away. The real surprise, though, was Lea, who fell for the place completely, saying she felt her roots here.

He had told his two sons up north that he would be moving to Palermo and dutifully sent his love to their mother. Didn't mention Lea to them—after all, that was *his* business. Anyway, he had never been close to the boys, even before his divorce, and now that they were adults, even less so. Did he love them? Yes, he supposed he did: his own flesh and blood. The question was, did they love him? The truth was he had been useless, a hopeless father, and they were far better off without him.

Dante watched the water disappearing down the drain, bending first to one side, then to the other, like the funnel of a hurricane. He placed the sole of one foot over the vortex to feel its pull the way he used to do as a child, then got out, stood before the full-length mirror, and started toweling himself.

Although he considered the aging of his body only a temporary state, which would revert back after a few weeks' dieting and sensible exercise, his reflection still managed to depress him. How was it those heavy rolls of flesh had somehow appeared on his lower back *without his realizing it*? He twisted round the better to see them, took a deep breath, and lifted his chest and chin. The rolls were absorbed. That was all you needed to do, just hold yourself properly: a question of deportment. But he knew it wasn't. And the realization pained him. How can she bear to make love to me? he wondered. He bent down to dry his legs, noticing not for the first time how thin they had become. A few more years and he'd turn into one of those barrel-chested, stick-legged dwarves. *For God's sake!*

At least his hair was still all right, he thought, running his fingers through the coarse gray mass; teeth as well. He bent nearer to the glass and stretched his lips in a humorless smile: hadn't been a bad-looking guy. Could get back like he was too. Lea said it was his own fault he had started to put on weight because he never walked anywhere. Perhaps she was right. He was really going to make an effort from now on.

Her voice came softly from the other side of the door: "Dante, have you nearly finished? It's after nine."

"Two minutes," he called back.

The party wasn't as bad as he'd feared, despite that old shit Fontanini hobbling about with a stick and telling everybody what a *spiritual* experience being confined to a hospital bed had turned out to be. Compensating for his lack of originality, for he wasn't a great writer and never would be. Some of his stuff was *passably* good but certainly no more than that. The man had always known how to sell himself, that was it; who to stay in with. Dante didn't blame him for that. After all, you make a choice in life. His own refusal of any form of political compromise hadn't got him anywhere in his career, had it? So there you were. Good luck to Fontanini. But as far as the book went, it was Lea's pictures—heartbreaking, delicate, searing, and extraordinary—that would make it, certainly not the man's text. Still, there had been some attractive women at the party and plenty of booze, which were always a bonus.

"Let me drive," Lea said now as they stumbled out into the silent three o'clock streets. He just muttered his dissent and climbed in behind the wheel.

"You've drunk a lot," Lea said.

"Yup." He fumbled at the dashboard. "Get in." They tore away from the curb, the left front tire flattening an empty plastic bottle with a deafening report.

"That bastard's going to get all the glory, thanks to you," Dante said suddenly as they swung round into Via Roma. "You realize that? I've always thought him a fraud." Lea didn't answer, just stared at the dead straight road unraveling ahead of them. Amber pools of light from the street lamps fell at regular intervals onto barred and shuttered shop fronts, illuminating unknown alleyways and teetering piles of black plastic-wrapped rubbish. Three tall Nigerians lolloped loose-limbed along the narrow pavements, punching each other playfully on the shoulders. One of them waved crazily at the car and let out a whoop as it shot past.

Dante's criticism was partly envy. When he spoke about his own writing, it was to say he was a journalist—a recorder and commentator of facts—nothing more. But she knew he tried to write, *wanted* to write. Novels—perhaps even poetry. Once—ages ago—when she had asked him, he said he had no time or inclination to indulge himself in that kind of thing, but she had found some pages of manuscript he'd been working on. Quite simply, he was jealous of Fontanini, of his success and of her working with him, and it suddenly occurred to Lea that he would like to have taken the man's place.

"I know he's not a particularly talented writer," she said. "I've never thought he was. But I think this book is good, and it *won't* be just down to me if it's a success. Okay, so he'll get most of the glory. I can't do anything about that."

Dante hawked noisily. He brought the car to a halt in the middle of the road, opened his door a crack, leaned down, and spat onto the road. "I wouldn't be so sure about that," he said, wiping his mouth, slamming the door, and accelerating. "You deserve recognition, and he bloody well knows it." He drew on his cigar and blew out a plume of smoke. "Too full of himself is Mr. Fontanini."

A skeletal dog stepped into the road, head and tail drooping. Lea let out a screech and they braked just in time. It stopped, lifted soulful eyes, and regarded them through the windscreen.

"I told you to—" she began.

He laid a warm, almost feverish hand on her thigh. "Never fear," he said gravely. "No man or beast will ever lose its life when I am at the wheel." The hand traveled up beneath her skirt and began massaging her thigh. "You were the most beautiful woman there tonight. Did you know that? I want to get you home."

"Dante . . ."

"Go on, get out of the way," he said to the dog and, when it still didn't move, pressed the horn impatiently in a double blast. "Shift your bony canine arse, will you!"

"Dante!"

Slowly the animal began to move, but before it had reached the sanctuary of the opposite pavement Dante put his foot down so that the car shot forward and began bouncing like a maddened toy over the cobbled surface. His right hand, freed from the gear lever, went back under Lea's skirt and resumed its climbing. She felt the hot nicotined-ingrained fingers reach her crotch, then slip underneath the smooth cotton of her panties.

"No, Dante, no. Not now. Not here."

The fingers went on exploring, and she turned her face imploringly toward him. "Look, don't . . . I can't."

He took no notice, the pads of his fingers now delving and stroking. She just managed to push his hand away before going under.

"I said don't, Dante. Not here. When we get back."

He said nothing, just transferred his hand to his cigar butt. They traveled on in silence for a few minutes. Then he said: "You're not going off me, are you?" It was said so gravely that she turned to look at him. "Not falling for that *coglione* Fontanini?"

"No," Lea said. "I'm not."

"Or for anybody else?"

The car swung left at the still brightly lit Politeama square, cutting across the 101 bus lane and turning left toward home. Lea had a sudden image of Nick and the way he unfolded his tall body when he stood up, the way he had looked at her in the café. Then the picture was gone. Dante was still waiting beside her for his answer.

"No," she said. "Nobody else."

They got back, put the car into the garage, and let themselves into the flat without exchanging another word. Dante went straight into the sitting room and poured himself a whisky.

"I'm going to bed," Lea said. "Are you coming?"

He shook his head and bent down to untie his shoelaces, his face turning crimson with the effort.

"Well, don't be too late."

"Mm?"

"I said don't stay up too late," Lea said again. She wanted to put her arms around him and lay her head on his shoulder but knew it wasn't the right moment. It wasn't quite the right sentiment either: an affectionate gesture rather than a sexual one. That was what had upset him in the car.

"Goodnight, then," she said. But he had already turned his back on her and switched on the television.

Lea knew she wanted to see Nick again, knew that if she didn't get in touch, he would, that it was a matter of days—tomorrow perhaps, or the day after. What happened after that she wouldn't think about. She turned a corner of the duvet down and slipped beneath its softness. She didn't want to think about Dante now either. That would all come later.

It was just the one room with a vast painted slightly concave ceiling. A curved wooden staircase led up to the bedroom on the open mezzanine. You could sit up quite comfortably in the double bed or lean on the balustrade and look down at what was going on below, but a tall person had to stoop when he straightened up—Nick had discovered that for himself. Mario was shortish, though, so this wouldn't have worried him at all.

The pair of French windows in the main area opened onto a narrow slab of white marble balcony measuring no more than two by six feet overlooking Corso Vittorio Emanuele. Below, the traffic roared and choked out fumes all day long, and pedestrians had to walk sideways like crabs along the strips of pavement. It was at night when the flat really came into its own, when the traffic died away and the floodlights came silently on, turning the cathedral and tall palms opposite into a thing of delicate and almost unreal beauty.

Mario had bought the flat (the smallest of six that had been created from the original patrician palazzo) several years before but only used it occasionally when he was in Palermo. He had been a student of Nick's back in the late seventies: witty, generous, good company, and hopeless at English. His father, who had a small business making wall and floor tiles, wanted his son to better himself and get a university degree, but Mario had no interest in tiles and even less in studying. He loved women and women loved him, and he was taking lessons from Nick so that he could impress female Anglo-Saxon tourists and get them into bed as quickly as possible. He forgot everything he was taught immediately after the lesson was over, so Nick had to write, "You have gorgeous eyes, like clear pools of water" and "Can I show you over the cathedral? Then we can have dinner and go back to my place afterward" phonetically in an old exercise book.

Then Mario's father died suddenly from a stroke, and his son had to give up his studies and take over the business. Soon after that Nick married, and they lost touch. It must have been about five or six years ago that they had met up again. Mario had turned out to be an entrepreneurial wizard and was now selling hand-painted Sicilian tiles throughout Italy and all over South America. "Argentina and Venezuela, mostly," he told Nick after they had embraced again. "God, those lessons were crazy, weren't they?" He had gone on to complete his studies, married, divorced, and now lived alone, dividing his time between a house in Buenos Aires, a large flat in Milan, and the pied-à-terre here in Palermo.

He told Nick that if he ever needed the flat ("for anything—you never know") it was his. They had a quick drink together, exchanged phone numbers, and then parted.

Nick invited him over to dinner a month or so later, where to his faint astonishment Mario completely won Paola over. Nick had never understood what women found attractive in his friend's short, almost stunted body and (to Nick) very ordinary-looking Latin looks. But Paola, quite uncharacteristically, melted before him and went on and on afterward about his intelligence, sense of humor, and lovely eyes. He made a great deal of her that evening, praising her cooking and God knows what. Nick had never seen her react that way to anybody. Over the next few months she asked Nick several times why they didn't invite him over again.

And now Nick wanted the flat to be with Lea. He dialed Mario's Palermo number twice but never found him in. The third time he got him. They chatted for a few minutes. Then Mario said, "I'm off to Lima, Nick. Come with me."

"Wish I could. Listen, Mario, I need the flat. Can I . . . ?"

"No problem. Now, let's think how I can get the keys to you. I'm off to the airport now, you just caught me." There was a pause. "I could leave them next door. Could you pick them up there?"

"Next door?"

"The souvenir shop. You know the one: painted carts, Jew's harps, Sicilian puppets—the usual stuff. Literally next to the front door. I'll give the keys to Toti there. You can keep the flat as long as you like—at least, I'll be away three weeks. Is that enough for you?"

So Nick had collected the keys from Toti's portly wife and let himself into the flat. Double glazing had been put in since he was last there, and it was eerie to watch the buses and cars passing noiselessly back and forth outside. Only his footsteps sounded on the parquet flooring as he crossed from one Persian rug to the next. Everything in the flat was gleaming and of good quality, from the wooden paneling and antique dresser to the bookcases and oval dining table. The tiny but beautifully equipped kitchen secreted beyond a little archway was in perfect order. Nick opened the fridge and found the door rack and shelves filled with bottles of champagne. There were two vacuum-packed containers of shelled, roasted peanuts, one of black olives, and another of succulent-looking capers.

He opened one of the wall units and was met by an impeccably drawn up platoon of fluted wineglasses. The next cupboard contained individual crystal fruit goblets, and the next, gold-rimmed bone china teacups and saucers. An extractor hood in matt-finished steel surmounted the pristine stove top on which stood—as though on display—two shining unused saucepans.

The only signs of recent occupation were one wineglass in the kitchen sink and the raised lavatory seat in the bathroom. It occurred to Nick that there was very little security here—leaving the keys downstairs in the souvenir shop and so on. But then Mario was a true *palermitano* and knew his way about. The locals would all know and like him (Nick remembered how the face of Toti's wife had lit up when he mentioned Mario's name), and this would perhaps act as some guarantee against burglars. An outsider—*uno straniero*—living in one of these flats would have to be far more careful.

Upstairs on the mezzanine, a thick quilt the color of peaches and cream embraced the king-sized bed. Nick picked up the book on one of the bedside tables: a Wilbur Smith in Italian translation. A cordless telephone sat next to it. He straightened up as far as he could beneath the low ceiling and opened the door of one of the built-in cupboards. It swung outward with a sigh and a small click, the light bulb revealing a suede jacket the color of freshly shelled horse chestnuts and a pair of Armani jeans. Gorgeous George they called the designer in England. Nick himself preferred comfort to elegance and secretly disliked exaggerated attention to chic. A throwback to his father's very English attitude to dress probably. Anyway, he was convinced that Englishmen, unlike Italians, didn't possess an instinctive gift for dressing well.

He closed the cupboard door. Shouldn't really be prying like this, although he knew Mario wouldn't see it like that—on the contrary: "Just make yourself at home," he had told Nick on the phone. "Use anything you like or can find in the fridge and don't bother about cleaning. A woman comes once a week when I'm away. On Wednesdays. So anything you want washed just leave out and she'll see to it."

No questions about why Nick wanted the flat, no nudge-nudge, wink-wink. That was the other man's business, not his. Again Nick was reminded of the differences between the two cultures.

Unlike the English people he knew (or had known), for instance, Italians were innately open, generous, and altruistic. It wasn't a case of consciously "sharing," the way he had been taught to do as a boy, but of giving naturally. He had seen it again and again. Well, perhaps he had just known the wrong sort of people in London. And yet he still believed he belonged to a not particularly *friendly* race. Okay, so the English ran their country far better than the Italians, were more law-abiding, had more respect for their national institutions, and so on and so on, but there was still something basically missing.

Suddenly there was a long, low *boy-ing!* then another and another. Somewhere nearby a church clock was striking midday. The strokes, only slightly muted by the thick plate-glass windows, rang slowly out, each one vibrating and trembling away into nothing before the next arrived. It was both a melancholy and a moving sound, and Nick found he was sitting on the peaches and cream quilt overawed.

From here he could see down through the French windows to the cathedral opposite—or part of it anyway. The spacious forecourt was dotted with figures, some moving briskly, others standing still in little knots as though waiting for something to happen. Some had raised their faces, perhaps trying to locate the church bell—those would be the tourists. Just then the figures were momentarily hidden from view as the top of an orange bus glided silently by.

Bus. Stolen wallet. Lea. A sudden desire to be with her made him pick up the phone. The twelfth stroke died away as he dialed her number. Of course there was nobody there at this time of day. He tried again that evening from home.

"Yes?"

"Lea? It's me."

A short pause. Then she said, "Oh, Nick."

"I want to see you."

Silence.

"Lea?"

"Yes. Yes. Okay. Listen, there's this . . . this *thing* tomorrow evening, a sort of exhibition where I've got two of my . . . of my pictures. At San Giorgio. Do you know about it already?"

"No."

"Oh, I thought you would. It's this exhibition on the English in Sicily. I thought you'd know—be involved in it in some way."

"Me? No. Should I?"

"I don't really know. No. I suppose not. I just thought the university might have . . . Anyway, the mayor'll be opening it and all that, so I'll have to be there, but it shouldn't go on that long. Why don't you come?"

"I will," he said. "Where did you say it was?"

"San Giorgio dei Genovesi—down by the port. It's meant to start at five, but you know what these things are. He'll probably roll up at about six."

"Who will?"

"Orlando," Lea said. "The mayor."

San Giorgio was a sixteenth-century deconsecrated church. Nick vaguely remembered going there once, or having it pointed out to him. He wasn't good on churches, and there were hundreds of them in Palermo.

"Lea, will you be free afterward?"

"Yes. I should be. Yes I think so."

When he put the phone down, he found Paola's stony face confronting him from the doorway.

"Who was that?"

He lied easily: "Someone from the university. What is it, Paola? You look dreadful."

"So would you if you knew."

"Knew what?"

"Sandro," she said and snapped her lips shut. She watched his expression.

"What about him? Look, would you mind telling me what's

happened instead of being so dramatic. Where is he?"

"If you took a bit more interest in your son, you'd know." She put her hands on her bony pelvis, leaned back, and gave him a withering look. "He's been stopped by the police, that's what."

Terrible things passed through Nick's mind: drugs, theft, violence, his son's body thrown into a prison cell, bones broken, covered in knife wounds.

"You come home at all hours," Paola was gathering momentum, "shut yourself away here, and never bother about me or the children—your own family. And now look—"

"Tell me what's happened to him!" Nick shouted, grabbing her by the shoulder.

"If you must know," she said quietly, shaking free of his grasp and brushing the part of her body his fingers had touched, "he hadn't paid the insurance on the Vespa, and now he'll—no, we'll—have to pay the fine. So now you know. If you'd taken a bit more notice of him—*reminded* him—this wouldn't have happened." She turned down the corners of her mouth in that way he had got so used to seeing and gave him a look of pure hatred. "You just don't *care*, do you?"

Nick was trembling and feeling slightly nauseous. He had always had a dread of the children getting mixed up with the Italian police—Sandro mostly. Young men were always being stopped, not just for driving offenses or for failing to pay their insurance or road tax—just hanging round bars at night would be enough. Then there were those horror stories of people being wrongfully accused, being flung into jail and left to rot there for months. A seventeen-year-old life irreparably ruined.

"Where is he now?" he asked quietly.

"I have *no idea*," she answered. "He asked where you were,

and I certainly couldn't tell him. So he went out again."

Just then they heard the sound of the front door opening. Nick pushed past Paola and went out into the hall. "Sandro?"

"Hi, Dad." His son hadn't put the light on and was only a dim outline. "Mum's told you, hasn't she? Look, I'm sorry, I didn't realize it had run out. I'll pay you back when I can."

Nick put an arm round him. "Don't worry about it. There are more important things than that, for God's sake." I thought you'd had an accident, he wanted to tell his son. I even thought you'd been killed. Tears pricked his eyes. "You're not hurt, are you?"

They were still standing by the front door. Sandro switched on the light and began unwinding his scarf. "What d'you mean?"

"Nothing: I thought you might have . . . I thought the police might have stopped you because you were going too fast or something."

"No, I was coming back here. Franco was with me on the back. They stopped us outside the Fiera." He flung his jacket on a chair and went into the kitchen, relieved that there wasn't going to be a showdown. Wrenching open the fridge he said, "I really will pay you both back. I'm starting this job at a pub tomorrow night."

"You're what?" Paola had followed them.

"Oh hi, Mum. What's for supper?"

"What job's that?" she asked again.

Sandro's voice came from inside the fridge: "A pub. They don't pay much, but we get free drinks and food."

Nick marveled at the way his son's humor could change from one day to the next. The other night he'd hardly spoken a word.

"Aren't you going to ask him where it is?" Paola said to Nick. "Don't you care what your son does at night?"

"It's all right, Mum. It's a place Franco knows. Dad knows it too." Sandro cut himself a hunk of cheese. "The one in that little road behind the Politeama. You remember it, Dad, don't you?" It was more a plea than a question.

Nick didn't. "Oh, that one, yes. What was it called?"

"Drake's."

"Mm."

Sandro turned round all smiles. After a quick grateful look at his father, he crammed the cheese into his mouth. "So you see, Mum, everything's fine. And that way I'll be able to pay you back the insurance and the fine." In a voice made thick with chewing, he said, "I think I'll make a plate of pasta for myself. Anyone else want some?"

In bed that night, Paola said, "You don't know that pub, do you?" She swallowed the laxative pills she took every evening, placing both on her tongue, throwing her head back, and gulping down half a glassful of water. Nick had said they completely messed up her system, but she told him it was the only way she could function and that he was lucky *he* didn't suffer like her, because chronic constipation was quite unbearable. "You were just helping him out, weren't you?" she said now. "I could tell." She climbed into bed beside him and checked the alarm on her clock. "He'll go off there and mix with God knows what types, not bother about studying and fall even further behind at school. I just don't understand you."

"I want him to feel he's loved." The words surprised him as they came out.

Paola turned to look at him. After a moment, she said, "What on earth do you mean?"

"I've just said," Nick went on. "He needs to know he's loved by us."

"Well, lying about a pub isn't going to help, is it?" she said with a twisted smile. "The best way you can show you. . . . *love* . . . him is to see that his marks improve at school and he gets through his exams. That's the best thing *you* can do."

"Don't try to tell me what I should or shouldn't do, Paola," Nick said slowly. "Can't you see Sandro's trying to ask for help? Can't you tell with your own son? He's unhappy."

The telephone rang from Paola's side of the bed and she clapped a hand to her cheek. "Giulia! I'd forgotten all about her." She turned away from him and picked up the receiver: "Giulia? Where are you? How is everything? We've been having a terrible time here. Your brother . . . caught for not paying his insurance on the—. No, no, he's fine, but—. No, nothing wrong, only—. Yes, because your father—. If he'd only—. Yes, but—. And now he's saying he's going to work in a pub that we know nothing about. . . . Yes, I know, but Giulia, don't you see that—?"

There was a ten-second silence while Paola listened. Nick glanced toward her back, saw the bony shoulder blades emerging from the blue brushed cotton nightdress, the phone pressed into the small, delicate ear. He tried to imagine what his daughter was saying. Poor Giulia, it wasn't right. It wasn't right for her either.

"But I can't help worrying," Paola got in. "If he fails and has to repeat the entire year again, he'll never get to university, he'll ruin his whole life. . . . It *does* matter, Giulia. Look at you, you'd never have got into Bologna if you hadn't—. All right, all right, I won't, but I still think—. Nick? Yes, he's here. Just a minute."

She turned abruptly and held out the phone, ducking under the wire and grimacing as he pulled the receiver toward him.

"Hallo, my love," Nick said.

"Dad? It's not all that bad, is it? Sandro, I mean."

"Not at all, he's fine. What about you? Enjoying life?"

"I suppose so."

He laughed. "It doesn't sound like it. Too much work?"

"No, no, it's not that, just a down period. It'll pass. What about you—lots of new jobs with masses of money rolling in?"

"Jobs yes, money no. When are we going to see you?"

"Not before Easter . . . unless . . ."

"Yes?"

"Well I might be . . . I don't really want to say anything about it yet, it's just an idea, but . . ." There was a short pause. "Dad, what would you say if I left Bologna? I'm not saying I am, and it's only a very vague idea at the moment, but just supposing I decided to do something completely different?"

He didn't have to think. "It's your life, Giulia."

Paola nudged him with her elbow: "What is it?" she hissed into his free ear, but he shrugged her off.

"So you wouldn't be angry, then?" Giulia's voice went on.

"Of course I wouldn't."

"And Mum? I daren't say anything to her."

"You mustn't let that worry you."

He suddenly wished his daughter were with him, wished he could clear the anxiety on her face and stop the worried way she turned the big silver rings round and round on her fingers. "We'll talk again. You can always call me on my mobile, you know. Or I'll call you." He'd do that. Tomorrow. "I'll hand you back to Mum now, okay, love?"

Paola almost snatched the phone from him. "What is it, what is it?" She sat bolt upright on the edge of the bed, tensing herself for the worst. "Giulia? What is it, what's wrong?"

Nick lay back, one arm over his eyes. He wasn't surprised, because he hadn't been happy about Giulia leaving Palermo in the first place. She had never seemed to want to go herself. It was as if she were doing it for Paola and him, as if it were what they expected of her. Looking back he could see the mistakes they had both made. Both of them? No, it was Paola who had gone on and on about Palermo being a dead-end city with no opportunities, about how Giulia was wasting herself down here and how much better a chance she would get in the North. It was *his* fault he hadn't *stopped* her from going. Well, now it looked as if his daughter was coming back, or thinking of leaving university anyway. Whatever she wanted or decided to do from now on was fine by him—anything, that is, except let herself be taken over by Paola again. But somehow he knew that would never happen.

He half-heard the phone being very quietly replaced on the bedside table. Then Paola's light was switched off. The sheet was pulled up just once, and her body lay stock still beside him. Whatever Giulia had said in those last few minutes had had a profound effect. He felt his wife lying there in the dark, eyes wide open, unable to come to terms with what she had heard. Well, it was done now. The lids slid down over his own eyes, and immediately Lea was there. He crossed his arms over his chest and squeezed his shoulders thinking of her. Tomorrow he'd be seeing her, tomorrow they'd go to Mario's place.

The next morning he phoned his daughter from work, but her mobile was switched off. He tried her again at eleven from the café across the road but still couldn't get through. There were three of them standing up at the counter: Pauline, who worked in the department above, Josh, and himself. Pauline had launched into her usual tirade against Italy and everything Italian. Why the fuck doesn't she go back home? Nick thought again. "Got a boyfriend here, that's why," another colleague had once told him. "He treats her like dirt, but she's mad about him."

Nick wasn't interested in other people's private lives and less so in gossip, but he disliked the Englishwoman intensely and would have offered the guy who treated her like dirt a large sum of money to leave Palermo and take Pauline with him. "If they can't get their act together," she was saying now, blowing cigarette smoke out of the side of her mouth, "I don't know what we're doing in Europe anyway." She took a large gulp of her coffee ("My God, I don't know how many times I've told them how to make it: two parts water and one milk. But do they get it right? Do they, hell") and tapped her cigarette on the saucer.

The young man behind the counter reached out to remove the saucer. He wore a maroon waistcoat and a boat-shaped hat cocked low over his forehead.

"Hey, I haven't finished with that yet," Pauline said, pulling the saucer toward her. She rolled her eyes heavenward. "Honestly."

The man ignored her, whipped some empty coffee cups away instead, and ran a cloth over the stainless steel surface all in one quick movement. "*Tre cappuccini!*" he called out to his mate behind the espresso machine as more customers came up to the bar.

Pauline had a large, heavy bust like two melons that she carried before her in a world-weary manner and covered in a succession of V-necked sweaters. She always wore her jacket (suede with greasy collar and cuffs) draped over her shoulders—probably because it wouldn't meet over the melons. Passable legs ended in thick ankles and scuffed low-heeled shoes, and her coarse yellowish hair was pulled back into a ponytail in the nape of her neck. Forty-one or two, Nick guessed the first time they met. He felt like saying now that smoking was a disgusting habit that had been banned from public places in Britain, and he was surprised she still did it. His distaste must have shown, for she now said: "Smoke bothering you, Nick? Filthy habit, I know, but makes no difference in Palermo, does it? The place is so foul anyway."

"Why do you stay here?" Josh suddenly asked, "if you hate it so much?"

Nick looked up in interest.

"Ah, that would be telling, wouldn't it?" Pauline said darkly. "Unfortunately, Josh, life isn't always a bed of roses. We have to do things we don't always like, and for my sins I am in Palermo."

Oh bugger off, Nick thought. He glanced at his watch. "I'll have to get back," he said to Josh. "Coming?" The other man nodded, downed his espresso, and the two of them crossed the road and entered the university building.

The Church of San Giorgio had been built by the wealthy and influential community of Genoese merchants who enjoyed a very comfortable standard of living in Palermo during the sixteenth century. It rose on the site of the old church of San Luca, which they had acquired in 1576, and was handily close to the harbor from which it took its name and where so much of their business was conducted.

Nick knew nothing about any of this but was struck by the church's massive facade, soaring straight up from the flatlands near the waterfront. Totally unencumbered by other buildings, it dominated the surrounding landscape with an almost proprietary air. The sea probably came up much closer then but had retreated like much of Palermo's coastline and was now separated from the church by the same divided highway Nick had driven along and by the jumble of harbor buildings over on its far side.

He had recognized San Giorgio straight away by the crowds standing on the flight of steps outside and by the policemen in their ceremonial dark blue uniforms with red and yellow braid and their white gloves. A long trestle table at the top of the steps bore a battery of champagne glasses and a huge display of crimson roses whose stems must have been a good two feet long.

Nick glanced at his watch: twenty past five. Experience had taught him that no public function ever began on time in Palermo, yet he had hurried just the same. He strode up the steps two by two, past the anxious-looking, shuffling group of men in suits outside, and into the cavernous interior, automatically bending the upper part of his body as he did so.

Fierce halogen bulbs illuminated a series of pictures around the walls, while the main body of the church was shrouded in a penumbral blur. Little by little he made out the barely moving mass of people in its midst, the whole thing looking, he thought, like the depths of a murky, weed-entangled pond. He began walking round in search of Lea, glancing only perfunctorily at the pictures as he went. The exhibition, he now saw, was a mixture of paintings and photographs. Hers would be here somewhere. A massive canvas depicting what appeared to be a Victorian mansion surrounded by a garishly colored tropical garden hung next to a grainy black-and-white photo of two men in crumpled white suits. Nick recognized the slim bearded one on the left as Luigi Pirandello. Both were standing on a veranda looking into the camera lens with deadpan expressions. A basket chair and a fern in a pot stood behind them. That certainly wasn't one of hers.

The soles of his shoes struck the marble flooring like pistol shots as he walked along, one image following another. What *was* all this anyway? Lea had said something about the English in Sicily. Could well be, he thought, noticing the plethora of flowery hats and low-slung Edwardian bosoms in the photos. Those fashions and smug expressions would be just right for that family (What were they called? The Whitakers, that was it). Canny Yorkshiremen who had made their millions from marsala wine and dined off the proceeds ever after.

He strained his eyes, still trying to make out Lea's figure in the swirling dimness, before realizing he had made an entire tour of the exhibition and was now back at the entrance. Well, it was still quite early, she'd probably got held up in the traffic.

A sudden commotion inside the church made him swivel round. Everybody started gravitating in his direction, and Nick looked out to see two shiny black saloon cars drawing to a halt at the curb. All eight doors seemed to open at once, and the pavement was simultaneously full of heavy-looking armed men in jeans and sleeveless jackets with wires coming from their ears. In among them Nick saw Mayor Orlando straightening up. He ran fingers through the lock of oily black hair falling over his high forehead, fastened the middle button of his badly creased jacket, and started ascending the steps. As he reached the top the police came to attention, a flashbulb went off, and various greetings took place. Nick noticed the sprinkling of dandruff on the man's collar

as he was shepherded inside. Smiling and nodding, he shook
hands with those whom Nick supposed must be the artists, and
let himself be propelled toward the pictures along the walls.

Still no Lea. Nick scoured the illuminated square for her but
it was now deserted except for the bodyguards leaning on the
cars chatting, and an old lady over on the other side walking her
Pomeranian. He heard the faint sound of a trumpet from the
nearby conservatory, then a piano. It was six o'clock now, so she'd
be here soon. Perhaps she had wanted to avoid Orlando, or perhaps she was stuck in the traffic. I've said that already, he told
himself. He wandered back inside, noticing the poster in the entrance for the first time. It was pinned to an easel: "*Un' epoca
gloriosa,*" it said. "*Gli inglesi in Sicilia*" An Age of Glory, The English in Sicily: "A collection of oils, watercolors, and photographs." Underneath was a blown-up shot of an ineffectual,
weak-looking young man in a bleak landscape holding a Greek
urn and with a dog at his feet. One of the Whitakers, Nick
guessed, probably the one who fancied himself as an archaeol-
ogist.

A few people who, like him, had already completed the circuit
were now hanging round the table eyeing the canapés. Nick
heard a sudden burst of laughter from within: Orlando had evidently cracked a joke. How the man managed to be everywhere
in Palermo was a mystery. Always turning up on the local news
at some function or other—schools, the naming of a new street,
parades, the lot—an activity that grew more frenetic as elections
approached. A wonder he hadn't pegged out from exhaustion.

I'll wait outside for her, Nick thought. That way I'll see her as
soon as she arrives. Surely she wouldn't have come early, not
found me here, and gone away again. Or would she? No, of

course not. He had only been about fifteen minutes late anyway. He stood at the top of the steps for a while, then went inside and began wandering round the pictures a second time. Once more he found himself in front of the Pirandello portrait.

> There once was this guy Pirandello,
> God help us, an effing old fellow.
> He wrote plays and a farce,
> A right pain in the arse,
> That boring old fart Pirandello.

He had composed that at college. The second line had never sounded right.

Just then Orlando's party came up, and Nick found himself face to face with the mayor. The man smiled vaguely at Nick as though he ought perhaps to know him, then smoothed his tie inside his jacket and moved on.

"In this one, *signor sindaco*," his guide was saying, "you can see the English queen, Queen Mary. It was taken when she visited Villa Malfitano. You can just make out the ficus tree there in the background. It's still there today."

Nick's phone rang from his jacket pocket. Lea! Standing on the steps outside once again, he put it to his ear. "Hallo?"

It was Paola: "Nick. Where are you, where *are* you? Mother has died."

Looking at the coffin in front of the altar Nick wondered whether hospitals accepted organs from donors who died of old age. He imagined not. Not that his mother-in-law would have considered the issue; that sort of thing hadn't concerned her generation at all. Yet in a few years' time, everyone who didn't want to donate their organs was going to have to sign a form saying so. Otherwise the lot would be whipped out before you were cold. He couldn't make up his mind whether this was right or not, whether it infringed on individual freedom. Would he want his insides removed after his death? Yes, why not? They'd be no good to him anymore.

He had left the exhibition right after Paola's phone call and, still longing for Lea, had driven straight home. From there he and Paola had gone to see the body.

This time it was a nun inside the glass booth in the lobby watching television. Without taking her eyes from the screen she motioned them toward the lift. Upstairs, his mother-in-law lay in her bed, a rosary entwined in her fingers. Nick's first thought was that she hadn't been a religious woman and that it was outrageous the nuns had presumed to place the beads there. They had left her hair unbrushed, which made this hurried pact with God somehow much worse.

Nick and Paola were told she had died in her sleep and hadn't suffered. How the hell did they know that? Paola wept and said she would have been visiting her that day. "I was going to bring her those cakes she liked," she sobbed.

A cleaner put her head round the door and disappeared again, old women plodded up and down the corridor, and staff bustled by, calling out directions without lowering their voices. Down in the atrium again, the nun switched off the television, called Nick and Paola over, and asked them to settle *signora* Lentini's bill.

"We have," Nick said tightly. "You wanted the month paid in advance." (That was in case patients died on them. Well, Ida had.)

Yes, the nun said, but the *signora* had used up two jumbo packs of incontinence pads and a bottle of sleeping pills and had had a visit from the doctor. She had also drunk three one-liter bottles of mineral water. Would he and Paola be seeing to the funeral arrangements? Because if so, the institute could recommend a firm of undertakers. She called them back just as they were going through the door and said she had forgotten to take into account a packet of water biscuits *signora* Lentini had eaten, and that would be another two thousand lire.

·   ·   ·

As in every Catholic funeral, there was a great deal of standing up and sitting down again in church. Seeing the waiting hearse outside, several of the regular parishioners had wandered in and stayed for the service, thus making the mourners seem more numerous. The priest gave a short tribute to "Ida" and prayed for comfort for the bereaved—in particular for her daughter, Paola. The organ broke into a loud wheezing dirge, Holy Communion was celebrated, and the chalice was raised.

As the Host was offered up, the sidesman nearest to them left off collecting and knelt reverently down, placing his basket of money beside him on the floor. A lump of chewing gum was adhering to the sole of his shoe.

Nick felt a sudden poignant sadness as the coffin was lifted up and borne down the aisle. Outside, relatives crowded round Paola and the children. They made clucking noises of sympathy and stroked Paola's hair. Giulia was weeping and Sandro looking stoically ahead. Difficult to know what he was feeling.

His mother-in-law had gone. Well and truly. Poor foolish unworldy lover of Christmas fare. He found he was crying as the coffin was lowered into the grave. The Lentinis had no family vault of the walk-in mausoleum type, common in Sicilian cemeteries, simply a marked shaft in the ground. Even this, however, required a good deal of chiseling, banging, and cementing up. Poor Ida was trussed up in strong ropes and lowered, dangling dangerously, to the bottom of the hole to the accompaniment of shouted instructions and warnings. A sweating workman in jeans and shirtsleeves who had preceded her now stood halfway down the shaft in a recess. "Come on, come on!" he bawled up. "Okay, okay, lower . . . lower it gently now . . . gently. . . . *Stop!*"

The other men, ropes braced over their shoulders, leaned over.

"Got enough room down there, Pino?" one of them bellowed.

"Acres of it!" came the reply. "Slack off up there. Okay, okay, that's it. *Hey, careful!*"

There was a crunch and an oath from below. Poor Paola. Nick glanced at her pinched face and drew her toward him. Tears now began to course down her cheeks too. Giulia, clutching a bunch of pink carnations, had turned away and was staring out at a row of cypresses creaking gently in the January wind.

Nick remembered the solemn decorousness of his father's cremation: the dutifully murmured prayers and smooth gliding shut of the curtain in front of the retreating coffin, the whispered expressions of sympathy.

"*Bloody hell!*" came suddenly from below, making Ida's seventy-three-year-old brother lean dangerously over the shaft to see what was going on. Nick had to clutch hold of his overcoat in case he stumbled. The remaining few mourners who had followed the hearse to the cemetery stood round in eager anticipation of the sealing process.

This began with the heaving and banging home of the flat stone slab.

"Turn it more this way—*this way*, for Pete's sake!"

"Listen mate, don't try and teach me my job."

The workmen went on jostling and shouting until Nick could stand it no more: "Take those cigarettes from your mouths," he said slowly and evenly. "And keep your voices down. This is a burial. My wife has just lost her mother."

Perhaps it was the word *mother* that struck home, or his dangerously quiet tone, or even his foreign accent, but all three men immediately took the cigarettes from their mouths and crushed them underfoot. Then they fetched the bucket of cement from the nearby parked truck and in total silence fixed the stone into place.

Nick was aware that Giulia had come to stand beside him and had taken his hand. As the men drove off with a respectful "*Buona sera, dottore*" to Nick (no hope of a tip this time), she began silently distributing the carnations among the mourners. When she had finished, everybody held a frail-stemmed flower. Then, taking their cue from her, they laid the flowers on Ida's grave.

Walking back past the towering presences of family mausoleums, Nick felt a sense of lightness, almost of happiness. "Committed to the ground" had a good, a *right* ring to it. A sense of a chapter closing and of new things about to happen. A strong feeling that the way he had been living up till then was about to change sent a tingle through his whole body. He didn't love Paola and it was no good pretending he did. He longed for Lea, longed so much it was painful.

She had phoned the day after the exhibition: "I tried to get you yesterday. The car broke down right in the middle of traffic and I had no way of letting you know. When I finally got there, you— everyone—had gone. I'm so sorry Nick. Was it awful?"

He told her he hadn't really taken much notice of the pictures, that his mother-in-law had died, and that he wanted to see Lea.

"God, I'm so sorry," she said again. Then quietly, "Listen, this is my fault. Can we meet on . . . on Tuesday? Will that be all right? Would you be free then? Oh no, but you'll have the funeral."

"The funeral's on Monday. Of course I can see you."

"Do you know Marconi's?"

He did.

Now, dutifully slackening his pace, he came level with Paola and took her arm. Sandro was on her other side and Giulia just behind. The cypress trees sighed as their untidy group made its way toward the cemetery exit.

"You'll never catch your plane if you have to start looking round for a parking place," Lea told Dante the next morning. "It's a quarter to nine already. I'll drive you there." He grunted, stuffed some papers into a briefcase, and looked distractedly round the bedroom.

"What is it?" she asked. "What do you want?"

"Socks."

"Over there. When do you think you'll be back—the last plane tomorrow?"

"An earlier one if I can manage it. I'll let you know." He shrugged himself into a dark blue jacket and wedged a pile of newspapers under his arm. "Try and finish these on the plane. Okay, that's it, we can go."

Now, driving back into Palermo, she thought of his retreating figure on the airport concourse. "Don't enjoy yourself too much," he had said, unsmiling, when she left him at the airport. "Will you?" and had strode away without another look at her. It was a mean thing to have done, waiting till he was out of the way to see Nick: underhand.

She sat herself down in front of her imaginary psychiatrist, something she hadn't done for years now.

Are you happy in your present relationship? (the questioning be-gan). *How would you describe it?*

I don't really think about "happiness" (she answered). It's

simply a background to my life. It's the way things are at present. I'm very fond of Dante. No, I've never loved him passionately. No, I've never thought of being unfaithful to him before. I've never met anybody I wanted to have an affair with. I think Dante needs me and loves me deeply. In his own way.

Are you attracted by Nick?

Yes.

What do you experience when you meet?

A sense of excitement and possibilities. I feel there's a lot there behind his gaze, but I haven't let myself think about actual sex with him yet.

Why didn't you get in touch after he bought you the book?

I kept telling myself I would but kept putting it off. I was scared.

What did you experience meeting him on Christmas Eve?

The same as every other time I see him. I went hot inside. I know he wants me.

Are you worried about what Dante would feel or do if you started an affair with Nick?

I don't want to face that yet. I'm not "worried"—more sad. And that can't be right. I'm sure he'd say we must break up straight away if I told him I was having an affair.

What made you ask Nick to the exhibition in the first place? Did you really want him to come?

I hoped he'd be there, I wanted to see him, then I got scared. I'd probably have made another excuse not to go off with him afterward.

How do you think it will go when you meet on Tuesday?

I don't know. I'm going to wait and see.

You're a coward.

· · ·

High above the island of Ustica some forty miles off the northern coast of Sicily, the plane began to climb. Dante watched as the thick gray cloud mass beyond the aircraft windows fell away and they emerged into the sparkling blue. The juddering and rattling of loose internal fastenings died away, and they were suddenly being buoyed along in magical smooth silence. Below them stretched the layer of cloud, a brilliant white from up here, as softly heaped as cotton wool. He watched a tiny silver speck cutting across the blue and heading in the opposite direction.

I am not a spiritual man, Dante said to himself, yet I find this beautiful and moving: the thought that clarity and light are always up here, no matter what the mess and foulness below.

Lea was drifting away from him—just like that tiny airplane down there. Ever since the beginning of December—before Christmas anyway—he had felt her changing: she had become overaffectionate toward him, trying to please, even humor him—a sentiment that didn't become her and one that had no part in their relationship. What was more, she had begun to bear his attentions with (he realized in horror) . . . with *good grace*. Not that she had ever responded with the passion he longed to awake in her. Always keeping part of herself back. But their lovemaking had been good at times, he knew it had. Was it habit then that was changing them, or staleness? On her part, not his. He wanted Lea with him forever. He loved her passionately and deeply. The thought of doing without her was unbearable. It was probably another man. Someone she worked with, some photographer or writer—maybe even that shit Fontanini, though somehow he thought not. She had said no, and she wouldn't lie to him, he felt sure of that. If she had met someone else, she would tell him.

The plane continued its silent path through the brilliant airy lightness. Below, the white blanket of cloud had flattened itself out into acres of ribbed sands stretching away to the curve, the very edge of the world. Dante drew the blind down a few inches against the flashing shards of sun. There was a trundling, and the trolley stopped in the aisle beside him.

"*Caffè, signore? Té, una bibita fredda?*" An almost hostile tone. Not the softly scented presence bending solicitously down that you got on foreign airlines. Alitalia staff were unfriendly, hardly bothering to mask their impatience. As though they couldn't wait to unload you at your destination. Passengers, you felt, were definitely a nuisance.

"*Caffè.*" He watched slim wrists handling the plastic cup, pouring the coffee, taking the cellophane-wrapped *biscotti* from the steward on the other side of the trolley. Dante took the offering in its minute paper napkin, aware for the first time that he was uncomfortable in the narrow seat. Lea was right, he had put on too much weight.

Lea.

Down below, sitting in the snarled-up traffic on the ring road, she decided to call in at Flora's shop—tell her not to bother about getting a copy of the Martinucci book. Probably long forgotten about it anyway. But first she drove home and garaged the car.

The pavements were wet and shiny with rain, so that the early morning piles of dog turds had collapsed into slithery slag heaps. Empty cigarette packets and candy wrappers gleamed jewel-like underfoot. These were real paving slabs with curbstones of heavy-duty marble from the quarries of Custonaci in northeastern Sicily. Their serviceability and solidity gave Lea pleasure, and she had photographed parts of them several times, with and without their scattering of litter. They didn't use these paving stones anymore, just drew pretend ones in the cement. She had watched workmen down on their knees stretching a string across the newly laid surface and then marking out the lines as though practicing elementary geometry. It seemed a completely pointless exercise.

Flora's window display looked unchanged since the last time she had seen it, with a ruched paper angel left over from Christmas still wedged between two of the brightly colored, rather dusty vases. Outside, the two dwarf firs shared their wooden containers with a collection of cigarette butts, used bus tickets, and crumpled-up paper handkerchiefs. The beveled glass door of the shop was closed, but Lea made out the blurred outline of two figures inside. She went in.

Flora was standing with a man who had his back to the door. She looked up when the bell tinkled, and an odd look came over her face. A mixture of worry and relief, Lea remembered thinking. The man turned round and smiled, showing even white teeth, and at the same time Flora stammered out: "Oh, Lea, it's you. I . . . I won't be a minute. I'm just—"

"Don't worry about me," the man said, still smiling. "I can come back later." He looked Lea up and down appraisingly. "A friend?"

Flora nodded. "Yes."

What is going on, Lea thought. A lover or what? He looked personable enough yet not the sort Flora would go for at all. And anyway, Lea had always imagined her friend as being a faithful wife; she had never given any hint of affairs, at any rate. Of course, they didn't know each other that well, weren't *close* friends at all, but still.

Flora was looking more and more uncomfortable, so Lea said, "Listen, I've got a few things I've got to do nearby. I only came by to see if you were in—for a chat. I'll come back later."

"Not at all," the man said warmly. "I can't make up my mind anyway with all this lovely china" (*China?* Lea thought). "I want to think it over before I make my purchase." He had a very marked Palermo accent, which she found disturbingly at odds with his formal, almost dapper appearance.

"How about this afternoon?" he turned to Flora. "About fiveish?" It wasn't really a question at all. "I'll see you then." Buttoning up his jacket, he said to Lea, "It's a present for my mother-in-law, and I want it to be just right." He gave her a conspiratorial smile. "Wouldn't want to get on the wrong side of her, would I?"

Odder and odder, Lea thought, as he left the shop. Her puzzlement must have shown, because Flora, who now lit a cigarette with trembling fingers, said, "Don't look like that, Lea, for Christ's sake."

"Sorry." She watched the other woman inhaling deeply. "I'd have come back, Flora. There was no need for him to go. It was nothing important anyway—just to tell you about the book."

"The book?"

"The book you were going to get for me. Look, what is it—don't you feel well?"

"Can we go out somewhere?" Flora said, suddenly crushing out her cigarette and reaching for her fur coat. "Get out of here for ten minutes or so." She swept up a bunch of keys. "I can't stand this place a moment longer."

Outside, Lea noticed that Flora ignored the rain. Normally she opened an umbrella at the slightest drop, or covered her head with her handbag and ran squealing for shelter. When they got to La Rosa's she ordered a vodka.

"I'm scared," she said to Lea. "And I don't know what the hell to do." She told Lea who the man in the shop was, about her husband saying she was to pay the protection money, about Maurizio down the road who sold oriental carpets and refused to pay up.

"He'll be killed, I know he will," she said. "Sooner or later they'll get him. He says we should all do what he's doing, but I'm terrified, Lea." Her fur coat, still glistening with raindrops, was draped over her shoulders, and she pulled it roughly around her. "I never wanted to have the bloody shop in the first place. I was quite happy living my own life. I've lost all my friends. I've got nothing to do all day except sit among those fucking vases and dishes. D'you know I sometimes never talk to anybody the whole day except the postman. The *postman*! If it wasn't for you, Lea, I'd go out of my mind."

This was overgenerous, as they rarely saw each other more than a couple of times a month and usually only briefly.

"It's all right for you," she went on. "You've got a job you like, you've got Dante." (She had met him only once, and neither had liked the other.) "*He* wouldn't put you through this, I know."

How could she "know" that?

"But the police? Surely your husband"—Lea couldn't remember his name—"could, well, do something. Why don't you tell him? Ring him up now. See what he says."

"I've told him a hundred times," Flora got out between clenched teeth. "But he doesn't care. Well, now I've had enough,

I'm not going back after lunch. He can do what he bloody well likes. I'm not going back there. They can burn the whole place down for all I care."

Lea felt for her distress but was inexplicably irritated at the same time. Of course she knew these things went on, but somehow she had never imagined Flora being mixed up in them. That just showed how little Lea took notice of the things around her, *on her very doorstep*. All tied up in her photographs. A sudden crystal clear vision of Dante up in the clouds somewhere overhead made her wonder what his reaction would be. Probably raise his eyebrows in that way he had, accepting reality and distancing himself from it at the same time. "I'm not in that position," he would tell her. "Everybody must make their own minds up." And when she pressed him: "If the state does nothing, how can you expect the ordinary man in the street to take a stand? Why the fuck should he?"

She laid a hand on her friend's clammy-cold fur coat and told her not to worry, to finish her drink, that somehow it would work out (senseless, perhaps even dangerous advice). Flora blew her nose and began ineffectually tidying her hair. "You're so lucky," she said again to Lea. "You don't realize."

"I've got other worries." It was out before she could stop herself.

"What worries have you got?" Flora sank her painted fingernails into her handbag and drew out a compact. She opened it and made a moue in the mirror. "You've even got that gorgeous man." She started touching up cheekbones and chin. "The English prof. Well, haven't you?"

Nick. She'd be seeing him at seven tonight. Must be mad. "I haven't got anyone, Flora."

"About a month ago, wasn't it? At Longhi's. Couldn't take his eyes off you."

They'd have a drink sitting up at one of those glass-topped barrels, Lea was thinking, then go off somewhere. Go to bed together.

"Listen, Flora, I'll have to go. Will you be all right on your own, or do you want me to run you home?" Lea stood up. "This is on me."

"No, I'll wait till the rain stops, then ring Biagio." She shut her handbag. "Thanks, Lea—for everything. You're a real friend."

Walking away, Lea realized she hadn't told Flora not to bother about buying the book.

She saw him leaning up against the bar. He looked all brown— jacket, trousers, sweater. There was ruby-red wine in the glass in front of him. Red wine guarded against heart attacks and enriched the blood. What had that to do with anything?

There weren't many people, but then it was still early. The place only started to come alive after eight. The top of the bar was brown too, she saw—well-worn wood, heavy and shiny. Nick lifted his glass to drink and as he did so caught sight of her in the doorway. He put the glass down again and came up to her.

"Lea," he said and kissed her cheek.

"Hallo. I came this time."

Bottles lined the floor-to-ceiling shelves: beautiful slim dark Latin wines, portly reds, skinny rosés. Warm concealed lighting glinted from alcoves onto oak tables and varnished barrels, onto the cartwheel suspended from the ceiling through an archway.

Marconi's was *di moda*, the place to go, a sumptuous, jeweled cave where you drank from long-stemmed glasses and grew mellow with the wines.

They sat on high stools at a glass-topped barrel where their knees pressed uncomfortably against the convex wood strips and there was nowhere to hang her bag. When she slipped her coat from her shoulders, Nick reached over and ran his hand softly once down her neck. They had a bottle of Sicilian white wine from Agrigento, and a quarter of an hour later a young man in a yellow sweater brought over a dish of savories.

"What do you call these in English?" Lea asked Nick, picking up a tiny scoop of pastry filled with blue cheese.

"I've no idea. Canapés maybe. What are they in Italian then?"

"*Antipasti.*" She closed her lips round it. "How long have you been in Italy?"

"Ages."

"Then you should know." She smiled and brushed the crumbs away.

"Yes, I should."

He couldn't take his eyes off her, could barely stop his hands from reaching out.

"What is it, Nick?"

"Mm? I just want to look at you."

She started pushing the fallen crumbs about on the tabletop with her fingertips, making symmetrical little heaps of them. Somebody laughed loudly over in the corner. Nick drained his glass.

"Was it difficult getting away?" he asked her.

"Difficult? No. My time's my own." She'd ask *him* now: "You're married, aren't you?"

"Uh-huh." He poured out some more wine for both of them. "I'm married, but it's not all that good, I mean not a good marriage. Anymore." He put the empty bottle down and twisted round. "Shall we have another of this, or something different?"

Her head was singing. "Another one? I ought to eat something first." She leaned across the table and put her hand on his cheek. "Nick. I ought to eat!"

He clasped her hand in his, pushing the plate toward her with the other. "Go on then. Finish them up."

"No more wine, though," she said, biting into a tiny *bruschetta* glistening with dark oil-soaked flakes of sundried tomato. "That's enough. If it wasn't so early, I'd like some real food."

"If you're hungry, we'll go and eat somewhere."

"No."

"Well, let's leave anyway." He stood up and handed her her coat. "Will you come back with me?"

He shrugged himself into the brown jacket, reaching as he did so into his back trouser pocket for his wallet. What other gestures excited her so much in a man? When he loosens his tie and leaves it slack round his neck. When he stands with both hands in his trouser pockets, pushing back the corners of his jacket with his wrists.

"Will you?" he said again.

"Back where?"

It never occurred to him to tell her a lie. "A friend has lent me his flat," he said. "Near the cathedral."

"Near the cathedral." She looked at him and gave a great sigh, which made Nick smile.

"Is it that bad?" he asked her.

She nodded. "Not the cathedral," she said with a little smile.

"The other. Yes, it's that bad." She drew her coat around her.

"What about my car?"

They were standing by the bar. Nick paid and stuffed his wallet back. "Leave it here—wherever it's parked—and we'll come back for it later. Mine's just round the corner." He pulled her to him and squeezed her gently. "Come with me, Lea."

The working day traffic had gradually thinned out and died away, leaving groups of people standing outside in the mild evening air with their glasses. Kids of fifteen or sixteen were draped over their scooters, drinking beer and holding their crash helmets under their free arms. There was always a dog in places like this, Lea noticed, always mangy and sand-colored, which relied on the charity of shopkeepers for its survival. This one was sniffing the back wheel of a battered gray Panda. Back and forth it went, as though chasing its own tail, easing its nose into the crevices of the hub until it found just the right spot, then lifting its leg against the tire.

Nick kept his right hand very lightly in Lea's lap as they drove. It was some local feast day, and the deserted side streets near the cathedral blazed under tunnels of arched lights. At either end of the arches was a stylized fountain with sequentially winking bulbs forming the curved jets of water. One of these had been mounted the wrong way round and the jets of water entered the basin instead of leaving it.

Nick parked under one brilliantly lit arch with its deep sizzling hum of electricity, and they let themselves into the building. Upstairs in the flat he closed the door quietly behind them and took both Lea's hands in his, pressing her gently up against the wall. Her face was half in shadow and half illuminated by the ghostly glow from outside.

"Don't look so serious," he whispered to her.

She looked back at him, her dark eyes huge, and slowly laced her fingers with his. They kissed, then he freed his hands and took the coat from her shoulders. It slipped off easily onto the floor. Still pressed close to her, he slid out of his own jacket, first one sleeve, then the other, then took her hand and led her toward the wooden stairs.

It was as though the cathedral opposite was watching them. Deserted by tourists and bored by solitude, it peered into the mezzanine, fascinated by what was going on. In a child's picture book it would have had a puzzled expression on its bricks and mortar face, with the Gothic portal of a mouth forming an open "O" and two of its arched windows the surprised eyes. This is what would have occurred to Lea at any other time, but now she noticed nothing—neither the cathedral nor the clipped box hedges and dwarf palms in its forecourt. She was conscious of nothing at all except Nick's presence. Sounds were blotted out, as were sensations of hot and cold, the feel of the polished wooden floor under her feet, and the soft sag of the bed. No awareness of any sort, just oblivion.

The closer they held each other, the deeper she fell, into darker and darker depths until her whole being turned inside out and she was rushed back up to the surface.

The noises came back into the room, the hum of the fridge downstairs, the muffled sound of a bus going by through the half-opened window. She saw the small red glow of the telephone on the bedside table and the strip of illuminated cathedral outside. Its floodlit facade threw light back onto the part of the smooth balustrade running along the mezzanine where it sloped down-ward into the bannisters. It slanted onto the painted ceiling above her head and picked out part of a dancing maiden's anatomy. Bare feet, flowing robes, arms balancing a lyre. Nick put an arm across Lea's body.

"What are those meant to be?" she whispered, still staring upward.

"On the ceiling? Goddesses, aren't they?"

"Maybe. They're watching us, and I'm not sure I like that." She turned her face toward him. "I want it to be just you and me. What time do you think it is?"

She heard the dull *tink* of his watch as he picked it up. "It's just after nine." He switched on the lamp and looked down at her. "Is it late? We'll go back now if you want."

"Nick."

They made love again.

She was already sitting there at the kitchen table with a cup of coffee and a propped-up copy of the scandal magazine *Chi*.

"Hi, Dad."

"Hallo, Giulia. I thought I'd be the first up." He looked at the bare table. "Aren't you eating anything? You should, you know."

"Mm."

"You need the energy."

She looked up from the magazine with a pained expression. "Dad!"

Nick ran his hand through his hair and pulled the faded sweater he wore a little lower over his pajama bottoms. It was cold in the flat, but his large feet were bare. "You're not off today, are you?" he asked.

"You know I am."

"Mm." He filled the electric kettle and stuck two pieces of bread into the toaster. "I wanted to talk to you, Giulia. Before you went back. What time's your plane anyway?"

She told him.

"Then we can have lunch out together." He got out a jar of marmalade and put it on the table with a butter dish, then laid a place for himself opposite his daughter. "Will that be all right?"

She didn't answer.

"*Giulia*."

"Yes, yes, if you want." She looked up impatiently from the magazine again. "Only Mum's probably expecting us to eat here, that's all."

Nick said nothing, just got down a bulbous brown teapot and slipped a teabag inside. The toaster gave a click and began to smoke. Making a dive for it, he whipped out two tortured-looking slices. They clinked onto his plate. Giulia gave a snort of laughter. "That ghastly old thing. Why on earth don't you get a new one?"

"Nothing wrong with it—just needs regulating a bit, that's all." He was pleased by her amusement and wanted to prolong it. "Now, look very carefully at this, please." He picked up two more slices. "If I put these other two in and then slowly. . . . slowly . . . turn the knob to the left"—he bent exaggeratedly forward—"they'll be absolutely perfect, done to a turn."

The kettle sent out a jet of steam and clicked off. Nick filled the teapot, brought it to the table, and leaned over the magazine. "What's that you're reading? Mm." He began to read upside-down: " '*un nuovo amante per Stephanie di Monaco*—A New Lover for Stephanie of Monaco.' Gripping stuff."

Giulia was smiling despite herself at the rich British voice he had put on. "It came free with the newspaper."

"That's what they all say," Nick went on, sitting down. "I've heard *that* one before. You just enjoy sensational gossip, that's all."

There was a loud twang of splitting metal and the front of the toaster fell off. Inside were two twists of disintegrating black matter. Nick sprang up. "Bloody hell! My toast."

Giulia was weak with laughter. "There you are. Now what?" She wiped under her eyes with a bent index finger. "God, Dad, if you knew what you looked like!"

He opened the window to let out the acrid smell and got himself some rolls from the bread bin.

"A new toaster it'll have to be."

She watched him spread the split roll with a thick layer of butter.

"You shouldn't eat that, you know. It's bad for you."

"What? Butter? Nonsense." He covered it in glistening marmalade.

"Cholesterol," Giulia said.

"I'm English, and I will not do without my butter," he said, taking a huge bite. "Or my marmalade. Did you know you can't buy marmalade in Palermo, that the Sicilians with their thousands of oranges and lemons *don't manufacture the stuff*?" He tapped the jar. "This comes from up north. Anyway," he went on, "you won't get me eating any of your revolting Italian slops. Biscuits dipped in milky coffee. It's obscene, that's what it is."

"The Mediterranean diet's the healthiest in the world," Giulia said, leafing though *Chi*, "and you know it." She watched Nick pouring out his tea. "So what time shall we meet then, and where?"

They heard footsteps in the corridor, immediately recognizable to both of them as Paola's.

"One. At Ciccio's," Nick said quickly and swallowed some tea.

"What a terrible smell," Paola said coming into the kitchen. "What on earth's happened?"

She wore her floor-length dressing gown of washed-out blue with a cord knotted round her thin form. Her slippers made a sound like sandpaper on the cold marble floor.

"Hi, Mum," Giulia said. "Shall I make you a coffee?"

"Hallo, Giulia." She glanced with distaste at Nick's breakfast. "Yes, thank you." She screwed up her nose again and looked about her, trying to locate the source of the smell. "What *is* it?"

"The toaster's had it," Giulia said, getting up. "Look."

"Well, that's not my problem," Paola said pointedly to Nick.

"I know it isn't," he answered. "How did you sleep?" He felt she would have preferred to ignore him but was making an effort for Giulia's sake.

"The bedroom's freezing." She went over and closed the window. "And so it is in here. The wind whistles through every chink. Now I've got this dreadful pain in my neck." She rotated her head with an expression of extreme suffering.

Giulia placed a plate, a bowl, and a spoon on the table for her mother and put a jar of biscuits next to them. "Shouldn't Sandro be up?"

"He most certainly should," Paola said, "but I'm not going to be the one to wake him."

"I'll do it," Giulia said, "if you keep an eye on the milk."

When she had left the room Paola said, "You were late back last night. I'd cooked that chicken specially."

"I did tell you—"

"I had to throw it all away. I never even heard you come to bed."

"Listen, Paola—"

"I'm not interested in what you do. All I'm asking is that you let me know beforehand if you intend staying out till all hours. That way I won't be wasting my time cooking for you."

The milk began to rise slowly in the pan, and she switched it off. "I've got better things to do—far better things—than wait in for you." She poured the steaming milk into the bowl and added coffee, then sat down and picked up a biscuit. "And if it's not too much trouble, perhaps you could tell me whether you'll be here for lunch or not. Giulia's leaving at six, in case you didn't know." She dunked her biscuit and sucked at the sodden mass.

On the way to the university he reflected on her bitterness and hate toward him. At breakfast it had taken great forebearance on his part not to grab her by the shoulders and shake her. In fact, he'd had to clench his fists to keep them at his sides. He could almost see her face under the force of his violence: the sallow cheeks ballooning in and out, the lips opening and shutting over rattling teeth, the wisps of hair flying back and forth over her forehead, the eyes staring at him in disbelief. And supposing he had actually done it? Supposing that was what she really wanted? Well, he certainly wasn't going to be the person to give it to her. Any display of affection was out too. So was sympathy—he'd proved it there at the graveside at Ida's funeral. When he put his arm around her he had felt her stiffening, as though she *resented* him. Yet he still hoped, in spite of everything, that one day she would be—if not happy—at least at peace with herself.

The faculty occupied three floors of a nineteen-seventies office block in a square crammed for twelve hours a day with triple-parked cars and scooters. The building had not been intended to house the university at all, and Nick's nine o'clock lesson was held in a stifling box room containing six fiercely contested desks. Once these had been taken, students had to either stand round the walls balancing their notebooks on each other's backs or try and hear what they could through the open door.

He shared the lift up with Pauline. Her armful of books projected beyond her massive front so that she took up two-thirds of the available space.

"Aren't you meant to be in Via Manzoni this morning?" she said accusingly. Via Manzoni, three miles away in the newer part of the city, provided a further four lecture halls and, like this place, could be reached only by tracing a zigzag though a maze of parked vehicles.

"No, I'm meant to be here," Nick said. "Odd though it may seem."

Pauline sniffed. "Then it's Josh. You've heard the latest, haven't you?"

"I don't know. What latest?" The graffiti-covered doors slid open at the fifth floor.

"Exams are to be the week after next. According to our delightful prof." She went out ahead of him onto the landing already crowded with students. The air was thick with cigarette smoke and the smell of sweat.

"Excuse *me*," she said loudly in English, elbowing her way through. "For Christ's sake, can't you all wait somewhere else?"

·   ·   ·

Nick met Giulia at the trattoria, where as soon as they had ordered, she told him she wanted to leave Bologna and go to Australia.

"Forever?" he joked, alarmed.

"No, probably just for a year." She said a friend of hers was working in a restaurant in Sydney and that the owner would sponsor Giulia for a year.

"To work in the restaurant?"

"Yes. Are you shocked?"

"Why should I be?" Nick asked. "If that's what you want."

"That's what you always say." She sounded irritated. "Aren't you angry I'm giving up my studies?"

"Listen, Giulia, it doesn't matter what I think. If that's what you feel you want to do, well then you must go ahead and do it. Anyway, who says you'll give up studying altogether? You might want to go back to it one day."

"And if I didn't? Supposing I decided to stay in Australia forever, get married there, never come back?" She took a roll from the basket on the table and tore it angrily in half. "Then what would you say? I don't like what I'm studying, Dad, I never have. I'm not happy there."

"In that case, you're doing the right thing," he told her. He asked whether Paola knew.

"I didn't really want to say anything, with Granny dying and all that, but then I thought I should. So I told her this morning—after you'd gone. I said I hadn't made up my mind yet, just that I didn't want to stay on in Bologna anymore."

When he made no comment, she went on. "I said I was sorry—and I really am, Dad—that you've both paid out all this money and everything for me, but that it's just not what I want."

He imagined the scene: Paola taking it in shocked silence—after all, she was losing her only ally in the family—or that's how she would see it anyway. "Did you say anything about Australia?" She shook her head. Just as well, Nick thought; having her daughter working as a waitress in the antipodes was going to take Paola some getting used to. Well, it was a lesson to her (and to him too, for that matter) never to try and fit your children into the mold *you* wanted for them.

A waiter put two steaming plates of *pasta alla Norma* down in front of them. "It won't be for a while yet anyway," Giulia said, picking up her fork. "I'm staying on there till Easter." She wound the spaghetti deftly round the prongs and turned to him with it poised halfway to her mouth. "Come on, Dad, eat up." And it was suddenly as though their roles had been reversed: he being the wayward son and she the understanding parent.

After lunch she told him she wasn't coming home with him right away. "Don't leave it too late," Nick warned her. "Your plane goes at—"

"I know, Dad," she said, as though placating a child. "Don't panic. I'm just going to say good-bye to a friend, that's all, then I'll be back. There's masses of time." She climbed onto her scooter and fastened her helmet.

So he left her in town and took the 101 bus back home.

What came first, he wondered or what *should* come first—the family, Giulia, Sandro, the hopeless situation with Paola? Or was it Lea? Was it sex? Was Lea more important to him at the moment than anything or anybody else? He glanced out as the bus passed the top of her street. Yes, she was more important to him. Giulia would find her own way, children did. He had always believed that. Just look at her: by the time he left her, she seemed to have forgotten there had been any kind of problem at all. She would go back to college—not now but in a few years' time. Needed to find herself.

"Has she told you?" Paola asked when he opened the front door. Wearily he put his briefcase on the hall table and went past her into the kitchen. She followed him. "Has she?"

"Yes. If you mean Giulia."

"So? What are we going to do?"

"Nothing," Nick said. "We're not going to do anything, Paola. We're going to let her do what she likes."

"I can't believe it." Paola's mouth dropped. "I can't believe you're saying this." She suddenly burst into tears. "Your daughter's leaving university, just like that, and you don't care! You just don't care!"

He watched the heaving shoulders for a moment, then went over to her. "Paola—"

"Don't touch me!" she screamed. "Don't you dare! After *Mamma's* death too. I don't know how you can do it. Instead of—"

"It's her decision, for God's sake," he shouted back. "She's not happy there."

There was a gasping break in the sobbing. "She loved her studies, she told me so. Something's happened, somebody must have done something to change her mind. She'd never have wanted to leave otherwise."

Nick made a supreme effort. "Just listen to me for a moment, Paola, will you?" he said slowly and evenly. "Giulia has thought about this very carefully." (Had she?) "She wants to take some time off—a year maybe."

Paola lifted a tear-streaked face, aghast. "A *year*?"

"Well, six months, I don't know. Does it matter how long?"

"Yes, it does matter! She's brilliantly clever."

"Oh, come on, Paola. She's just like everybody else."

Paola came menacingly toward him, her arm lifted. "Don't you *dare* say that! She's a brilliant student, I tell you, and she's got a wonderful career ahead of her!"

He caught the arm in midair as it descended over his head. "Paola!"

"Let me go!" She struggled, teeth clenched, breathing heavily. *"Take your hands off me."* She broke free and rubbed her elbows. Her voice dropped: "And if you think I don't know about you . . ."

Now what?

"I know all about her."

Nick turned away.

"Yes, you may well walk away." She followed him into the bedroom.

Is this really happening? Nick wondered, getting out of his jacket. He remembered Ida once telling him. "She's not the same, my Paola, Neek. Not like she used to be. I don't know what has happened to her. She won't talk to me, but she loves you very much, you know." Putting the responsibility well and truly on his shoulders. As though it were his duty to get her back the way she used to be. She was standing behind him now.

"Of course it's up to you whether you take a lover or not," she said in the same quiet voice.

"Oh, for Christ's sake."

"Yes, for Christ's sake, for Christ's sake. That's all you can say, isn't it?"

He sat down heavily on the bed and began undoing his shoes. She couldn't possibly know. No way.

"I have to put up with that as well," she went on. "A husband with a *mistress*."

Still he ignored her, reaching for the pair of old tennis shoes he wore about the house. Infuriated by his calm, she snatched them from him. "A fucking bloody *cunt* of a mistress!" She hurled the shoes across the room. They thumped one after the other against the far wall and slid to the floor.

Genuinely surprised by her swearing, Nick experienced the same unnerving sensation he had had on the bus that morning: that she was taunting him, pleading for violence. It scared him.

"And don't try and tell me it's not true," she said, thrusting her chin toward him, "because I've seen her!"

"You haven't seen anyone."

"Oh, yes I have. Oh, yes I have." The spit flew from her mouth. "On the bus!"

Nick went to retrieve the shoes from the other side of the room, and as he straightened up he felt her arm come down hard across the back of his neck. In sudden fury, he caught hold of her wrist and bent it back, then turned his face toward hers. For a split second he saw the triumph in her eyes.

"Go on, hit me! Hit me!" she panted. "If you dare!" She tried to break free of his grip, but he kept an iron hold on her. Breathing heavily to control himself, he pushed her slowly backward toward the bed. Just as they got there she made another attempt to free herself, and this time he let her go. Her arm shot up and backward and hit a small ceramic bowl on the shelf. It traced a graceful arc through the air and fell with a splintering crack onto the marble floor. Paola let out a scream. "Giulia's bowl! Giulia's bowl! Now look what you've done!"

It lay in burnt orange and powder-blue fragments around their feet.

At the same moment the bowl shattered, Dante was walking up the steps of the newspaper offices. He pushed open the double glass doors and entered the lobby, greeting two colleagues going the other way. The porter came out from behind his desk and took Dante conspiratorially aside, telling him his brother-in-law had been fishing and come back with six *totani*, several calamari, and a handful of small octopus. "And I've kept these two for you, *dottore*," he said. "Freshly caught last night. Beauties."

Dante bent toward the oval dish the man was holding. "Hey, they're wonderful, Turi." He poked the tentacles admiringly. They shivered imperceptibly and then lay still.

"I know you like them, *dottore*. They can be done fried or else boiled with half a lemon. The wife does them that way the day before, then we have them cold in a salad." He winked and made a sucking sound of relish. *"Fa-vo-lo-si."*

He waited while Dante straightened up. "I'll keep them here in the fridge until you go," he told him, taking the dish back reverently. "Then they'll keep fresh. Got the car nearby, have you?"

Dante nodded and asked where the fish had been caught.

"Off the Trapani coast, *dottore*. My brother-in-law was out all night. Didn't catch them till four in the morning. Dolphins wouldn't let him get near them."

"Dolphins?"

"Swam round and round and underneath the boat. Protecting

the fish, they were. Followed the boat everywhere."

When he went home, Dante told Lea about the dolphins. She had been horrified by the huge tentacled squid on the oval dish, and he hoped the story would bring her round. But the dolphins' courage and sense of brotherhood and their thwarted attempt at salvation had the reverse effect.

"It's terrible," she said. "A terrible story."

He told her that sentimentalism had no place in man's search for food. "It's us against them," he said about the fish. "They do exactly the same themselves. It's survival: each eats the other. Besides, they have the chance to escape, and millions do."

He brought the squid over to the sink. Each was well over a foot long and as thick as his forearm. "I'll show you how to clean them," he said, rolling up his sleeves.

"No, Dante, please."

He ignored her. "I used to watch my mother doing it. It was always fresh stuff then, like this. Nobody dreamed of going to a fish shop. We'd go down to the beach early in the morning about six—"

"Dante, I don't want to watch."

"Come on, you're a photographer, for God's sake. They're beautiful, magnificent creatures."

He turned on the cold tap, letting it dribble down in a thin stream, and hung a plastic bag on the hot one. Then he got hold of the first gleaming brown and white mass. Lea saw the squid's huge pleading eyes turned toward her before Dante thrust thumb and forefinger into the flesh and gouged them out. They were perfectly spherical, the size of a large marble. He dropped them into the plastic bag one by one, wiping the slime off his fingers onto the sides of the bag. Next he grasped hold of the tentacles growing out of the head.

"That's right," he grunted, pulling and twisting. "Come on, now." With a slow *shluck!* the bunch came away. He held it under the tap, pulling at the thick ribbons one by one to clean them.

"You can tell how fresh it is," he said, putting the pads of his fingers on the rubbery suckers running up the underside of the tentacles. "Just look at that."

Lea watched the nodules cleaving to his fingers, a disturbingly sexual union. As though showing him they were still alive and able to function. Or perhaps begging for mercy.

The two fleshy lateral tubes that had come away with the bunch of tentacles were now being cleaned. Dante ran his fingers firmly up and down these several times, then put the whole lot aside.

"You see, there's no smell," he said, thrusting his hand up to the wrist into the now open-ended body. "Fresh fish hasn't got a smell. It's only when it's old that . . ." He screwed up his face in concentration, searching around inside. "Here we go . . . that's it." He pulled out a dripping white handful and dumped it in the plastic bag. "Eggs."

So it was pregnant. The poor animal.

Humming softly to himself, Dante continued to clear the body of its internal organs. Various small lumps and nodules swathed in slime were drawn out and placed in the bag, and when the cavity was completely empty, he rinsed it out thoroughly. Turning it upside down he began rubbing at the thin covering of red-brown epidermis with his thumb. It came away like sunburned human skin.

"See that?" he said to Lea. "Just rolls off. Only does that when it's super fresh."

He went on worrying the flesh until it was quite clean, then thrust his hand inside again, this time easing and stretching his fingers as though testing the quality and wearability of a glove. A white rubber mitt, Lea thought. Shiny, faintly medical, aseptic.

He was now at work on the triangular tail fins, rubbing and smoothing until those too turned a moonlit tombstone white.

"Right. How shall we have it, Lea: in rings, then fried, or stuffed in the oven?" He reached for a large knife.

"I told you, Dante, I don't think I can eat it."

"It's a fairly tough fish," he went on, ignoring her. "Not like the calamari. But the flavor should be excellent." He brandished the knife. "Fried?"

She nodded in mute misery and watched the gleaming wet blade sinking into the mitt and transforming it into perfect rings.

"May I go now?" she asked him.

"Yes, you may go, *signora*," he conceded graciously. "I shall see to the other one all on my own." He sliced up the tail fins and started on the tentacles. "We dine at eight."

Over supper she told him that the book launch was now definitely set for the end of the month and that the invitations had gone out by express mail that morning. It was the only possible time they could have it because then Fontanini was off to Argentina for three months.

"Not exactly the best time of year for promoting a book," Dante said. "And what about the football match? It's an important one. You knew about it, didn't you?"

"Yes, but what could we do? Just have to hope the sort of

people who come to a book launch wouldn't watch football matches on the box, that's all."

He saw her crestfallen face. "I'm sorry, love. After all that work. But wouldn't it perhaps have been wiser to wait till Easter? Or even better, just gone ahead and done it without him?"

She gave a wry smile. "I know you can't stand him, but he *is* the author, you know. Anyway, don't let's talk about it. If it's going to flop, it's going to flop, and that's all there is to it." She put a ring of squid into her mouth. "These are gorgeous. I'm sorry I was rude about them."

He gave a grunt of satisfaction.

"I just can't take those bits, though." She gave a slight shiver and pushed one of the tentacles to the far side of the dish with the back of her fork. It was a terrible twisted parody of its former self.

"They're the best of all," Dante said, skillfully spearing one with his fork. "Don't know what you're missing."

He was feeling particularly at peace with himself, soothed into mellowness by the steady domestic ritual of preparation and cooking, and proud of his success. Lea had left him to it, only once putting her head round the kitchen door when the coated fish began exploding in the pan with a series of loud reports. She laughed when she saw him sheltering from the scalding missiles of flour and oil behind a saucepan lid.

When they had finished the fish and Dante had opened another bottle of wine, she told him about meeting Flora and about the man in the shop and how Flora had decided to go home rather than having to confront him again. Dante listened with a grave expression, then shook his head. "Bloody stupid thing to do."

"What?"

He took a cigar stub from the ashtray and relit it. "You don't bugger around with people like that."

She told him about the owner of the carpet shop in the same street who refused to pay the *pizzo*. This time Dante got up and started pacing the room. He wanted to know whether Lea had met him. When she said no, he seemed pleased, then said Flora was risking her life thanks to that shit ass of a husband of hers.

They drank their way through the wine. Then Lea told him she would be starting to photograph the tree the next morning and wanted to get off early.

"Tree?"

"I told you: the rubber tree—*Ficus magnolioides,* if you want its proper name—for that Norwegian magazine."

He repeated the Latin name slowly to himself, rolling the diphthongs over his tongue, then took a long pull at the cigar. "I remember them as a boy." He let his head drop back and blew out a funnel of aromatic smoke. "The one in Piazza Marina. It seemed quite magical to us, this massive great—*cathedral* of a tree. Hardly real at all." He reached for the bottle of *amaro*. "So it's for the Norwegians, is it? What is it, some botanical journal?"

Lea stood up yawning. "No, not really, more a general interest magazine. The journalist spent a holiday here and was fascinated by them."

Always *fascinated,* Dante thought to himself angrily. Foreigners are forever fascinated by Sicily. The Scandinavians, the Americans, the British—even the Milanese, like that God's-gift-to-women, Fontanini. What was it that arrested their attention? The island's beauty, poverty, corruption, decadence, violence, its *trees*? No, more likely its insistence on not conforming, on doing things *its* and nobody else's way. The kind of life everybody secretly craved and hadn't the courage to lead. He poured out a tiny glass of the *digestif* for himself and held the bottle inquiringly up toward Lea. She shook her head and began clearing the table. "I'm off to bed, Dante. You don't mind, do you?"

He did, rather. "If you're tired."

"The squid was wonderful."

When she had gone, he wandered out onto the terrace. It was cold, the sky studded with millions of stars. That must be the British warship down there in the port; lit up from end to end, massive great thing. He had seen the sailors wandering in twos and threes round town. Who knows what *they* thought of Palermo.

He knew that the popular image of Sicily abroad—threatening and corrupt on one side, mysterious and indolent on the other—hadn't entirely disappeared, and maybe never would. The majority of northern Italians he had known subscribed to it too, although they would certainly never admit as much—considered themselves far too "open-minded" for that. As long as he could remember, he had always experienced a polite but definite distancing between himself and his colleagues, especially from the Emilia-Romagna region. Mistrust, basically. The island simply wasn't taken seriously. Things were changing, of course—at least for the tourist trade. Now it was the wonderful Mediterranean food they were furiously peddling, the heady southern wine, the back-to-nature way of life—the wholesomeness. Cooking and corruption, violence and vineyards: there was something for everyone. Well, balls to the lot of them.

He wondered whether he could be bothered to get down to a bit of work on his article. He had dropped in on the Andreotti trial that morning—only stayed an hour or so, chatted to a couple of friends, lent an ear—no more—to the prosecuting counsel. No way of knowing how it was all going to end, but he could speculate. That was his role, after all, wasn't it? An observer. He looked at his watch. Lea obviously didn't want to be disturbed. He knew the signs. Hardly ever did these days.

With a final look at the starlit heavens and the twinkling harbor lights, he came back indoors and fastened the French windows behind him, then went into the little room they called the study. The computer was humming softly. He sat down and opened his file.

Half an hour later, finding himself unsure of a word spelling and opening the weighty dictionary he kept beside him on the table, he experienced the familiar leap in his loins. Funny how it had never left him. It went back to early adolescence when he used to look up dirty words in his father's dark blue dictionary. That trembling anticipation and hardening between his thighs as he drew near the letter *B* (breast), *I* (intercourse), or *V* (vagina). The release of frenzied rubbing, the emptiness afterward.

Well, that was far away and long ago. He found the word he was looking for: *sovraccarico,* overfull. A double *c* followed by a single one. He corrected his text, yawned, and switched off the computer.

Lea was turned toward the bedroom wall, just as he had expected. Somehow he knew she was only feigning sleep, but nothing on earth would have persuaded him to disturb her. He might be losing her, but he was a proud man. A *Sicilian.*

·   ·   ·

After their row Nick had shut himself in his study. In a way, he thought, it had made things easier, because after an outburst like that, things could never be the same again. She just wasn't the same person anymore, nothing remotely like the girl he had married. After the bowl had shattered, she had thrown herself face downward on the bed and shrieked at him like a madwoman to go away and leave her alone. So he had.

Then Giulia had come back, and Paola had reappeared, washed and tidied up, and said she would drive her daughter to the airport. Ignoring Nick completely, she took the car keys, picked up Giulia's case, and opened the front door.

"Good-bye, Daddy," Giulia said, eyes wide with worry. "Say good-bye to Sandro for me, won't you?" She kissed him and threw a quick nervous glance at Paola, waiting stonily on the landing for them to finish. "I'll phone you this evening."

Nick nodded. "Good-bye, my love, and everything'll be fine."

"I know," she said unconvincingly.

When they had gone he went into the bedroom and sat down, wondering how to fill the evening. There was no trace of the broken bowl anywhere. Just then the entry phone buzzed, and he got up thinking Giulia had probably forgotten something, but there was a man's head and shoulders filling the little video screen. God almighty! He'd completely forgotten.

"Good evening, professor," the face said. "This is Goffredo Di Marco."

I can see that for myself, for Christ's sake, Nick muttered, and in a loud voice, "Hi, come on up." He pressed the button to release the catch on the downstairs entrance door.

He had never wanted this student in the first place and had

quoted him an exaggeratedly high price, but Di Marco had accepted with alacrity. At the time he had been working in the local branch of Nick's bank and was keen to better his career prospects by learning English. In taking him on, Nick had broken his own golden rule of never accepting hopeless learners as private students. Strictly speaking, the rule applied to the dire type of schoolkid you handed back to parents after months of tuition in exactly the same state as he had come to you. The kid's inevitable failure in examinations would of course be seen as your fault or, at the very least (if parents were generous-minded), caused by your "wrong approach" as a teacher. It just wasn't worth the hassle.

Di Marco was totally unable to grasp the simplest grammatical concept. Added to this was his appalling rendering of the English language. Nick had wondered whether the man suffered from slight deafness, but he seemed to have no trouble in his own language or in dealing with his customers at the bank. What made the whole thing so ridiculous was Di Marco's conviction that he was making progress. He came to Nick for two hours every Thursday.

The doorbell rang.

"Good evening, Professor Stirling," Di Marco said in English. This came out as "Could eevening, Profficer Steerling" and was accompanied by a very slight inclination of the head.

After the first half hour Nick heard a noise out in the hall. A moment later Sandro put his head round the study door. "Oh," he said and withdrew.

Nick excused himself and went into the kitchen. "Everything all right?" he asked his son. "I completely forgot about"—he jerked his head behind him and made a face. "I'll be finished in an hour or so." Sandro nodded cheerfully and opened the fridge.

When Nick went back into the study, Di Marco was bent over his textbook. "I no *under*stand dis ward."

Nick told him its meaning. "I'm going to give you a short dictation now," he continued. "The first time I'll just read through the piece and you listen. The second time, you'll write." Di Marco started fussing around with pen and paper. "I am reedy. Pliz not fast."

At the conclusion of the exercise he handed over his work eagerly for Nick's perusal. The first sentence read: "Hawe cam it it so difialt faind English fud in Enland?" Interestingly, Nick thought, the whole thing looked slightly Irish or Gaelic. It certainly bore very little resemblance to modern-day English.

"I'm afraid it's not gone very well, *dottor* Di Marco," Nick said. "Take a look at it," and he handed him back the book. The page was scored from top to bottom in red. Di Marco took it with good grace. "Eet iz diffical always understand der wards," he said, frowning at his work.

"Yes, well," Nick began, "you must try and understand the *sense* of the piece: *il senso,*" he added in Italian, hoping this would drive it home. "Then there wouldn't be so many mistakes. Take this sentence, for instance." He twisted the exercise book round and showed Di Marco "Der britisch haf alwais imported fud from a bboad."

"Now what does that mean? Who are we talking about here?"

"British people."

"Yes," Nick went on encouragingly. "British people what?"

"People import food."

"Import food from . . . from . . . ?"

"Import food from. . . . I no understand 'a bboad,' " he finished.

"No, you can't, because it's written incorrectly," Nick said. "The correct spelling is *a-b-r-o-a-d,* and it means *estero.*"

"*Ah, l'estero, ora capisco.*"

When the two hours were up and Nick was showing him out, Di Marco settled his coat more comfortably over his shoulders and with evident satisfaction said in Italian, "I think I'm improving, don't you, Professor Stirling? I feel I made considerable progress this evening. Perhaps we'll be able to move on to Book Three soon."

It wasn't until nine o'clock, when Paola was still not back, that Nick suddenly realized Thursday was her opera night. After the theft of her membership card, she been issued another one and had started going again with a colleague from the office. She would have gone off to the theater after leaving Giulia at the airport.

He made a plate of pasta for himself and opened a bottle of beer. Sandro was on his way out. "Working in the pub tonight?" Nick asked him.

"No, I've finished there. They never paid." He turned up the collar of his jacket against the cold out on the landing. "See you later, Dad."

Nick sat on his own at the kitchen table thinking of Lea and the quarrel with Paola and wondering how it was all going to end. Too early to try and work things out yet. He was seeing Lea tomorrow. At the flat. What was *she* thinking about it all?

There was nothing on television, so he decided to watch the video his sister had sent him from England. "You're always saying you're forgetting your English," she had E-mailed him, "so I've sent you a tape. It's a mixture of stuff I recorded and thought you might like. The program at the beginning is hilarious."

He slotted in the cassette and flopped down on the sofa. The first item his sister had found so irresistible turned out to be *Have I Got News for You*. Nick sat through it from beginning to end stony-faced, not understanding any of the topical references. Only one or two of Paul Merton's deadpan deliveries raised a smile from him.

That was the trouble with living abroad—you lost touch. You forgot the subtlety of British humor. Italians laughed at quite different things. He was suddenly homesick for old friends, for pubs, the cinema, the theater (not that he could afford to go often then), parties, discussions, even BBC television. He realized he missed sending up people, the pricking of overblown theories, pompous ideas, plays on words. For all their shortcomings, the English were witty. Their adverts were brilliant to start with. Every time he went home he was full of admiration for them.

He missed the British papers; on-line ones he found a poor substitute, as he did BBC World Service. Edward Greenfield on Sunday mornings playing an Elizabeth Schwarzkopf lieder for a faithful listener in Sierra Leone wasn't really his kind of thing at all, never had been. Nor were women's problems in Eastern Europe. How on earth had he crossed the barrier from real to ersatz Englishman? Come to that, how had he finished up here?

One thing was certain: wherever he was in the world, he'd always want Lea. He craved her body, her eyes looking into his as they lay together, her hair, the scent of her. Everything about her. They had arranged to see each other at five tomorrow at the flat. Still meeting during the day. Not evenings yet. Not yet.

He heard the front door opening. That would be Paola, back from the theater. She must have seen the light from the sitting room but didn't come in. He heard her moving about, going to the bathroom, then switching on the light in the kitchen and opening the cupboards. Still she ignored his presence. Well, better that way. He lay back and closed his eyes.

"I'm just telling you I shan't be in to lunch tomorrow." She was standing there in the doorway, looking down at him as though he were something dirty on the carpet. "So don't wait for me. That's all I wanted to say." She turned on her heel and was gone.

He gave her a good half hour, then went along the corridor and slipped quietly into bed.

The most important thing was the light, and it was just right that morning: mostly a clear blue sky with just a few fine-weather clouds. As long as there was no wind it would be ideal. She told Dante she was going to the botanical gardens first. "There's that very old tree there," she told him, "which I want to do first. Then I'll probably go on to your one in Piazza Marina after lunch."

"*My* one?" He smiled. "Where'll you eat? Shall we meet somewhere?"

"No, no, better not. I don't know when I'll be finishing. It all depends on what the weather's going to do. I might not even get to Piazza Marina today." Already starting to hide things from him.

He nodded. "Okay then. So you won't want a lift either?"

"No. I'll need my car today." She had to load the tripod and everything else into the back. "But we'll eat together tonight. Or go out somewhere nice if you want."

"You don't have to placate me or make atonements for your absence." He smiled.

"I know I don't. I wasn't. I just thought we could go and have a pizza somewhere."

Dante put his head thoughtfully on one side. "A pizza, mm? Very youthful idea. Yes, why not?"

"Even old men eat pizzas," Lea said, rinsing their cups under the tap. "I'll ring you anyway."

"You look very nice today," Dante said appraisingly. "I don't really want to let you go."

"Well you must." She put the cups above the sink to drain.

"Yes, I must," he said heavily. "Have to wait until this evening."

She found a parking space right outside the botanical gardens, which was a good start, but immediately realized that the tree was going to present problems. To start with, it grew near an ugly perimeter wall, which was overshadowed by a gas tank, and was also very gloomy beneath its crown. As well as all that, it was going to be difficult to get far enough away to photograph it in its entirety. It was only when she had set up the tripod for some preliminary shots that she became aware of yet another inconvenience: the olivelike fruits, which fell without warning all around her, hitting the camera with little *thuts!* and catching her on the back of the neck quite painfully.

"This spectacular tropical tree was wrongfully attributed to the magnolia family because of the similarity of its leaf," she read on a metal sign fixed into the ground. "It can grow to a great age and its foliage may spread over one thousand square meters." Never having bothered much about plants or trees of any kind, she marveled now at the massive central trunk and muscular horizontal branches. Aerial roots in different stages of growth hung from these—the most recent suspended in a solid tangled mass of fibers above her head, the oldest hardened into secondary and tertiary trunks in their own right. Other horizontal roots raised some two feet above the ground snaked away elephant-gray and solid like the rest of the tree.

The only way she was going to be able to photograph it was from high up. It would either have to be from the roof of that little building nearby—it looked like some sort of a laboratory— or else using a special gantry. And, she realized, there would also have to be human figures underneath the tree to show its size. In the meantime she started taking close-ups of the interlacing bright orange fibers hanging from above, the smooth gray bark, and what the description had called the tree's "columnar and tabular" roots.

One or two people came and stood round watching her, and when a child ran up and sat astride one of the overland roots, she photographed him too. The father hung back watching, then when Lea straightened up asked what newspaper she worked for. The little boy left the root and ran up to peer at the complicated camera. Lea said that if he wanted to climb a little way up the trunk, she'd take another picture of him. "If that's all right," she added to the father.

"As long as none of the gardeners comes up," he said. "Go on then, Salvo. The lady wants to do you again."

By two o'clock she had finished. Walking back past a bamboo-fringed lily pond, she felt the sun warming her back. Under the dense canopy of trees it was cooler and smelled of damp earth and leaves.

She decided to get something to eat in the little snack bar opposite the gardens so she could keep an eye on the car. The weather was holding and the light still good, so she'd be able to go on to Piazza Marina afterward. It would only take her three minutes by car from there to Nick's. That's why she had planned it that way round.

There were no spare tables, so she stood up at the crowded bar and ate a slice of pizza held in a paper napkin. Too late she remembered she had arranged with Dante to have pizza that night too. Well, that could be changed. Anything could be changed. You could change your whole life if you wanted to.

She watched two sailors on the pavement outside. They conferred together for a few seconds, then came in, first looking Lea up and down, then turning their attention to the food. She saw they were English—HMS something or other on their caps—and very young. Must be from that ship Dante had pointed out to her this morning. One of them tapped on the glass-fronted counter to show he wanted an *arancina* displayed on the shelf inside and was told in sign language to pay for it first. He went over to the till, and both sailors bent their heads over a handful of notes. She heard muttered words between them. Then the money handed over, and they started to eat.

"Beer?" the first one said to the barman. "Two beers?" He pointed to himself and his shipmate and mimed drinking.

With the glasses in their hands they became bolder and began sizing the place up. Lea got another, longer look from them, and so did another woman who had just come in. They couldn't be more than twenty or twenty-one, Lea was thinking: her son's age.

He was coming over for the book launch. Well, not especially for that—it would have been far too expensive—but tying it in with the film and other things. The thought filled her with pleasure. He'd be staying the two or three days with them—more if she could persuade him to. He and Dante got on well.

Just then one of the seamen caught her eye, held it for a second, then seeing her spontaneous smile and realizing he had miscalculated her availability, looked away again. She finished her bottle of mineral water and left.

The square known as Piazza Marina, at the lower end of Corso Vittorio Emanuele, had been designed and laid out with its central *villa*—or garden—in the second half of the nineteenth century soon after Garibaldi's triumphant passage. Before that, in Arab times, the place had been used as a communal rubbish dump. This was not wholly unsurprising, as it lay where the river Kemonia flowed into the sea and, like other urban river deltas, was probably foul-smelling and infested by mosquitoes. Lea remembered sombody once telling her that a gallows had stood nearby in the seventeenth century and that the notorious murderess Francesca La Sarda, who dispatched her victims by means of poison, had been hanged there. The river had long since gone underground, and the piazza was now mainly cited in guidebooks for the historic buildings round its perimeter and for the magnificent examples of *Ficus magnolioides* in its central garden.

In point of fact, these trees were even more impressive than the one in the botanical gardens, Lea decided. Maybe it was their setting in the decadence of broken fountain basins and cracked statuary that gave them their dignity. They rose, massive cathedrals of vegetation, proclaiming their sheer size and power over the faded, dusty garden. Everlasting! Which one was Dante's tree? She guessed it was probably the larger of the two, the one with branches that soared above and beyond the broken, rusty garden railings. The most exciting one for children, the one you could actually *walk into*.

She set up the camera and began working from a distance, then from different angles, pleased by the passersby. A woman walking her dog, oblivious of Lea, steadied one foot on a wall-like root and stooped to tie her shoelace. Some minutes later two tourists stopped underneath, threw their heads back, and pointed up into the crown of leaves. One dropped her spectacles, and Lea got her as she retrieved them. Next an old man shuffled by and drew out a handkerchief. Something caught his attention as he was about to blow his nose, and she froze him turning round with a startled expression on his face and the white handkerchief open in front of him.

The relationship between human being and tree was exciting and beautiful—the patterns they interwove with each other, the colors of clothes against the gray, the movement and the static. Dogs trotted into the cavern of branches with their noses to the ground, and out again. Children grasped the hanging roots and tried to swing on them Tarzan-like.

She had been so intent on her work that the fading afternoon light surprised her. Irritated at being interrupted she looked up into the sky and saw cauliflowers of storm clouds billowing and merging together. Beyond and between them the slivers of sky were still a primose gold, so they might yet clear and let her go on working a little longer.

But it had gone quiet in the garden. Everybody suddenly seemed to have left with the sun. Lea glanced at her watch: half past four. A gust of wind lifted the strap of the camera bag. Well, if it was going to get blustery and start raining, that was it. She began packing everything away, her mind still swirling with images.

A hot wave washed over her as she remembered she was seeing Nick, and that he was just up the road. Waiting for her.

"I almost forgot I was seeing you," she told him half an hour later. "I was so tied up in those trees."

"Tied up in the trees!"

"You know what I mean."

"Your invitation came this morning."

"Did it? It's going to be a farce."

"What is?" he asked "The presentation?"

"Nobody wants to buy books at this time of the year—right after Christmas."

"Why not? There're birthdays and things. Don't despair."

"I do despair."

He reached over and touched her face. "I love you, Lea."

After a moment she said, "You don't know anything about me, Nick, nothing at all."

"It doesn't matter."

"Yes, it does matter. Besides, I live with someone else, you know that. I've got a son."

"I've got a son *and* a daughter."

She gave a sad, crooked smile. "Don't try and humor me. I don't know what to do."

She turned toward him. "I only know I like being here with you." She squeezed him to her. "Help me, Nick."

It was as though they were lying in a cave cut off by the rising tide. She was aware of the water coming closer and closer, swirling round the entrance, licking the rock floor and trying to get to her, while above their heads, the wind tore and roared through the coarse grass. She knew she had to get out quickly because the waves were swelling, crashing, and thudding against the rock. And then, just as they were about to break through the entrance and flood it completely, she felt herself pulled strongly and smoothly into the very depths of the cave. Darkness, smoothness, and peace.

Later, she felt him turning toward her. "That's seven."

"What?"

"Seven o'clock. Striking."

"It can't be." She had to phone Dante.

"It is. I didn't know whether to wake you."

"I've got to phone." She grabbed her phone and ran naked down the stairs. He heard her speaking into it from the kitchen.

"You see," she said to him when she came back. "You see what happens?"

She began picking up her clothes. "It's useless."

He came up behind her. "It isn't useless, Lea. Anyway, I'm in the same boat." He stroked the nape of her neck, watching his hand as it ran lower and lower down her back. She didn't answer, just gently eased away from him and went down to the bathroom.

Outside on the very grand marble landing, he ducked beneath the waxlike leaves of a towering pot plant and said, "So we'll go out there on Wednesday then."

"Oh, I don't know, I don't know. Yes, all right. But if something happens and I can't come . . ."

He drew her head toward him and kissed her. "If it does, it does."

· · ·

That evening she and Dante ate at Lillo's in a little street behind the theater. Inside, the walls were covered with signed photos of famous stage and screen personalities. "To Lillo from Bob," Lea read scrawled across a photo showing De Niro with his arm slung round a sheepish-faced and much thinner Lillo. Another had a terrifyingly chic Sofia Loren raising her glass with a slightly more portly version of him, while he gazed into her cleavage. "*A Lillo che sa far 'a pizza migliore del mondo!*" she had written.

Dante followed her gaze. "She may have said he makes the best pizzas in the world," he said drily, "but I'm wondering if I really want one now." He squeezed Lea's arm. "I know I said I would."

"Have what you like," she said. "Do you think they're authentic?"

"The photos? You should know. Yes, I should think they probably are. He had a place in New York for years. What are you having?"

She said she wasn't very hungry. "A salad perhaps . . . no, I won't, I'll have the grilled vegetables."

Dante said, "And I'll have the pasta with clams." He put the menu aside. "The book's in Feltrinelli's, you know."

"Is anybody buying it?"

"I didn't see. I was only there a few minutes."

"Oh Dante, for God's sake, tell me. Nobody was, were they?"

He lifted his hand to catch the waiter's attention. "You haven't had the launch yet; what do you expect?" He recognized some friends at another table and waved.

When they had started on the wine, Lea had a sudden overpowering desire to say she had fallen for another man and what did Dante intend doing about it?

"What's wrong?" Dante said, looking at her curiously. "You look odd."

"This wine's quite strong." *Coward.*

"Do you want to try a different one?"

She shook her head. "No, just give me some water. So Wednesday you'll be in Milan then? Don't smoke that thing here."

"I'm not," he said. "It's not even lit." He stuck the cigar butt between his teeth. "Milan? Not if I can get out of it, no. Ah, here it comes. *Real* clams, I hope, Lillo?"

"You'd prefer pretend ones?" Lillo said, putting the steaming dish in front of him. He told Lea hers was just coming.

"Dante . . ."

"For Christ's sake, Lea, what is it? Are you trying to tell me you've got a lover, or what?" He lifted his fork and, when she said nothing, put it slowly down again. "Well?"

"I've met this man."

This time he said nothing.

"This man. There's nothing serious yet, just that . . ."

He waited.

"Well, just that I wanted to tell you."

"Right, you've told me. Who is he?"

"You don't know him. There's nothing really yet."

"You've already said that. Okay, what am I supposed to do about it then?"

Lea's vegetables came.

"Haven't you started yet?" Lillo said to Dante accusingly. "It'll spoil. *Buon appetito!*"

"Listen, Dante," she began softly when Lillo had gone. "I

wanted you to know. I want to be honest with you. We said we always would be."

"Do you want to go off with him, or what?"

"*No*. It may not come to anything." But she knew it would.

Dante picked up his fork and began playing with the strands of spaghetti. He lifted up a tiny clam, shelled it, and put it in his mouth. She watched him, her own food untouched.

"Dante . . ."

"It's not that shithead Fontanini, is it?"

"No, it isn't!" The couple at the next table turned round startled, and Lea lowered her voice. "Why do you go on about him? For Christ's sake, he's gay anyway."

This seemed to cheer Dante up, and he took a large mouthful of pasta. "You haven't said what you want to do. Do you want me to clear out—leave you *campo libero*—leave you to fuck in peace?"

She looked away in distaste. "Of course I don't. Anyway it's your place, not mine."

Dante took a long drink of wine, then leaned forward over the table. "Look, Lea, eat up, will you? You've told me and that's that. And have some more of this, for God's sake." He slopped the wine into her glass. "Go on, drink up."

By midnight they had finished their second bottle. Dante called Lillo over to their table. "You fat slob, you. Why the hell did you leave America and come back to this hole, eh? Italy's the pits."

Lillo humored him. "The wife's family. Missed her sisters. If it wasn't for her I'd still be there." He winked. "Know what I mean?" He turned to Lea. "Was everything all right?" he asked. "Anything else?"

She shook her head, fuddled by the wine.

"Is this the bill, you old so-and-so?" Dante asked, picking up the saucer and holding the piece of paper almost at arm's length. He stood up rather unsteadily and ruffled the man's sparse hair so that it stood up clownlike all over his head. "You're a great guy, you know that? A great guy."

They walked home, the cold, clean night air blowing into their eyes and nostrils. When they were halfway back, Dante put his arm roughly round Lea and pulled her toward him, and she let her head drop onto his shoulder. Neither of them spoke. That night they made love passionately, and it had never been like that before.

They didn't speak much over the next few days either, just greeted each other politely in the morning and—if Dante came back for supper—made small talk in the evening. A couple of times he phoned saying he was working late, and she didn't ask any questions. At nights he kept to his side of the bed and made no attempt to touch her. It was as though he were waiting for her to make a decision, waiting for her to tell him what she intended to do. There were times, of course, when they had to communicate, and then he would be very polite and formal, asking her if it was all right if he asked her to see to the insurance payment on one of the cars because it had run out and he was tied up all day. The morning after they had eaten at Lillo's, he told her he had decided to go to Milan after all on the Wednesday, then turned away before she could say anything.

Lea was desperately hurt by all this and knew she was handling it wrong. The mistake had been to tell him in the first place—so early on. You didn't do that until you were absolutely sure and had made up your mind what to do, and she hadn't.

Telling him was just a salving of her conscience—a terrible thing to have done. She put herself in Dante's place: supposing *he* had suddenly told her he was in love with someone else? The thing was, she knew he never would. He was in love with *her*. And that made what she had done seem even worse. She got on with her work and tried not to think about what was going to happen.

The last tree she wanted to photograph for the Norwegian assignment was at Villa Malfitano. The house had belonged to the Whitaker family (the same family that had inspired the English in Palermo exhibition) and was now the headquarters of the foundation that managed and preserved their various properties in Sicily.

The gardens were spacious and disappointingly dull. It looked as if the owners had simply insisted on every known species of Mediterranean shrub and tree being planted there without giving a thought to its shape, potential growth, or color. Lea found herself unable to find anything of harmony or beauty there. Even the ficus tree had been planted too near the villa and had to have the branches on one side lopped off as a result. The tree's fame nowadays—as a gardener told her—rested not so much on its tremendous girth as on the way its horizontal branches appeared to defy gravity.

She could see that for herself now. Looking through the lens from the wide gravel drive in front of the house, it was as though they were arms reaching out in supplication. Lord, let us stretch and grow! She took several shots of them, then moved round to the other side, humming "Don't Fence Me In" as she worked. Watching two children playing under the tree, she remembered how she used to take Roberto to a garden a bit like this in Rome when he was small. He had a yellow bicycle with an extra pair of little balancing wheels attached at the back and would go pedaling furiously off ahead of her. He was always falling off it too because the paths were rutted and full of holes, and she would clean up his bleeding knees by dampening her handkerchief in the drinking fountain and smoothing the grit from the wounds. The next day the cuts would grow crusty scabs, which she would run her fingertips over and will herself not to pick off. He would have loved climbing this tree.

When Roberto was sixteen, she and Lucio had divorced. They had agreed that he was old enough and that once he had finished school he could go to a university in the States and live with his father. And that was what happened, in part anyway, because Roberto chose to go to drama school, not to Columbia University where Lucio was doing research. It was probably much better that way, Lea thought. Not that the two of them didn't get on, but at least Roberto was doing something he wanted, not what they wanted for him.

He would be in Palermo the day after tomorrow, and although they had masses of room at the flat, she had put him in the smallest bedroom at the back: This had a little spiral staircase going up through the ceiling onto the roof, which she knew he would love.

What Lea hadn't told Dante and certainly couldn't now was that Fontanini also wanted to be put up. He had phoned yesterday.

"This is it at last, eh? Got your speech all worked out like a good girl?"

"I'm not speaking," she said. "It's your book."

He didn't question that. "Still, you must say something intelligent and touching about your pictures: like why you took them at that hour of the day and so on. You can't leave it all to me."

"Photographers don't speak, they *show*. Anyway, you'll love it, you know you will."

"Mm . . . uh, you couldn't put me up for those two nights, could you, Lea? I hate to ask, but I get in so late."

"Oh God, I'd love to, Giorgio" (have to be quick), "only unfortunately—I mean, not really unfortunately!—I've got my son over from America, and . . ." He'd never know how many rooms the place had.

"Dante—is it?—doesn't like me, I know."

"He does," she lied. "It's nothing to do with that."

And yet she would have liked him to stay. He was good company, and they had worked all those months together, but there was no way she could broach the subject with Dante. And it was true, he did dislike Fontanini intensely. Unjustly, but still. So she had to tell him it couldn't be done.

That afternoon she went to the two main bookshops along Via Ruggero Settimo to see how the book was doing. In the first, copies were stacked up in a neat heap on a central table. There must have been about forty of them. No special sticker on them saying *best-seller* or anything and no copy propped up to show the cover. She hung around for a bit to see if anybody was interested. A couple of people leafed through the top one, then put it down again.

It was slightly better in the next shop, as they had put a copy in the window. The rest had been placed with the other glossy art books on Palermo, which were nearly all photographic impressions like hers. A couple of these had forewords by well-known writers and (she had to admit) were better produced. She glanced at the prices inside. More or less the same. It had been a mistake to have given it to a publisher here. Fontanini was going to realize that too. It had seemed a good idea to her at the time, but it just wasn't going to get the boost it needed. Not even with the launch. Far, far better to have had it done with his usual publisher. What was he trying to prove, anyway: a magnanimous gesture of love and solidarity toward the Sicilians? Nobody cared about that sort of thing anymore. Disconsolately, she went out into the street.

Although Lea hadn't mentioned it to him, Dante was certain Fontanini had asked to stay and, much as he disliked the man, would probably have agreed for her sake. But that was before all this happened. No way now, though, *Cristo!* It was perfectly all right for her son to stay, of course, whatever might happen and whatever she decided to do afterward. They looked very alike, the two of them. Dante had met Roberto twice—once when the boy was about sixteen and then last year when he was over from the States and they had all spent a weekend together in Lucca. He liked him a lot and even felt protective toward him, rather to his own surprise. It was a bit like the way he felt toward Lea.

It was his concern for Lea, in fact, that had made him want to find out more about the man Maurizio, who sold the carpets. It wasn't difficult—everybody knew about him at the newspaper, and anyway he'd heard most of it himself.

"The guy who has the oriental rugs business, you mean?" His colleague had shaken his head at the hopelessness of the case. He told Dante about the times Maurizio had been targeted by the Mafia and how he insisted on holding out. "Says nobody listens to him and that the police couldn't care less. Says he re-

fuses to give in: 'over his dead body' more or less." Maurizio had
a teenage son—his daughter had died from leukemia two years
ago—and was apparently a very religious man. Had the sympathy, if not the concrete help, of the Curia. Dante had known
neither of these last two facts.

"You're sure of that?" he asked.

"I remember perfectly. There was some statement made by
the cardinal when that bomb went off behind his shop. His Em-
inence stuck his neck out, saying it was the government's duty
to act, etcetera etcetera. You can look it up."

Dante discovered that, as a high-risk element, Maurizio was
understandably unpopular with the other residents in his apartment block. He suspected they had nothing personal against him
but were simply scared for themselves and their families—
although it was highly unlikely that he would ever be harmed
inside his own home. Dante had become more and more interested in the case and had almost decided to interview the man
when Lea came out with all this about this guy she'd fallen for.

He tried to analyze his feelings. If she was being sincere, if
she really believed herself to be in love—*really* in love—there was
nothing he could do about it. A tiny seed of fear stirred inside
him. He was going to give her all the time she needed, let the
book launch go by and so on. Her son coming to stay was a good
thing, it would help her to. . . . to what? Well, to decide. Then
tomorrow Dante would be going off to Milan. He had tried to
think who it could be. He thought back to the last party, the one
Fontanini had been at, but couldn't remember her talking to anybody in particular. Lea was beautiful and desirable and intelligent.
Any man would be mad for her.

The following evening, with a two-hour wait ahead of him for his return flight, he wandered over to the bar in Milan's Malpensa Airport and ordered his fourth coffee of the day. Dog-tired and aching from travel, he rested his arms on the stainless steel countertop and stared at the few remaining pastries in their glass case.

"*Il suo espresso, signore.*"

Dante slowly stirred in a heaped teaspoonful of sugar and lifted the scalding cup to his lips, and as he did so, he was roughly shoved from behind.

The coffee leaped devil-like from the cup onto his white shirt.

"Oh, I'm so *terribly* sorry," a woman said in an American accent. "*Mi dispiace tanto.*" She looked in dismay at the slowly widening stain on his shirtfront, a hand over her mouth.

It was such a bloody awful end to an awful day, and the woman looked so aghast, that he shrugged it off. "Don't worry," he told her in Italian. "It'll wash out."

"But I do worry," she answered in Italian. "Mee pree-uck-koo-poh molto."

Her atrocious accent was too much, and he had to smile. "Really. They make rotten coffee here anyway."

"You must let me buy you another," Stella said. "Or something else anyway." Her tenses were wrong, and she used the familiar address instead of the formal *lei*. She also confused the verb *buy* with *sell*, so the sentence came out as "You will must allow I to sell you more. Or other thing."

"Your Italian is charming," Dante said laughing. "I'll buy *you* something."

They chatted for the next half hour. She introduced herself and said she was on her way home to the States. She had been to Palermo, Rome, Florence, and Siena.

"And which did you enjoy most?" he asked, genuinely interested.

"*Enjoy* perhaps isn't the right word. I felt very at ease with myself in Sicily. Especially Palermo."

"You say that because I'm Sicilian," Dante joked. He liked her immensely, although he couldn't say why. Her open face, perhaps, and lack of any kind of pretense.

"Not at all, no. It was a feeling I got, a very special feeling. My father was from Palermo, maybe that's part of the reason."

She didn't look Italian, or maybe yes, she did . . . something about her eyes. She was his age more or less, carefully if unfashionably dressed. He had a sudden absurd desire to tell her about what had happened between him and Lea, and had actually opened his mouth to do so when she started to get up.

"I have to go now. My flight has just come up." She looked him full in the face and smiled. "Will you do your coat up so the stain doesn't show? I still feel guilty."

"You've left your mark on Italy," he joked again. And this time he used the informal address too.

"He's getting the last plane back," Lea said, "so he'll be home about midnight." She started picking her clothes up off the floor. "I'll have to go."

He watched her. "Me too." He yawned, got slowly out of bed, and cracked his head on the ceiling.

Lea's body crumpled from laughing. "Sorry, really. Are you okay?"

"Bloody house." He rubbed his head. "I'm going back to live

in England where they have proper ceilings. The Sicilians are too small. A race of midgets."

Lea slipped her sweater over her head and freed her hair. "Would I like it there? I'm not a midget."

"England? You might, I don't know." He sat down and started pulling on his trousers. "The weather's foul."

"I'd get used to that."

"Mm, maybe. There are other things, though." He remembered the successful, rather haughty British writer who was constantly traveling the world in search of inspiration. "It's hard to engage with any originality in the England of nineteen ninety-nine," she had told her interviewer. The words had stuck in his mind. Was it really like that now? "Maybe it's become too predictable," he told her. "Dull."

"But they have nice high ceilings." Lea zipped up her jeans and started combing her hair.

They had been out to the country to pick up some wine—a gift from a grateful friend of a friend. Nick had translated a complicated legal document for him in record time and asked a very modest fee.

"If you're ever in the area," the recipient, who was a *barone,* had said, bending close and tapping Nick confidentially once on the shoulder, "you must come to the house so I can give you some bottles of my rather special wine." He had explained how to get there.

Nick hadn't had the time or any particular desire to go; he preferred beer to wine anyway, and Paola didn't drink at all. Now, though, he wanted to take Lea and spend a whole morning in the country with her. When he rang to say he was coming, the *barone* said what a pity it was he wouldn't be there that day but that he would leave the wine ready for Nick.

"Another time, *professore,* you must let me know in advance so that I can have the pleasure of you and your wife's company at dinner. I shall not be modest: I am an excellent cook."

It turned out to be a massive eighteenth-century manor house still in fairly good condition overlooking a flattish, treeless countryside. The paved courtyard had an ancient, weather-beaten eucalyptus in the center and was surrounded on three sides by shuttered stone outbuildings.

Nick told a young man in rubber boots struggling with an armful of long grass what he had come for: "The *barone* La Licata told me he had put the wine by. This *is* the right place, isn't it?" There were lemon-yellow wildflowers mixed in with the lush green grass, and the whole bundle drooped like an upside-down U. The man shifted its weight so that the long willowy stalks brushed the ground.

"The English professor? Yes, the wine's over there." He nodded once to indicate one of the buildings on the far side of the courtyard. "Can you wait a moment while I get rid of this?"

Obviously one of the family, Nick thought, the son perhaps. Lending a hand. He knew from translating the document that the *barone* was selling off some of his land and that the potential buyer lived in the States. What would they use it for?

"Build a campsite there?" Lea had suggested. "A disco, a *water* park? May even get down to planting more vineyards. This is wine country after all."

Nick somehow thought not: too much hard work for too little return.

The boy opened a stable door and dumped the grass inside,

then came back wiping his hands down the sides of his trousers. "Over here," he said to Nick. The eucalyptus leaves stirred and shivered in the wind above their heads as he pushed open another heavy wooden door with both hands. It grated on its hinges, and they saw a dim, cavernous interior. A strong smell of mold exuded from the walls, and an icy draft whooshed out to meet them. Nick saw that the place was on different levels, with a sort of raised walkway above and a sunken part in the middle containing two flat circular stones as big as cartwheels. Obviously the oil press. Only it looked as if it hadn't been used for centuries.

"Do you want any help getting them to the car?" the boy asked, picking up two sealed cardboard boxes by the door.

"No, no, of course not," Nick said, taking them from him. "It's only just over there."

Lea asked whether they used to press the olives here, and the boy nodded, in no mood for reminiscing with nostalgic city dwellers. "Once."

He waited politely, but impatient to be off, until they were out in the courtyard again, then dragged the door closed. This time it gave out an agonized, strangled cry.

Driving away, they decided the boy had been unfriendly but that physical work was unrewarding when you didn't enjoy it or intend making a living from it. "I always think it's what I want— to live in the country, growing my own grapes, working in the fields and everything," Lea said, "but I know I could never do it. The countryside makes me melancholy in the evenings."

Nick brought the car to a stop on the deserted road and switched off the engine. It was perfectly silent, with just the soft rustle of wheat by the roadside as it moved with the wind. Far away over the vineyards and fallow fields they saw a tiny train moving across the landscape. The sun came out for a moment and lit up the swathes of wood sorrel staining the countryside a brilliant yellow. Nick took her in his arms. "The seats of these cars are meant to tip right back," she whispered, "so that you can make—"

He didn't let her finish, bringing his mouth down on hers. Slipping his hand beneath her sweater and running his hands over her bare skin, he wondered how he was going to be able to stop. She was all over him too, pressing her palm against the front of his trousers and running the fingers of her other hand again and again through his hair. He pulled at her jacket, and she tried to help him by easing out of it. Then she unzipped her jeans and he slid his hand inside.

Now, back at the flat, he remembered how her skin had felt there in the car: warm, silk-like.

"Come here a minute," he said.

She looked down at him, her hand still holding the comb to her shiny curtain of hair. He stretched out an arm. "Come on."

She took the three steps toward him. "I've got to go."

Outside, a bus passed by in a flash of orange on its way to the port. She made out the vertical exhaust pipe on its roof spurting out a funnel of used diesel. The saint's day illuminations had been dismantled, and the darkness was now broken up by pools of warm yellow light from the wall lamps all along the street.

She let him pull her down into a sitting position beside him. He lifted her sweater and began massaging the bare skin above her trousers.

"Nick . . ."

"We're going to live together," he said.

. . .

Nobody was home when he got back. Normally this would have been unusual for Paola, although it was only just after nine, because neither of them went out much during the week—often not on weekends either—but she had been keeping away from him as much as possible for the past few days. The concerts she went to were only once a week, and he vaguely wondered what she had been doing with herself on the other evenings. There was no Giulia anymore and no Ida. A colleague? Must be, he supposed. He pictured his wife's sour expression. "Don't think I'm going to stay in for you every bloody evening. I've got far better things to do. At least I've still got friends, thank God."

He went into their cold, unwelcoming bedroom and stared round in dismay. The green chenille bedspread and the wall crucifix stared back at him. Brown rosary beads had been draped round the arms of the cross as though it were a coat stand. "Do we have to have that thing behind our heads," Nick had joked when they were first married. "I'm an old atheist, you know." She had put her head on one side and chided him, not actually wagging a finger but almost: "Well I believe in God, and I want to keep it there." It had seemed charming to him then.

There was no spare hanger for his jacket in the wardrobe, so he opened Paola's side and immediately noticed a small plastic bag, like the ones they used for freezing food, on the shelf above where she kept her scarves and gloves. There used to be a woolen hat up there too, but he had made her throw it out, saying that she was far too pretty to stick that black chamber pot on her head. She had pretended to be offended, then had laughed, pleased that she was still pretty to him. That had been eons ago too.

He lifted the plastic bag down. It had something hard and quite sharp inside. Opening the little wire tag at its neck, he recognized the broken shards of the pottery bowl that had got smashed during their row. He felt a sudden sadness as he looked down at the pale blue and orange fragments. It must mean a lot to her if she couldn't bear to throw it out. Poor Paola: it could never be mended in that condition.

He replaced the bag and lifted a coat hanger off the rail for his jacket. Should he feel responsible for what had happened, what she had become, or would it all have happened anyway, in spite of him? Repentance was a useless excercise unless you happened to be a Catholic—a practicing one at least. Yes, they had been married in church but only because she had insisted. He had wanted a civil wedding. Luckily Nick's mother, an Anglo-Catholic, had had him baptized and confirmed when he was a kid, so if that was what Paola wanted, he was quite happy to let her have her way. She wore white and carried pale cream and white flowers.

Nick put on the old tennis shoes without laces and went into the kitchen to unpack the wine: eight bottles of white in one case, eight of red in the other. He didn't know the label but was sure it was one of the best. He put two of the white into the fridge and the rest but one into the bottom of the cupboard. He had wanted Lea to take half, but she had said no right away. Stupid idea of his. How would she be able to explain it away?

The figure of Dante made Nick rather uneasy, especially as he had the uncomfortable feeling the two of them might get on together. Any man who chose Lea must be okay, and she had never said anything unpleasant about him or given any hint of his being unreasonable or difficult to live with. Nick felt he would even enjoy sharing a bottle of this red he was trying to open with the man.

"Bloody fool," he muttered, meaning himself, and twisting the corkscrew deeper and deeper into the cork. "What would you say to him? 'Listen, I'm in love with your wife and I want to take her away from you. Another glass? Yes, it's excellent isn't it? Perhaps we can share another someday.' "

The cork came out with a gratifying pop, and he poured himself a generous glassful. It was rich and warm. A journalist, wasn't he? Writing about what? Went up to Rome and Milan, so was probably the correspondent in Palermo for some national papers. Lea had never mentioned how old he was or what he looked like. Who gave a shit what he looked like? The one thing she *had* said was that Dante wasn't the father of her son. But Nick hadn't asked her any more about that.

He took bottle and glass into the sitting room and slumped down in front of the television. Ten minutes later he heard Paola and Sandro coming in.

That afternoon she had gone into the church and prayed to Saint Anthony of Padua for guidance and grace on the same two things: first that Giulia wouldn't give up her studies and would stay on in Bologna and then that Nick wouldn't leave home.

Kneeling down in the single pew in front of his statue, she told the saint that if Giulia wanted to take some time off, she could, but please not to send her to Australia because Paola would miss her too much and she might never want to come back. "I'm not saying I want her to be with me all her life," she reminded the statue. "I didn't want her to stay in Palermo anyway, did I? I said she had no future here. But I want her to have a university career. I'd be happy if she married the right person when she'd finished, someone who really loves her, but"—she sniffed back a sob—"I need to know she's near me when I want her. And now I've broken the bowl she gave me. I feel lost." She blew her nose and dried her eyes with a corner of the handkerchief.

The statue stared down, a very slight smile on the delicately rosy cheeks. "I hadn't seen any woman on the bus, it was a lie," Paola went on after a minute or two. "So I don't know whether Nick's seeing another woman or not. But I think he is. He comes back late and doesn't want to talk to me. He doesn't care about Giulia either, like he used to. He even said, Anthony, that he can't see anything wrong in her going off to Australia."

"He was very good about your mother," the saint seemed to remind her. "And understanding and kind with you."

"I know he was," Paola answered. "And I wish he was always like that to me. He used to be. We always used to be happy." She closed her eyes and concentrated. "Please make my life get better and back to the way it was. I don't want to lose him."

She lit a candle and stuck it in a metal holder with the others. A creamy blanket of melted wax covered the base. Then she slipped a five thousand lire note into the slot of the battered old collecting box. It had a shiny new padlock on it. On the way home she met Sandro, and they walked back together.

Roberto leaned forward and picked up one of the oblong cards on the table. " 'On Friday the twenty-ninth of January, nineteen ninety-nine, at five P.M.,' " he read in a pompous voice, " 'Professor Ignatius Bladderwrack of the University of Western Samoa will introduce the book *Walls of Dreams* by Giorgio Fontanini and Lea Maselli.' " He looked up. "I see they've put his name first."

Lea gave a small resigned shrug. "It would have been odd if they hadn't," she said. " 'At Palazzo Fringuelli,' " Roberto went on. "Where's that?"

"Not far from here. A medieval building, all restored and everything. It's lovely."

He put the invitation down on top of the others and swung his legs over the arms of the sofa again. "Are you nervous?"

"A bit," Lea said. "I wish it were over." She yawned. "It's

been a long day. Do you want some more wine? I'll start getting supper in a minute."

Roberto held out his glass and she topped it up. "Thanks. I love the bedroom, by the way—the whole flat. Nothing like my evil hole."

"Why evil?"

"It's tiny, dark, and unhealthy, and it's all I can afford until I get rich and famous."

"Which will be very soon, of course," Lea added.

"Mm. Will you make a lot of money from this book?"

"No."

"And I won't be rich and famous from this film either."

"You never know," Lea said.

"I do know. With a part as big as mine—two whole lines, mind you—it's either instant stardom or total obliteration from the collective consciousness."

"How did you get the part?" Lea asked.

"Because of the way I look probably."

He was right. "Sicilian guys or lookalikes," the director had said. "Shortish, eighdeen, ninedeen, twenny, Banderas-type. Brooding, good teeth. Good-looking but not great-looking. We don't want to be watching *him* all the fuckin' time."

"And my accent," Roberto went on. "Not that they'll keep that—it'll all be dubbed out."

They heard the front door opening, and Dante walked into the room. Roberto sprang up off the sofa and they embraced.

"Hey, Dante!"

"*Ciao,* Roberto!"

Lea watched their obvious pleasure at seeing each other again, the way Dante touched her son's cheek very lightly just once with his knuckles, as though assuring himself Roberto was actually there.

She got up too. "I'll make a meal then."

Over omelette and zucchini Dante asked how long Roberto would be able to stay with them.

"Only until Saturday. The crew are arriving on Sunday, and we start filming the next day. But I'll see you on the way back." He told them they were shooting in a tiny isolated village somewhere way up in the mountains, although the Mafia boss (his elder brother in the film), who had of course actually existed, came from a fishing village near Palermo. "Still, they think it'll look more authentic choosing some godforsaken place up in the mountains—sorry, Mum."

"Why sorry?" Lea asked.

"Well, you're Sicilian."

"So what?" She laughed. "Dante is, too, aren't you?" She touched him on the sleeve, but he wouldn't look at her.

"You may call the whole of this island godforsaken or worse," he told Roberto. "I give you my express permission. In fact, it will give me infinite pleasure if you do. What's the name of this village anyway?"

"I think it's . . . Tesoro. Yes, that's it. They've been there this past week taking all the television aerials and dishes off the roofs and making it look all filthy and primitive nineteen-fifties again."

"Shouldn't be too difficult," Dante remarked drily. "Any more of these potatoes, love?" The endearment was out before he remembered, and he lowered his eyes, confused for a moment.

"Probably." She got up.

"So, you're the younger brother then," he went on quickly to Roberto. "*Was* there a younger brother? I don't remember one."

"I've no idea. The story we've been told is that Giacomo's—*Jake's*—father went to the States ahead of the rest of the family with *him* and that the mother and brother were to come on later, only she died and the brother stayed and grew up in Sicily. Then Jake comes back in the early fifties—that's the bit we're shooting here—to collect his baby brother." He jerked his thumb at his chest. "That's me, little Salvatore."

They all laughed.

"And did he go on to become a gangster like Jake?" Lea asked, helping Dante to more potato salad. He drew the plate toward him with muttered thanks.

"No, that's just my effing luck," Roberto said. "He got shot on the boat going over. Not only that, though, they're not even bothering to film that bit. At least they might have let me die on camera. I'd have enjoyed that."

"Do you know, I don't remember any of this," Lea said. "I mean this Jake whatsisname. Al Capone, yes, and"—she gave the name an American twang—"Joe Bananas. But not him. What did he do?"

"Whatever it was, it'll be different in the film," Roberto said. "All changed. Beautiful sexy childhood sweetheart waiting for him in Sicily"—he told them the name of the actress—"*la nonna* with a heart of gold, the usual. And you can't go wrong with a star like that, can you?"

"I suppose not," Dante said yawning. "Christ, I'm tired. Had this bloody day in Milan yesterday. So what are your lines then?" He smiled at Roberto. "What immortal truths do you utter in this sensitively directed, authentic movie?"

"I shall keep you in suspense over that," Roberto said. "Suffice to say they're deeply felt and majestically delivered."

Dante stood up and stretched. "I'm sure they are. Right, that's it; I'm off to bed. Leave these," he said to Lea, meaning the dishes. "I'll do them in the morning." He squeezed Roberto's arm.

When he had gone Roberto asked Lea if everything was all right.

"Why shouldn't it be?" She watched as he lit a cigarette. "You're not still smoking, are you?"

"As you can see, Mum, but only after meals. Well?"

"Well, what?" He looked so much more grown-up since the last time—and handsome, leaning back in his chair, blowing out smoke. Tired as well, though. "You mean with Dante? Good and not so good. What about you? Have you got a girlfriend?" It sounded ridiculous.

"Hundreds. Won't leave me in peace. Terrible, terrible." He leaned forward and stroked her arm. "So what time's this thing tomorrow then? I suppose I'll have to get all poshed up."

So he wasn't going to tell her anything, not yet at least. "Go just as you want," she said. "I suppose your English is fluent now, isn't it?"

"More or less, only it's nice not having to speak it."

"I never learned," Lea said. "I chose French instead at school." She eyed the cigarette longingly. "Give me just one drag, will you—just one." She took the cigarette, closed her eyes, and inhaled. "Mm . . . reminds me of when . . ." She handed it back.

"Your wicked past. And now you don't smoke, you don't speak English, you don't . . ."

"Is it a difficult language to learn?"

"Not really. The Americans swallow half their words anyway and speak through their noses all the time—they sound like foghorns." He twisted his mouth in an exaggerated parody: "Eee-owww-wraaaww. The best way to learn is to get an American—or English—lover. I mean in my case, of course," he added hastily with a smile.

He wanted to know what this *stronzo* Fontanini was like.

"Why do you call him that?" Lea asked. "You're just like Dante. He's not a shit at all."

"He thinks he's more important than you," Roberto said. "When your pictures are streets ahead of his stuff."

"How do you know?"

"Because I've seen it, I've read it. Hang on." He got up and came back with a copy of the book. "Just listen to this." He opened the first page and Lea saw her photograph of Piazza Pretoria in the early morning mist. She had got up at five o'clock to take that one. The top part of the statues were swathed in white, and she remembered the pigeon that had come just at the right moment and settled itself onto one of the marble heads.

" 'Palermo is like a wanton woman,' " Roberto began to read, " 'ungenerous, a temptress, taunting and full of fire. When I wander her streets and alleyways it is as if I am being drawn into her very heart. Torn remnants of cloth hang out above my head—the shreds of her cruelty. Cats slink away over century-smoothed stones or hiss at my intruding steps.' "

He looked up. "Mum, *really*."

She found she was a bit hurt by his scorn. "Perhaps that's not one of his best," she conceded.

"Then you look at your beautiful photograph," Roberto turned the book toward her, "and think, Well God, *this* is Palermo. *This* gives a real idea."

"You really should read it all through before judging," she

said. "Some of his pieces are superb." (Did she really mean that?) "Besides, you don't know the place at all. This is the first time you've been here."

"I know," he said. "Anyway, Mum, I don't mean to criticize the book or anything." She smiled at this. "It's just that I don't like to see him taking all the credit."

"He isn't. Wait till tomorrow before you make up your mind. Anyway," she went on, getting up and starting halfheartedly to pull the plates toward her, "what about Pacino getting all the hype in the film, mm? Doesn't that make you furious?"

He laughed and stubbed out his cigarette in a saucer. "Not exactly a good comparison." Lea regarded the soggy mass of ash with an expression of distaste. "That's disgusting," she said. "You can get rid of it yourself."

He made her show him the view from the rooftop before they went to bed. They climbed up the iron stepladder, pushed open the little square of trapdoor, and stepped into the night air. Although the roof was tiled, a small flat space had been left free for positioning water tanks and television aerials. Lea hadn't been up there for years—maybe not since they moved in—and had forgotten how much wider the view was than from down on the balcony. She pulled her long woollen cardigan about her against the cold.

"Look, you can see right over to Cefalù there," she said, pointing obliquely across an ink-black sea. "Those are the Madonie Mountains behind there, see? They go right back, then become the Nebrodis. If it were daytime, you'd be able to make out the Aeolian Islands straight ahead. That other way's Castellammare and San Vito lo Capo."

He listened to the magical names of the distant shapes and

they seemed to promise unimaginable wonder. Their lights twinkled and trembled under the stars. "Where would Tesoro be then?"

"Tesoro?"

"The village where we'll be filming," he said. "I think Dante said it was near Ragusa."

"Oh well, you won't see it from here then." She turned round and traced a quick arch in the air, toward the steep rise of tiled roof. "It's that way, down south. Miles away."

Lying in bed Roberto felt strangely excited by the prospect of seeing the mysterious, far-off villages and landscapes—more, in fact, than of shooting the actual film.

"Your name, please, sir?"

"Giorgio Fontanini."

"Ah yes." He checked his register, peeped over the counter to see the extent of the guest's luggage, and satisfied there was no need to wake the porter, handed over the key.

"Two-oh-seven, sir. On the second . . ."

But Fontanini was already striding toward the lift. The receptionist closed his eyes briefly, to show anyone who might be watching how he suffered at his job, and bent to retrieve his cigarette from the ashtray under the counter. He'd have to get him—*what* was his name?—to give him his ID tomorrow morning before he went out. He watched the tall, broad-shouldered figure being swallowed up behind the sliding metal doors.

The next morning he caught him as he crossed the hall on the way to breakfast. "Excuse me, *dottor* Fontanini? Could I have a document for registration?"

The man turned toward him a bit irritably. "Eh? Oh, yes." He reached into his breast pocket and handed over his driving license. "Give it to me afterward."

An overhead notice in three languages warned guests to look out as they entered the lower-level breakfast room. The English translation read "Watch Your Steps." Fontanini just managed to save himself in time. He took rolls, jam, and fruit juice from the L-shaped serving table and sat down. Bloody nuisance this trip had been. He had no further interest in the book, which had been completed ages ago and from which he now felt totally estranged. It was true he had been enchanted the first time he came to Palermo but only because he had been with Leandro. On his own it would have been like any other city. In fact, his lyrical outpourings that now accompanied Lea's photographs were sonnets of love, not eulogies to this (he glanced out of the window at the column of traffic crawling by) filthy, noisy, southern city. "Oh come on now, it wasn't ordinary, you could never call it that," he could hear Leandro protesting.

The two of them had shared a hotel bedroom, large, airy, and with its own balcony overlooking the old roofs and churches of the city. For three whole days. Fontanini had felt like the man in *Rolla,* that supremely beautiful painting by Henri Gervex, with Leandro the splayed nude on the bed. Except, of course, that Leandro was *not* a prostitute. Fontanini still felt the pain of the boy's absence. But then, experiences like that could never be repeated. God, if only all this were already over and he were on his way home!

"*Signore?*" The waiter was standing at the table.

"*Cappuccino.*"

When it arrived he crumbled the first roll, teaspooned some

plum jam onto a bite-sized piece, and dipped it into the milky coffee. He disliked hotel food. That's why he had hoped Lea would invite him to stay the two nights with her. He had this vague memory of someone telling him she was an excellent cook. Then he liked family life—never having known it himself—and would have felt more *protected* with her. But there was Dante: unlikable man. Couldn't say why exactly. It was as if he were always on the lookout. Cynical. You felt he was always gazing inside you, trying to expose you. Trying to show people you were a fraud.

He dabbed his mouth with the napkin (paper, he registered with distaste) and prepared another piece of the roll. If he hadn't already been at Rome airport last night on his way back from Bologna, he would have flown into Palermo at lunchtime today. As it was, he had the whole morning in front of him. Well, maybe it wasn't so bad after all; he'd have a walk and then at one meet Lea and the prof who'd be introducing them. They were going to have lunch together and work out what each was going to say. He had persuaded Lea to make a short speech because it was right she should. Half the book was hers after all. Well, perhaps not half—a *third*. The presentation was at five and would last at least a couple of hours, so he'd never be able to make the last plane home. And that meant a second night in the hotel. He'd try and get the early one back tomorrow morning.

The Giardino Inglese glowed almost sensuously beyond the bare branches of the plane trees along Via Libertà, showing off its luxuriant display of mop-headed palms and vivid lawns. The sparkling jets of water from the fountain leaped into the air in unison like ballerinas—no, he thought, like those synchronized swimmers he had once seen on television. Ghastly, but fascinating at the same time—couldn't take his eyes off them.

He remembered the kiosk there, over on the opposite side of the road, where he and Leandro had had those luscious lemon ices, and the stall farther on selling chilled prickly pears. He saw that the stall was barred and shuttered this morning; perhaps it wasn't the season for prickly pears. It had been late summer when they were here just two years ago. Aside from that party at the beginning of the month, Fontanini hadn't been back to Palermo. Only came *then* to cheer himself up after the accident. Luckily, his legs felt perfectly okay now.

The next couple of hours were spent wandering round the old city trying to recapture some of the magic. But it was useless. The little alleyways and squares seethed with people—many of them Asians or blacks—and cars were piled up just anywhere so you had to keep stepping round them. Hens pecked at the filthy cobbles under the stalls in the markets, where the once beautiful fountain basins were hidden under grotesque displays of women's underwear.

In a narrow alleyway he came upon a pulsating heap of something living, right in his path—an animal of some kind. As he drew nearer he saw it was three dogs. The bitch in the middle had been mounted from behind by a male, which had then turned round, leaving the two of them joined rump to rump. A second male, evidently unable to control himself any longer, was pumping away at the female from the front. His body thumping against her chest had forced her head upward, and she was staring about her in mute agony and despair, entreating rescue. The whole thing was horrific to behold, with the attached male barking frantically as he tried to free himself and the second one desperately trying to find an entry.

The rape of Palermo, Fontanini thought in distaste, turning away. Yet the city had been beautiful to him once: the crumbling piles of baroque masonry looming eerily in the moonlight, the washing hanging motionless on the line far above his head, a woman's singing coming from a barred window, the sounds of crockery and murmuring voices from the trattoria tables laid out in the night square. It just showed (in case he hadn't already realized it) that places could take on an entirely different aspect depending on whom you were with. It was like anything else you subjected to the senses—food, music, a famous picture, you were always influenced in some way.

How would Buenos Aires appear to him, he wondered, as he made his way toward the lunch appointment. Ah, but who would he find there as a companion? Leandro had gone his own way, and perhaps it was right that he should have done—right for both of them. Still, South America was full of beautiful people. Fontanini couldn't wait.

Lea was on the pavement outside the restaurant talking into her mobile phone. She was still so attractive and so *graceful* in her movements, it gave him pleasure to watch her. Beside her stood the little professor staring at the passersby with a copy of the book (*their* book, he now saw) under his arm. Fontanini waited till he was nearly upon them before calling out.

Over in the shop, Flora sat reading the latest copy of *Chi*. Slowly turning the pages, she pulled her coat more closely about her and crossed her ankles in their fur boots. So bloody cold in here. A couple more minutes and she'd try Lea again. She'd had three customers so far—two Japanese and a man from. . . . where did he say? Detroit, that was it. He bought three of the large dishes with the traditional figures painted on them, and she had been able to explain the water carrier, the knife grinder, and the chair mender to him. Wanted them really well wrapped as he was taking them back to the States on the plane. The Japanese women spent ages looking around, then bought the pale green and mauve coffee set: the two cups and saucers and the sugar bowl with the tray underneath.

She lifted the receiver of the cordless phone in front of her and pressed the repeat button.

"Hallo?"

"Lea? It's me, Flora."

"Flora! How are you?"

"That's what I'm calling about. Have you got a minute?"

"Well . . ."

"I wanted to tell you . . . well, you remember the last time we met—when you came into the shop and that man was there and I was in such a state? You do remember, don't you?"

"Of course I do. It was the day Dante went to Rome."

"Yes, well, when you left me, I did as you said and phoned Biagio, and he came to collect me, and we talked and talked and decided to go back to the shop together after lunch. So we did. And the bloody man turned up."

"And what did you do?"

"I paid him. Biagio was there with me in the shop so the guy could see we were . . . yes, well, husband and wife. Anyway, the upshot is that we're selling out. I can't tell you what a relief it is, Lea. I feel born again."

"Oh good, I'm glad for you, Flora, really. When will it be?"

"As soon as bloody possible. It's not actually selling; we're going into voluntary liquidation. But I don't care which way it's done so long as I'm out."

"So you're not phoning from the shop then?"

"Oh yes I am. I'm staying until the end of the month—the beginning of next month at the most. Then it's away!"

"I'm so glad," Lea said again. "Listen, why don't you come to the book thing this afternoon? Then we can celebrate together."

"Oh, I wish I could," Flora said, "But we agreed I'd do a full day here today and tomorrow. No, really, thanks anyway. By the way, I meant to tell you—"

"Listen, Flora, I'll have to go. I've just seen Fontanini coming across the street."

"*Who*? Where are you?"

"I'm outside a restaurant with . . . with professor . . . and Font—the author of the book. We're having lunch and discussing this afternoon."

"Lucky you. You have such an interesting life. Hey, it's not that *English* professor, is it, Lea? I don't believe it!"

Flora heard a man's voice, then Lea came back on the phone. "I'll have to go now, Flora. We'll be in touch very soon, okay? Bye, love."

Paola sat in the kitchen finishing her lunch. Nick had said he'd be having a snack out after work and was then going on to a book presentation. She had seen the invitation lying around somewhere—something to do with Palermo, photographs maybe, she couldn't remember. Being at the university he was always getting invitations to go to this and that—art exhibitions, conferences, seminars. There were leaflets about newly published teaching manuals and text books, which Nick told her were full of authors going on about their revolutionary new methods and heaven knows what. She didn't need any of that, thank you very much. It was a thorough waste of time.

She pulled a wad off the loaf of bread and started mopping up the juices from the tomato salad, feeling the little crescents of raw onion lodging between her teeth. The dentist had told her always to use an interdental brush as well as the ordinary one. "That way, *signora*, you'll avoid that nasty inflammation of the gums all over again." She sucked at her teeth now and twisted the nail of her little finger into the crevices.

After her rest she'd get down to tidying those books. Then she'd be off. Should be finished by sixish. Get the bus straight there. She was taking just one shard with her to show the woman, just in case she couldn't explain the design properly. After all, she might not have another one in the shop but would be able to order it for Paola.

She finished off lunch with a Golden Delicious apple, peeling and coring it and cutting the lifeless, oversweet flesh into quarters. The peel came off in one single spiral, which always used to amuse the children when they were small. Look at this, she told them, holding up the long worm in her finger and thumb. Then she would let it fall to the table and pretend it was alive while they screamed in delight.

At the end of her meal she stirred a teaspoon of bicarbonate of soda into half a tumbler of water and drank it down. Then she rinsed out the glass, washed up the two plates, and went along the passage to the cold bedroom. Lying under the chenille bed-cover, staring up at the molded ceiling, she thought of the row with Nick. It was her own fault; she was forcing him further and further away and couldn't stop herself. Then she thought of Giu-lia, who was going to leave Bologna and go to Australia, maybe forever. She thought of the broken bowl at the top of the ward-robe and how prophetic its destruction was. But when she slept, her dreams were of her mother, who bent over her and said in that infuriating voice, "You should eat turkey, you know. It's good for you." Only suddenly she wasn't at the dining table anymore but looking up at Paola from the bottom of the grave in the cemetry, and was wearing a paper hat.

When she woke at four, Paola heated up a thimbleful of the coffee she had brewed at breakfast, then settled down at the kitchen table to sort out the books. Sandro came home, made himself a sandwich, and went out again. By twenty past five she had finished. She peered out at the weather and decided to wear her brown jacket and skirt, hoping it wouldn't rain and she wouldn't have hours to wait for the bus. She took her umbrella along anyway because the last thing she wanted was damp shoul-ders and another bout of rheumatism. Slipping the plastic-wrapped pottery fragment into her handbag with wallet, keys, and handkerchief, she left the flat.

It was a lucky thing, she told herself, that Giulia had left the little gold-edged label on the Christmas present and that Paola had kept it. Otherwise she wouldn't have known where to go for the replacement. *"Flora's Place,"* it said above the address. *"Sicilian ceramics, pottery, and knick-knacks."* Not the sort of shop she would ever go to herself. No need. She sat on the bus holding her bag against her with both hands, staring out into the early evening. Replacing the bowl would make Giulia seem nearer, even though she wasn't, and she'd be able to look at it every night before going to bed, the way she used to do. They spoke less together on the phone now, and Paola had never felt more alone.

A third of the way down the street she realized she had got off the bus one stop too soon and would have to walk several hundred yards farther. Instead of going back, she might just as well carry on down, turn right at the bottom, and come up to the shop that way. All these roads looked alike to her, all with the same kinds of buildings and all sloping gradually down toward the port. She could see cranes and a ship's yellow smokestack there at the end. Although it had started to drizzle, it was hardly worth getting out the umbrella as she'd be there in a few minutes. Made the pavements a bit slippery, though.

Smoke rose from a makeshift stall on the street corner selling deep-fried chickpea fritters and potato croquettes. They were laid out on the counter on oval metal dishes next to slices of fried eggplant, trussed-up sardines, and florets of batter-covered cauliflower. Paola wrinkled her nose in distaste as she passed. *Fritture*—deep-fried snacks—were the very worst thing you could possibly eat, with all that oil and grease. Anyone could tell you that. Deadly for the digestion. Two or three men stood round the stall eating out of little paper cones, their collars turned up against the veil of fine rain.

At the bottom end of the road she crossed over and turned right so that she was walking parallel to Via Libertà. The road she wanted was just ahead. She checked the name: yes, she should have got off the bus at *that* stop, not the other. Still, it didn't matter. The rain was a bit heavier now, and she opened her umbrella and quickened her pace. It was quite dark along here, with only a few shops selling hardware, housewares, that kind of thing. There wasn't much traffic either. A dog lifted its head from its paws and looked up at her from a doorway as she passed, and a woman walked by dragging a sniveling child by the hand: *"Voglio la cioccolata! Voglio la cioccolata!"* it whined.

Paola saw the brightly lit shop as soon as she turned the second corner. It had two little trees in tubs outside and the name Flora's Place clearly visible on the front. A woman stood in the doorway. The window was full of colored dishes and spaghetti bowls, those old-fashioned urns her mother used to keep umbrellas and walking sticks in, statuettes of boy goatherds and laden mules, and wooden panels with Sicilian scenes painted on them. It looked well stocked anyway, which meant they just might have the bowl she was looking for.

It was unusually quiet in the street. That's exactly how she was to put it later—*unusually* quiet, as though it had been closed to traffic. And yet there were cars parked all along one side, so it couldn't have been cordoned off. Besides, she knew the places in town that had been made into pedestrian precincts, and they were always well lit and full of strolling couples. Not like this place at all.

Apart from the woman in the shop doorway, Paola seemed to be the only person about, although just then she saw a man coming out of another shop two or three doorways up from Flora's Place. As she got closer she saw that the shop sold Persian rugs. She could make out the rich colors and heavily fringed fabrics quite clearly in the window. And there was a moving car after all, reversing slowly out into the road that ran along at right angles at the top. But instead of changing gear and moving forward into the line of vehicles, it stopped, effectively blocking any oncoming traffic. God, she thought, parking like that! You couldn't believe it. No wonder Palermo was in such a state. No traffic police anywhere. Now, in Milan things were different. Just then another man crossed the road obliquely in front of her.

A deafening report rang out accompanied by a blinding white flash, then another, and Paola saw the first man crumple. He doubled up as though suffering from terrible stomach cramp, then slumped onto the pavement face downward. She clearly heard the crack as his forehead hit the stone. There was a loud shout from somewhere, and the other man sprinted up the road and disappeared round the corner at the top. She heard the revving of a motorcycle followed by the roar of its engine. For a split second she stood utterly alone in the street, watching in incredulous horror as a stream of blood curled slowly down toward her like molten lava. She tried to move, to reach the shelter of the pottery shop, but just then someone screamed piercingly right into her left ear. A woman's scream, and Paola froze. With the inside of her head momentarily deadened, she looked down and saw in terrible fascination that the crimson stream had reached her shoes. She tried to move out of its way, lifting first one foot and then the other, but the pavement was wet and slippery from the rain, and the blood was already beginning to form a pool round her feet. She felt as if she were on a skating rink, desperately trying to keep her balance and knowing she was about to fall and that it was only a matter of seconds before the ground rushed up to meet her. Her arms flayed, the umbrella whirled away, her legs shot from under her, and she came crashing down onto the pavement, striking the back of her head on the curbstone.

As she fell she remembered seeing two things with absolute clarity: the car at the top of the road leaping forward and disappearing across her line of vision, and a dog coming out of a doorway and sniffing the prone body outside the carpet shop. Then, just as the books say, all went black.

. . .

Nick took his time getting to Palazzo Fringuelli, not wanting to arrive before things got properly started. He didn't really know why he was going at all—not to hear Lea speak, surely. Or was it? She wouldn't expect him to be there. In fact, she had told him not to bother. Was it perhaps that he wanted to get a look at the men he had only heard about, the ones who revolved round her like planets?

He waited for a gap in the traffic and crossed the busy main Via Cavour. Twenty past five: they'd have started by now, and he could slip in at the back. Ahead of him, the severely unembelli-shed facade of the palazzo glared down, forbidding and un-friendly. Not surprisingly either, given its history as the seat of the Court of the Inquisition. As Nick knew, it contained a torture chamber somewhere deep in its bowels, the site of unspeakable practices, and a dungeon where the wretches were thrown after the clergy had done with them. A terrible fascination surrounded the scrawls the prisoners had left on the walls of their cell, and Nick couldn't make up his mind whether the huge sums of public money spent in restoring both chambers along with the rest of the building was morally justifiable or not.

An open RAI television van stood outside the massive portcullis-like doorway, and nearby one of the technicians was chatting up a policewoman. Her blonde hair had been carefully arranged to flow down her uniformed shoulders from under her cap, and she was well aware of the effect this was having. Long blonde hair was a way of getting her own back at having to do such an unglamorous job.

Nick took the lift up to the top floor as directed. There must have been over two hundred people in the long cream-colored room. A low roar rose from the tightly packed seats, and a smell of expensive scent hung in the air. He eased his way sideways along the wall toward the front to get a better look at the group of people by the table.

Once there, the sight of Lea surrounded by four unknown men provoked a not wholly unpleasant feeling in him of knowing *she was his* and that not one of the male presences was aware of the fact. At any moment, he thought, she'll look up and see me. And she did, raising her eyebrows and giving him a quick smile before turning back to the man at her elbow.

He was a thickset, gray-haired type in a dark brown corduroy jacket. As Nick watched, he removed the cigar butt from his clenched teeth and made a wide gesture in the air with it. Nick couldn't hear the joke he obviously made, but the others round him laughed. A much taller man with receding hair laid a hand paternally on Lea's shoulders and leaned forward to say something to her. He wore a light-colored suit and a shirt with no tie and kept darting glances at the fourth person in the group, a very handsome boy of about twenty or twenty-one.

Right, so the gray-haired guy with the cigar was Dante (quite a lot older than her, Nick noticed with surprise), the dark boy in the black polo shirt was Lea's son, and that tall old lecher must be Fontanini. Just then the professor of literature (who Nick recognized) half rose from the table, said something to Fontanini, and the group dissolved. Dante and the son sat down in the first row, and the other two took their places behind the table. The professor rapped on the glass-topped surface to quell the noise in the room and, when that had no effect, stood up and clapped his hands like a spoiled child. As a last resort, he bent forward and cleared his throat into the microphone. Gradually the roar subsided. There was coughing, a shuffling of chairs, and finally silence.

"Ladies and gentlemen," he began. "I was delighted to have been asked here this afternoon to present this beautiful and very moving book on our city. As soon as I picked it up I realized that here was something special: a tribute, a labor of love." He paused for effect. "A true *love letter*."

Nick noticed Fontanini leaning back and looking up at the ceiling.

"Palermo is not an easy city to live in, as we all know—perhaps, with all its problems, it is one of the hardest—yet it is a city people return to again and again because it is a city with its own particular magic. Of course, like every metropolis, it's home to people from all over the world, people who have chosen to settle here: Europeans, Africans, Asians. . . . But unlike so many other cities, Palermo has always shown great tolerance toward its citizens wherever they come from. Racial discrimination is not a Sicilian characteristic, and I think we should be proud of that fact.

"Maybe that is the reason foreigners—and"—he smiled self-deprecatingly—"we tend to think of *anyone* who is not from Palermo as a foreigner—are attracted to our island. We only have to think of Goethe, Wagner, or the English humorist and illustrator, Edward Lear, to see how artists, musicians, and painters have all found inspiration here. So when an author of the caliber of"—he turned to his right and inclined his head deferentially—"Giorgio Fontanini chooses Palermo as his muse, we perhaps feel there may be more to the city than we Palermitani ourselves realize. Perhaps it holds secrets and mysteries we are unaware of, that only outsiders (and I put the term in metaphorical inverted commas!), only *'outsiders'* can perceive and enjoy. Perhaps it reveals something very special and out of the ordinary. Happiness is, after all, a temporary state."

Nick noticed that the professor's slight speech defect prevented him from pronouncing the consonant *r* correctly and that the word *temporary* required considerable sideways creasing and elongating of the lips. He found himself fascinated by these labial contortions and wondered how the man would manage the word *fotografia*, for he was now turning in Lea's direction.

"A temporary state," the professor went on, "a *subjective* state, and that is why the work of"—again he inclined his head—"Lea Maselli is so significant."

Say it, Nick willed him, say it.

"For it is the art of photography . . ."

Nick found he was curling his own lip in sympathy.

". . . that so captures the fleeting moment—that which can never be repeated." The professor fingered his bow tie and looked round the room to give his delivery an air of casual spontaneousness. "I think you'd agree with me that several of her images have a slightly disturbing quality about them, as though they are showing us something we would rather not see. Yet at the same time they manage to capture the quintessential spirit of . . ."

Somebody's mobile phone started playing "Colonel Bogey" from the body of the hall, and there was a localized scuffling as the owner attempted to silence it. It must have been deep inside a handbag, for it tinkled insistently and gaily on while the professor forged ahead regardless. Nick saw Lea pressing her lips together in an attempt to keep a straight face.

The phone was finally suppressed, and the speaker's voice swelled in triumph. Looking round the hall, Nick mused on the Italians' phenomenal capacity for self-inflicted boredom. It may well have been a case of wanting to be seen in the right places, but practically all the so-called intellectually orientated conferences he went to were well attended, no matter how obscure the subject under discussion. How many people here this evening, for instance, were really interested in yet another book on Palermo or for that matter were going to bother reading it? The photographs (thanks to Lea) made it more palatable, but in this case it was evidently Fontanini's presence that had packed them in—the chance to get their copy signed by the man himself. Well, that was the whole point of book presentations, wasn't it?

Nick glanced at the man now, leaning back in his chair, legs crossed, dutifully following the professor's words and nodding sagely at a point made. Farther along, Lea sat studying the tabletop and twisting a large silver ring round and round on her finger. He felt a lurch just looking at her, at her wrists emerging from the black sleeves and the way her long purple earrings shook when she looked up. Mentally, he slowly peeled off the jacket to bare her shoulders, slid his arms round her waist, and undid the button of her skirt. As it rustled sighing to the floor, she turned to him . . .

"So I want to wind up by saying that everybody has their particular Palermo," the professor was saying. "Each different, each personal, and each jealously guarded."

Lea had told him that she had no idea what to wear for the occasion and that everything would look wrong so it didn't matter anyway. "I like the black dress," Nick told her, "but you'll look far better than everyone else whatever you put on." She was looking slowly round at the audience now, but wouldn't meet his eye.

"So we can be immensely grateful," the amplified voice went on, "that Giorgio Fontanini and Lea Maselli have shared their own personal Palermo with us in this book. Lea?" He turned to her, waited until she was on her feet, and amid the applause sat down and took a long drink of water.

"This isn't something I do very often," she said smiling as an RAI cameraman zoomed in on her. "Photographers like to be behind the lens, not in front of it. Apart from the fact that I never know where to look. Should you look into the camera or should you pretend it's not there? I'm still not really sure.

"Presumably, a good photograph is one in which the subjects are unaware of the camera's presence and go about their business or do whatever they were doing before you came along. And yet I've discovered something very interesting and for me exciting— that a symbiosis exists between camera and subject, which you can't, which *shouldn't,* be ignored. Being aware of this is what creates a good—even a great—picture." She stopped and smiled apologetically. "I'll try and explain what I mean: whatever you do, even the simplest thing like—I don't know—opening the car door and getting out, is never done without being aware, firstly of where you are and then of who's around you. It's probably a very vague or even an unconscious awareness, but it's there. And the camera is part of that . . . that background if you like. So in a way, you can say we are always *acting a part.*"

Nick noticed that the professor of literature was wearing a politely attentive but mystified expression, as though this were not the kind of thing he had been expecting at all. It wasn't exactly what Nick had expected either. Fontanini, on the other hand, was listening intently, chin resting in his cupped hand.

"I don't mean by that," Lea went on, "that people need to look the camera full in the face, as it were, to feel its presence; it may be invisible, but I believe we're never wholly and completely isolated. Or unobserved. When I manage to be behind the camera and be part of that experience, I feel I've made the picture live."

She stopped again, perhaps, Nick thought, to gauge the audience reaction. There was absolute stillness in the room, whether from puzzlement or interest he couldn't say. She went on.

"Another thing: when Giorgio and I decided to do the book, we agreed that image and words should complement each other, but that didn't necessarily mean that the photograph should *illustrate* the words or even vice versa."

Nick remembered her attempting to explain this to him at La Rosa's.

"What we tried to do—or what *I* tried to do anyway, because the text was already there—was to see what the words suggested to me and then take my photograph. That's why you've got Giorgio's description of, well . . . walking down by the docks in the early morning, for instance, next to a picture of mine of a child standing in church yawning. He describes the overnight ferry to Naples—the part where the cars drive on—as looking like a huge black mouth. And that gave me my idea." She smiled round. "There. Now you know."

The audience laughed, relieved that she was now making sense and was including them in this easy first-name relationship with the great writer. Nick, who had never heard her speak in public and hadn't fully understood her theory of camera awareness, still felt ridiculously, almost painfully, proud of her.

She went on to describe how she had set up her camera in a *quartiere popolare,* a working class area of the town, and how a woman there had refused to have her picture taken. "I asked whether she'd allow me to take her if I let her photograph me first. She could have me where she liked and doing what she liked. I set up the camera for her, and she put me sitting on a chair outside her front door, holding her baby girl. By that time there was quite a crowd round us, so I told them to come and be photographed too. You can see them in the picture I eventually took."

She told them stories behind some of her other photos, and when she sat down flushed and smiling, it was to loud applause. Nick again tried to catch her eye, but she was leaning across the table, saying something to Fontanini. He seemed very impressed and grasped her hand in both of his. No point in staying any longer, Nick thought, certainly not to listen to *him*. Besides, Lea had told him that afterward, when it was all over, they were all going out to eat somewhere. "Although I'd much rather not," she had added loyally, in case he felt left out. He did.

A police patrol car went by, its siren neighing, then another, and Nick was vaguely aware he had been hearing them for some time now. He stood up just as Fontanini got to his feet, and this time Lea saw him. He smiled to let her know how well it had gone, then left the hall. As it wasn't raining anymore and he was in no hurry, he decided to walk some of the way home. See how far he got anyway.

Fifteen minutes later he had reached the top of Lea's road. Something had obviously happened a bit farther ahead, as there were crowds spilling out into Via Libertà. Probably an accident. Then he saw that the top of Via Tarquinio was cordoned off and that people were lining the balconies of the buildings, all looking down. A sure sign of some disaster. A policeman was directing the traffic. It must be serious then.

"What's happened?" he asked a man who was straining to see over the shoulders in front of him.

"Hanno sparato ad uno." Someone's been shot. Words to send

a shiver through you, words outside your realm that told you violence and murder had crawled out of their lair and overlapped your own world.

"Avanti, avanti!" The policeman, legs martially apart, dark uniform trousers disappearing into knee-length boots, made hysterical shepherding motions with his baton. He stuck a whistle between strong even teeth and emitted a shrill screech.

"Chi era?" Nick asked when the whistle was removed. Who was it?

"A guy who had a shop," the policeman answered without taking his eyes off the traffic. He raised the baton above his head and strode, *duce*-like, out into the middle of the road, giving another piercing whistle.

A shopkeeper who perhaps hadn't paid the *pizzo*, Nick thought to himself. A Mafia killing then. Unusually shaken (for he had never come into close contact with murder before), he walked rapidly on, leaving the tense, excited buzz behind him. Italians loved a shooting, loved the drama of violence. Loved the huge public funerals, the speeches, the flower-laden coffin being borne from the church on the mourners' shoulders. They wept with the grief-stricken relatives and condemned the perpetrators of inhuman suffering. Actors, the lot of them.

The phone was ringing as he stepped out of the lift but frustratingly stopped the moment he opened the front door. He wandered through the empty, cheerless rooms for a few minutes, his mind still full of the unseen murdered shopkeeper, imagining the sense of loss, the forced separation and the pain such a killing would create in the man's family. This led him to the realization of his own unhappiness. Nobody, he told himself, nobody was going to force him to live a life he found miserable. He no longer loved Paola and couldn't, *wouldn't*, stay with her. The decision was such a relief that he sat down at the kitchen table in astonishment. Hundreds—thousands—of people had done it before him, and nothing disastrous had happened; things went on. He just had to find the right moment and tell her.

The phone went again. It was Sandro saying he was at the Civico Hospital with Paola, who had had an accident—*un incidente per strada*—which Nick took to mean a road accident. She had regained consciousness but had a broken arm and possibly two fractured ribs. His son's voice was carefully controlled, but Nick could tell that panic was very near the surface. Apparently she had fallen down outside some shop (so it hadn't been a car then). Somebody had been shot. There were police everywhere, and was Nick coming right away?

What did Sandro mean, "somebody had been shot"?

"I don't know, I don't know. Are you coming, Dad?"

He found Paola in a tiny room of her own on the second floor. Sandro had been right about the police. The two armed officers lolling about in the corridor outside looked up when Nick approached and asked his identity before nodding him in. Paola lay on her back, eyes closed, a huge bruise covering her left cheek.

"Your phone was always switched off," Sandro said accusingly when Nick had given him an encouraging hug. "I didn't know where you were."

"I'm here now." He bent toward Paola, who was breathing quietly and regularly. They had put a rough white nightdress on her, and one arm was in plaster. The hand emerging from it was thin and blue-veined.

"Paola?"

"She was awake just before you came," Sandro said, still making it sound as if the whole thing was Nick's fault. "She was speaking to me."

"Paola?"

She opened her eyes slowly. "Nick."

"How are you feeling?"

"Not too bad."

It was the first time for years he had heard her uncomplaining.

"My head still hurts a bit. They said I was concussed, so that's probably it." Two tears brimmed over and ran slowly down her her cheeks, one more quickly than the other. "I'm sorry, Nick."

"What do you mean?" She looked so pathetic he felt he was going to break down himself.

"For everything." She turned her head very slowly on the pillow to see where Sandro was. Satisfied that he had his back to them and wasn't listening, she said quietly, "You know, for the things I said. I didn't mean them."

He caught sight of her shoes under the bed. They were stained over the instep with what could have been congealed blood.

"What on earth happened?"

She told him everything, right up to where she had lost consciousness. "I've got this broken arm," she said, wincing and trying to raise it, "and they think a couple of broken ribs. I must have fallen very badly."

He didn't say he had passed by the very street only an hour or so ago. There didn't seem any point in it. He just sent Sandro off to phone Giulia and get something to eat for himself and, when his son came back, went in search of a doctor.

.   .   .

They sold a lot of books, just how many Lea hadn't asked. Giorgio spoke for too long, and she noticed several people in the audience growing restless and looking at their watches, so what with that and the police sirens screaming by outside, it wasn't exactly a successful conclusion to the evening. Still, he seemed quite happy with how it had gone. Afterward they went off for drinks and dinner, and by midnight she had had quite enough. Giorgio, though, all hyped up, asked them if they were ready to go on somewhere else.

"No?" he said, seeing her's and Dante's face. "What about you, Roberto? You wouldn't let me down, would you?"

Lea wondered how her son was going to deal with this one.

"Well, it depends," Roberto said.

"Depends on what?" Fontanini asked, bending toward him. "Don't you want to see the delights of Palermo? An actor should, you know. Isn't that right, Dante?"

"Sure, sure," Dante yawned. "Except that I'm off." He pushed back his chair. "Has he got a key, Lea?"

"I don't know." She turned to her son. "Has he got a key?"

"No, he hasn't got a key. But he has decided to come home to bed and sleep," Roberto said, getting up. "Like a good boy." He smiled sweetly at Fontanini. "Another time, Giorgio. You don't mind, do you?"

Fontanini did, very much. "Not at all. Perhaps I'll take another couple of days and come and watch the filming instead. When did you say you start?"

"Monday. I've got a very important part, you know."

"I'm sure you have."

"Mm." Roberto helped Lea on with her jacket. "Come on,

Mamma, I'm tired." He put an arm round her and laid his head on her shoulder. Dante asked whether they could give Fontanini a lift to his hotel.

"Well, yes, I suppose you can now. In the circumstances." He looked wistfully at Roberto. "Having been let down by this young lad here."

When they had dropped him off, Dante said he wondered how anyone could stand the man.

"He's harmless enough," Roberto said.

"Wouldn't be so sure about that," Dante rejoined. "I'd watch out for him if I were you."

Lea said, "Oh really, Dante."

"The theater's full of them," Roberto said, yawning hugely.

"I'm sure it is," Dante said drily. "I'm just glad I'm not in the theater."

He stayed up to watch the news after the other two had gone to bed. Ten minutes later he came into the bedroom. "You still awake?" he said into the dark, and when Lea muttered something, said: "They've shot that guy in Via Tarquinio, the one who has the shop near Flora."

Lea sat up abruptly, switched on the bedside light, and stared at him in horror. "Who, the carpet man? The one who wouldn't pay up?"

"I thought you should know," he said. "Forgive me for disturbing you."

There was no mention in the press of any passersby being injured as a result of the shooting. Paola's name was not released, nor were those of other potential eye witnesses. Maurizio had evidently been watched by the criminals over a period of months and his movements carefully noted. From his family and his assistant in the shop, the police learned that he went in every afternoon but that his times of arrival were rather erratic. The shop opened from four-thirty to seven-thirty every day, but it was his assistant's job to open up after lunch, and Maurizio would arrive anywhere from ten minutes to half an hour later. On other days it might be he himself who opened up. He drove to work, leaving directly from the underground garage in his block and driving the half mile or so to the car park in town, then walking the few hundred yards along the crowded Via Libertà to the shop. He had a monthly arrangement with the owner of the car park, who would also wash the car once a week.

The only day that followed a precise pattern was Friday, when Maurizio left the shop punctually at six to go and pick his wife up from her weekly concert. His assistant would then close up at the usual time. On those days Maurizio would walk the short distance back to the car park, then drive to the concert hall. Depending on the traffic, this took him from fifteen to twenty-five minutes. Husband and wife would then return home. It transpired that the couple rarely went out in the evenings.

Although the shop was located in a busy part of town, Via Tarquinio itself was comparatively quiet. This was because the short stretch between Via Libertà and the first intersection was open to one-way traffic only. Cars could enter from above but were then obliged to turn right at the intersection. As the parallel was again one way, this meant they were effectively retracing their steps, and as a result the road served little useful purpose. In fact, it was mainly used for parking.

It became clear why that particular Friday had been chosen

for the killing. Italy was playing an important qualifying football match, which was due to be televised live by RAI Uno at five-thirty. So by six the streets and shops were almost empty. That explained why, in spite of the rain, Flora was standing in the doorway of her place, looking out when Paola turned into the street: she was bored out of her mind. Flora remembered actually hearing footsteps coming along the pavement, something, she said, that hardly ever happened. There might not be a great deal of through traffic, but the continuous roar from Via Libertà meant you always had to raise your voice.

The car Paola saw reversing into the lateral lane of Via Libertà was not parking, as she thought, but purposely blocking oncoming traffic, and it was doing this so that once Maurizio had been shot, the gunman could dash toward the waiting motorcyle at the top of the road, leap on behind his accomplice, and have a clear route ahead. The car followed immediately in its wake. The police wanted to know whether Paola had heard revving from the motorcycle or just its roar, whether she could identify the make and color of the car blocking the oncoming traffic, and most important, whether she would recognize the man who had crossed the street and shot Maurizio. She could do none of these things. She told them the car might have been black or maybe gray ("I don't know what make") and that she thought the tone of the motorbike's engine had changed but it might not have. After all, she was already losing consciousness at that stage.

This confusion arose, the police decided, because Italy had scored a goal at two minutes past six—exactly the time the motorbike would have taken off—and a tremendous cheer had gone up from all the houses in the street. Paola didn't remember cheering of any kind, but she did seem to recall seeing flickering lights in a lot of the windows round about, which might have been coming from television sets. She had no recollection whatsoever of the man crossing the street other than he might have been wearing a dark jacket, but she wasn't even sure about that. She didn't notice his face.

In fact, there were far more reliable witnesses than her to the killing. Two women had been standing on their balconies bored by the football match their husbands were watching and had seen practically everything. Then there had been three passersby who had noticed the motorbike tear away from the curb, and there had been the man stuck behind the dark car. He was listening to the match on his car radio and was beside himself at being held up, especially as Italy scored at that precise moment. And then there was Flora.

She had been the one to let out the scream. She had waved to Maurizio as he came out of his shop and was getting ready to stand aside and let Paola into *her* shop when she saw the second man approaching diagonally across the street. Maurizio had just time to close the shop door behind him and turn round before the bullets caught him. "Yes," Flora shrieked hysterically to the policeman, "there were two shots, *two*! I heard them!" Even her husband couldn't calm her.

"I told you, I told you! Nobody would listen to me! I said he'd be killed! I told you we were all in danger! And now they've got what they wanted. He's dead! *Dead*!" She had to be given a tranquilizer, and it was another whole day before she could speak to anybody. Even then it was only to tell them about the blood pouring from the body and coursing down the pavement and how it had come up to that woman's shoes and seeped into the suede and stained them bright red. And then how the woman had slipped and cracked her head on the curbstone. Yes, the man had run off, what the fuck do you think he did, waited around and had a cup of coffee?

"Calm down, Flora," her husband told her gently but firmly. "You'll make yourself ill if you go on like this."

"Ill, for Christ's sake! He's dead, and we let him die." And she burst into tears. "If we'd stood by him, none of this would have happened."

If you'd stood by him, it'd probably be you in a coffin now as well as him, her husband wanted to tell her. But he kept prudently quiet. There were things in Palermo—dangerous things—one should never, never try to change.

Although his widow tried her hardest to respect Maurizio's wishes and have a small family funeral, the press were on her back that same evening, and the three intervening days before the funeral were quite unreal to her. She told her local priest not to let outsiders into the church, that the service was to be strictly for her, their son, and Maurizio's brother's family. "Nobody else, *padre*," she told him, dry-eyed. "Please. It's what he wanted."

"I'll do what I can," he answered, "but everybody wants to pay their respects. Everyone wants to pay homage to a courageous man."

His widow wanted to know why homage to this brave man couldn't have been made manifest during his lifetime, and what she was supposed to do with the scores of wreaths and massive bouquets that were piling up. To her they were obscene and their scent sickly sweet with insincerity.

"They're a gesture of solidarity, Lucia," the priest said, "and you should accept them as such."

On the day of the funeral the church was packed, and the crowds spilled out onto the pavements. The pew directly behind the family's was lined with solemn-faced members of the Sicilian government (one or two of whom had Maurizio's oriental rugs on their polished parquet floors), the mayor, and representatives from the Home Office. The widow and her son were filmed being embraced by the President of the Republic. Outside the church, television cameras waited for the coffin to appear and then filmed the crowds applauding and crying, while a few chosen words were gravely imparted to the cameras by politicians in scarves and overcoats anxious to be on their way back to the airport and Rome. It was rumored that the widow and her son were to be received by the Pope.

Flora was there with Olimpia from the shoe shop and their respective husbands, none of whom felt they could face Maurizio's widow. She didn't see them and wouldn't have recognized or cared to speak to them anyway. On the way to the cemetry she remembered Maurizio saying that if he were to die at the hands of the Mafia—and they both knew very well that one day he would—what counted was that justice was done. Looking out at the crowds she suddenly believed it would be; not now, perhaps not in her lifetime, but one day. Not everybody is courageous after all—she herself wasn't, for one—and it took time. He had also said never to forfeit freedom or lose faith in God. The last thing was the most difficult of all.

9

"He looks very like you."

"Does he? Yes, I suppose he does, in a way. But his character's completely different. He's not dithery like me. He knows what he wants."

"You're not dithery."

"I am, Nick. It takes me ages to decide anything, and I never want to hurt people. Roberto seems so much older than I was at his age. I suppose it's because he left home so early. I mean, for one thing, I'd never have gone on the stage like him."

"Is his father an actor?"

Lea smiled, "God, no. Was yours?"

"An actor? Dad?" Nick laughed at the idea and rolled over onto his back. "And yet, you know, he could well have been. He was creative, he invented things. But no, not really, he was far too *reserved*. Liked to be on his own too much."

"Did he speak Italian?"

"He could manage about two or three sentences," Nick said. "Anyway, why all this interest in my father? He wasn't like me at all. *My* Italian, for example, is faultless."

"Like everything else about you," Lea said, turning over and wrapping her arms around him. She laid her cheek on his chest.

"Of course," Nick continued. "In fact, my Italian was so good I remember translating Hemingway's novel as *For Whom the Doorbell Rings* when I first started teaching. The students just fell about. Why the hell can't you use the same word in Italian?"

Lea was laughing. "Because a bell in a church is one thing and a bell on your door—"

"Shut up," Nick told her softly, gathering her to him. "I love you."

"The English aren't a proud race, are they?" she asked after a few minutes, trying to extricate her face from his shoulder.

"What do you mean, proud?"

"Well, like the Italians being pleased they come from—or rather, were born in—a certain place rather than another: Tuscany, Naples, whatever. You don't feel that, do you?"

Nick thought it over for a minute. "I don't, no."

"You're not pleased you were born in London?"

"No, not at all. Cornwall would have done just as well."

She pondered this for a moment. "It's strange. I mean, isn't there anywhere in Britain—an island like Sicily—which is part of the country but different in its own way too?"

The only offshore island Nick could think of was the Isle of

Wight. It had vaguely the same shape as Sicily, but he somehow couldn't see its inhabitants demonstrating pride in their birthright. "I am first and foremost an Isle of Wighter and secondly an Englishman" didn't sound right at all.

"No, not really. We don't seem to care that much. Why, are you proud to be Sicilian then?" he asked her.

"It's a nice feeling of things being as they should be, of being a southerner. Of having a very long kind of history."

He gently stroked her neck, shoulders, and breasts and felt himself stirring again. She made a feeble attempt to free herself, "You're not listening to me."

"I am, I am. Go on." He knew so little about her after all, yet felt more complete in her arms than he had felt with any other woman. *Those whom God hath joined together* . . . Afterwards he lay gazing at her, trying to make out what it was about her that he needed so much.

"Why are you looking at me like that?"

"Somebody once said you could drown in a woman's eyes," he told her. "That's what I want to do now; climb right into yours, get deep inside you."

"Don't," Lea said, and told him about the squid's eyes being gouged out of its head and how they had rolled like marbles into the plastic bag.

"That is the most unromantic thing you could have said," Nick told her. "You have utterly destroyed my poetry. I shall now get up and leave you."

"And the worst thing of all is that I ate it," Lea wailed. "I ate the poor thing cut up into rings."

Nick shivered in sympathy, remembering Paola's predilection

for offal and how her own eyes would light up at the sight of a plateful of ribbed tripe and brains.

"Talk about something else, please, before I throw up."

"Okay," Lea announced, "I will. I shall now get up and have a shower, after which we shall have a glass of chilled wine together." She leaned over and kissed him tenderly. "Is that all right?"

"Yes, that's very all right."

Two days before he was due to give up the flat, Nick had received a phone call from Mario in Lima saying that he wouldn't be back for another month at least and that Nick could stay on at the flat if he wanted. Mario also said he was thinking of getting married again. Nick congratulated him and said that yes, he would like to stay on a bit longer if that was okay.

"Who is it?" he asked Mario. "Is she Peruvian?"

"No, Italian," Mario answered. "Beautiful."

Like Lea then, Nick thought, watching her now as she bent down to pick her shoes off the floor, making a perfect curve with her back. She straightened up and pushed the thick curtain of hair off her face. "Are you having a shower too?"

"In a minute."

It was after Paola had come out of hospital that Nick told her about Lea. She had already guessed.

"I knew there was somebody."

"I'm sorry, Paola."

She still had her arm in a sling, and with the bruise on her face fading into lemon yellow, she looked what Nick's mother would have called "really in the wars."

"It's a relief in a way," she said, "because we couldn't have gone on. You don't feel anything for me anymore, and I . . . I can't seem to *relate* to you at all. I know I haven't been an easy person to get on with. I don't know exactly what happened to make me that way, or why, but now I feel quite different, you know."

"Paola . . ."

"No, really different. And Sandro's changed too. Have you noticed?"

Nick had.

"He's suddenly grown up. He's going to be a great help to me." She took a sip of her chamomile tea and replaced the cup carefully on the saucer. "So, are you going to tell me who she is then?"

He did.

"What, you mean that woman who found my *wallet*?"

"It wasn't her, it was her . . . her partner."

"So she's not married to him then? At least that'll make things less complicated for you." She shook her head in wonderment. "Well, well, who would have believed it? So what are you going to do then, leave right away, or what?"

He told her he would be moving out as soon as he found a place. "But not until you're quite well again."

She said she would probably never be "quite well again" and that Sandro would see to everything.

"*Mamma* was very fond of you, you know," she said suddenly. "In fact, she preferred you to me. Did you know that? When she gave us the flat she made it quite plain that it belonged to both of us. So . . ." She opened her one good arm in a gesture of acquiescence. "One has to be honest. It's yours as well."

"I haven't said anything to the children yet," Nick said, who hadn't got as far as thinking about buying or selling flats either.

"Well, you'll be able to now, won't you? Now that Giulia's back."

Their daughter had left Bologna for good, Paola's accident providing her with a perfect excuse not to return. She had told them both that as soon as Paola had fully recovered, she was going off to Australia. And she's going. Nick had decided, no matter what.

"What does this woman's . . . partner say about it all?" Paola asked.

Nick opened his mouth.

"No, don't tell me, I don't want to know. I shouldn't have asked. Forget it."

He looked at her empty cup. "Do you want some more tea?"

She shook her head. "You'd better be going. You will be going out tonight, I suppose?"

Lea came back upstairs toweling her hair. "Still there? Do you want me to bring the wine up?"

He pushed back the duvet. "No, I'm coming. Look, can't we eat out together tonight?" The idea of having to go back home and climb into the cold bed in the spare bedroom was odious, unbearable.

"I can't, I told you. Dante wants to talk to me."

"Talk to you about what?"

"Things: arrangements." She looked him up and down, the towel still gently massaging her hair. "You look all cold and forlorn."

"Mm. Don't let him be nice to you, persuade you, that sort of thing."

She started to dress. "He won't. He's accepted it." She suddenly sat down on the edge of the bed and said in a small voice. "Don't talk about it, Nick, please. It upsets me so much."

The church clock began its measured solemn chimes, and they waited in silence until the last stroke had died away.

"It makes me uneasy," Nick insisted. "Dante does, I mean. I don't feel you're safe with him."

"Safe? Of course I'm safe. He's going to be hurt—well, he's hurt already. It's horrible, the whole thing's horrible for him, and there's nothing I can do about it."

"Do you want me to come with you?" he asked, putting out his hand and running it slowly up and down her arm. "Sort of, I don't know, talk to him?"

Lea gave a sad little smile. "What would *you* feel like if your wife's lover came along to 'try and explain things'? No, Nick, let me deal with this myself."

Dante heard her key in the front door and lifted the newspaper so that he wouldn't have to look at her when she came in.

"Dante?"

"Mm?"

Her voice came from the doorway: "It's dark in here. Don't you want some more lights on?"

He didn't answer.

She repeated his name.

He lowered the paper, folded it once slowly, and put it on the floor beside him. He saw Lea looking across at him, the long rainbow-colored scarf draped over the front of her black coat, one end hanging lower than the other, her bag clutched in both hands as though she were afraid it would escape. Beneath the smooth high forehead her eyes were wide from the cold outside air.

"Am I late?"

"Late for what?" he asked.

She looked anxious, almost frightened. "You know, we were going to talk. I said I'd be back at . . ."

A body so soft and pliable, you'd just have to touch it with your fingertips for it to collapse warmly, snugly, heavily into your arms.

"Come in properly and take your things off," he told her. "Your nose is red."

The corners of her lips went up in a small relieved smile. "It's cold outside." She started shrugging the coat off her shoulders. Underneath she had on that soft black sweater with the polo neck and a long orangey-brown skirt he hadn't seen before.

Leave everything, for God's sake, he wanted to tell her, and come over here, but instead he said: "Is that a new skirt?"

"This one? Fairly. I thought you'd seen it." She put the coat over her arm. "Why didn't you light the fire? It's all gloomy in here. I'll do it now."

He watched her crouch down before the grate and start fussing about with logs and newspaper for a few seconds, before getting up and pushing her gently aside. "Go on, I'll do this. You go and get us something to drink."

Flames were soon dancing up, licking the back wall of the chimney and suffusing his face with a warm glow. It reminded him of his grandmother's house in Turin where he used to go as a boy for Christmas. She always had a coal fire going (or would it have been logs?). Anyway, it was magical to him, and he'd sit staring into the flames, feeling his bare knees growing hotter and hotter and watching the shifting, falling embers. His grandmother would sometimes turn off the light so they could watch the shadows leaping over the walls and ceiling. She said they belonged to the *befana*—the old crone who brought presents—who was on her way. Under his grandmother's supervision he was allowed to jab at the red-hot center of the conflagration with the long iron poker so that the irridescent lumps scrunched together and fell rolling and crumbling to the bottom of the heap. Then sparks would fly up and the whole structure rearrange itself into a new shape.

It was Lea who had suggested they have a fireplace put in here. The flat had been without any central heating before, and Dante remembered how when he was young, in spite of the little electric fires people used to put in the corners of rooms, Palermo houses were always so cold in winter. It was the marble floors and thick walls. Well, it was much better now, thanks to Lea. He straightened up with a little grunt, first one knee, then the other, pressing the deep upholstered armchair for leverage. Yes, and now what? *Now* what? No Lea, no house. No anything. No bloody anything.

Yet he felt no animosity toward her, just a nagging sadness and sense of loss. It was strange, but in a way it was almost a *relief*—something you always knew was going to happen and that had finally come about—something you wouldn't have to worry about anymore. A bit like the falling coals in the fire: inevitable. He'd known from the beginning that their relationship wouldn't last, he had told her so. It wasn't just the age difference (although that counted as well) but his own godawful character, his moodiness and fatalism, his disappointment as youthful hopes of a socialist society collapsed, his disillusionment with the way the country was run. Then there was the conviction that happiness was just not his lot. So persuaded was he by this that it had never seriously upset him. He accepted it as others might accept being an only child or having an allergy: something you learned to live with. Lea had been—what was it?—a wonderful light, a *spark,* wonderful, yes, but doomed to go out.

And yet, and *yet,* he told himself, giving one of the logs a vicious kick with his shoe, I am but a man, and I want to know who the bastard is. I've waited nearly three weeks to find out. Who is it who has won her away from me? What does she see in him? Bound to be younger than me anyway. He realized in mild astonishment that he had never been jealous before—never even thought she might have had somebody else. It was probably because they had been wholly honest with each other. Okay, they might have had other difficulties, but at least (as far as he knew) they had never concealed anything of importance from each other. Well, he hadn't, and in fact Lea's blurting it all out in that restaurant shouldn't have been a shock at all. But it had.

So who is it then? he would ask her. Someone I know? Okay, and when she told him, how was that going to help? What was he going to do when he did know? Or more to the point, what was he going to do *anyway*? Hadn't got that far, hadn't really worked that out yet. Just then Lea came back into the room.

"That looks better," she said, about the fire. She had put on some flat shoes and loosened her hair so it hung down her back. She handed him a glass of wine and put a bowl of water biscuits and cubes of cheese on the table in front of the fire. Then she switched on two table lamps and drew the curtains. "Is that all right for you?" she asked, meaning the wine. "There's white as well, but there was this bottle already open, so I used that up first."

Changed her shoes before telling me about her lover, Dante was thinking. And loosened her hair.

"So?" Lea said softly.

"So?" he rejoined.

"You wanted to talk to me."

He said nothing, just looked into the fire.

Lea studied the contents of her glass. "I should start, I know I should."

"As long as you don't begin by saying you're sorry or any balls like that."

"Dante . . ."

"Who is it? Who is it you've fallen for? I'm really fascinated to know." His voice came out sarcastically, not at all how he'd planned it.

"You don't know him," Lea said. "Or at least . . ."

He was immediately on the alert. "At least?"

"Well," she began softly, "he's the man who came to pick up that wallet you found."

"Wallet? What wallet? What are you talking about?"

"Don't you remember? At the end of November you found a wallet in the street and telephoned the owner, and then he came round and you weren't here?"

He did remember now. "So?"

"Well, I was here," she finished.

He was puzzled. "What, you mean you had it off while I was out?"

"For God's sake, Dante! We—"

"Anyway, who is he? What does he do?" He suddenly connected. "So this man's the *husband* of the woman who lost the wallet, is that right? A married man?"

"Yes, he's married. And he's English."

"*English*? Lea!"

"What's so strange about that?"

This was a quite unexpected turn, and he looked at her with renewed interest. "Nothing. Just that I'd somehow never have thought you'd have chosen . . . What does he do? How long have you been seeing each other?"

He listened to her explanation, watching how her mouth moved on the half of her face illuminated by the fire, the way she kept pushing her hair behind her ears. He would have been less surprised if it had turned out to be somebody from her own circle, a photographer or some publishing type. A university lector. Well now. What *was* the name in that wallet? Couldn't possibly remember now, and surely he would have done if it had been foreign. But wait a minute, no, no, it belonged to his wife, didn't it? Perhaps the wife was Italian then.

"And so that's how it went," Lea finished. She frowned. "What's so funny?"

"Nothing," he began. "It's just the irony of the whole thing. I actually go to the bother of telephoning this . . . this *man* to tell him I've found his wallet, and he thanks me by taking my woman away from me. Well, nobody can say that's not a slap in the face, mm? What about the famous English 'fair play'? Fucking hell, I should have left the bloody thing lying in the gutter."

She didn't say anything for a moment, so he finished off his wine and leaned forward to cram some water biscuits into his mouth. When he looked up again he found her watching him.

"So when do you plan to go off with him then?" he asked. "Not that it's any of my business." But he felt it was. Very much.

"Soon. You won't want me round anymore, will you?" She fingered her wineglass. "Dante, I'm so sorry. I never meant it to happen."

"People never do. It just does." Perhaps she was really in love this time, and at the thought, his throat contracted and his eyes began smarting.

"Dante?" She came over and knelt beside him on the rug. He smelled her skin and clothes and hair and tried feebly to push her away, but she got hold of his arm with both hands and laid her head on his shoulder. "Don't hate me. It's diffcult for me too. I wish it hadn't happened. I don't want to hurt you."

He let her talk on, telling him how happy both of them had been for these three years. "Don't make it sound so idyllic," he managed to get out, willing himself the while to stay stock still when all he really wanted to do was to pull her to him. "I've been a bloody awful person to live with and you know it. I'm surprised we lasted so long together."

He had warned her, hadn't he, told her to think things over very well before agreeing to come down to Palermo with him? Bloody hell, why hadn't she listened to him? In his misery he was suddenly reminded of a film he'd seen on television the other night where the lovely youthful Guinevere agrees to marry Sean Connery's very mature King Arthur while all the time lusting after dashing Richard Gere's Launcelot. For Christ's sake, what could you expect?

"Do you believe in King Arthur?" he asked her. It worked well, a bit like practicing reciting the alphabet backward when you were trying not to come, and she drew back.

"King Arthur?"

"I was just thinking," he told her, relieved she wasn't touching him anymore. "How this man of yours is like Sir Launcelot and you are Guinevere."

"*Dante.*"

"And I'm that old fart Arthur," he went doggedly on, "who watches you being swept off on another man's white steed."

It was a good move because she threw him a rather hurt look and got up off the floor.

"It's not like that at all," she said.

But he knew, like it or not, that the image had gone home. She knew his fondness for *cappa e spada*—cloak-and-dagger— films and would realize this was his way of trying to make things easier for both of them. That night, though, as he lay on his side of the bed listening to Lea's steady contented breathing, he saw the future stretched out ahead of him—bleak and totally empty. This time the image was from another film, Chaplin's *Modern Times*. Again he was the pathetic, slightly ridiculous guy, only in this version he was toddling off into the dawn without the lovely Paulette Goddard beside him. Entirely on his own.

10

With their bodies shaking in unison like strung-up mail sacks he stared out at the blackness rushing past the windows and wondered what could be a madder form of existence than this. The rows of bent heads, folded-back paperbacks and open newspapers and ungainly splay of shoes were just as he remembered them. Gloved hands twisted handkerchieves round dripping noses, lips moved furtively round chocolate bars, and eyes stared glassily ahead at their reflections. Nick kept one arm tightly round Lea swaying obediently beside him, while the other grasped the metal upright bar near the door. A black youth nearby with a woolen cap pulled low over his forehead threw Nick a single hostile glance before squirming out at the next stop. Seats emptied and they sat down.

At Green Park the doors drew back to admit a curved bundle.

This unfolded itself like a chrysalis to reveal a girl of perhaps twenty-two or -three, wrapped in layers of fringed clothing and carrying a guitar. Pale yellow hair emerged from a chimneylike collar. She dumped a small rucksack proprietarily down on the floor.

"Good morning, ladies and gentlemen. I'm going to play a few songs for you. If there's anyone here who would prefer me not to, they only have to say so, and I'll leave the carriage."

Silence.

"You are under no obligation to give me anything. If you want to, you can, if not, that's fine." She strapped the battered-looking instrument round her thin body. "Okay then, I'm going to start with one you probably all know."

Nick, to whom this was quite a new occurrence, was interested to see that nobody was taking the slightest notice and that newspapers were still open and eyes dutifully down. He tried to imagine one of the morning travelers standing up and telling the girl to go to hell. Unlikely in London, where people were too accommodating, too willing to forfeit their right to peace and quiet, and loath to make a fuss. He supposed it might also be deep-seated fear of reprisal, or even a genuine Christian there-but-for-the-grace-of-God conviction. Would *he* do it, would he raise his voice and let her know he wanted to be left in peace when he traveled on public transport? Probably not. You tended to fit very quickly into the ways of a country. And besides, he didn't know whether he qualified as a Londoner anymore. In Rome gypsies would often board the underground and deliver a sob story in a toneless shout before passing through the passengers with upturned palm, and he had never told *them* to bugger off. Perhaps because he didn't feel wholly Italian either.

This skinny little thing, he thought, looking at her, had obviously chosen the particular line and time of day with some care, for the carriages were not too crowded and not too empty and the stations fairly far apart.

He nudged Lea: "Mm?"

She made a face to show how awful she thought it, and he smiled in sympathy as the wailing Americanized voice tried unsuccessfully to keep company with the twanging guitar strings.

Lea had wanted to see England, despite saying she couldn't speak a word of the language and that Nick would have to do everything for her. She told him she was scared stiff.

"Scared? I don't believe it."

"It's true. I've only ever been out of Italy once before—to France. I'm a terrible coward. The paper wanted to send me to Chile once, but I refused."

"I thought the Italians were great travelers," Nick said, having always found one—usually a Sicilian—wherever he went in the world.

"Not really. We pine away from home, miss our food, our friends, the sun, everything. At least I do."

"And now you want to see England? Is that wise? Who knows what dreadful things might happen to you?"

"Yes, who knows?"

The girl stopped singing, and Nick was surprised for the second time when the carriage broke out into a polite round of applause. Still nobody looked up or showed they were aware that anything out of the ordinary had taken place. The girl came swiftly along the aisle between the seats. "*Thank* you, thank you so much, *thank* you, thank you so much." A litany to match the rhythm of the rails beneath the racing train. People must be contributing then.

"And now, as you've all been so generous," she announced, "I shall sing one last song for you." She stretched the guitar strap round her neck again, and Lea pressed her face into Nick's shoulder to hide her laugh.

They wandered along the Embankment, fingers laced like young lovers, went down into the cold silence of Southwark Cathedral and up rickety stairs in Doctor Johnson's house behind Fleet Street. It was a completely different London from the one he had shown Paola years ago. Then, she had wrinkled her nose at the noise and traffic fumes and wanted to see Madame Tussaud's and the Tower and buy a cashmere cardigan and a teapot at Harrods.

"So there you are," he said to Lea. They were sitting in the old kitchen at Kenwood House. "Observe this typical English scene before you and tell me what you think."

She looked obediently out over tables filled by families with their well-controlled toddlers, the Jewish matrons, intellectuals, and loners, all of them united in their unswerving devotion to afternoon tea. "It all looks so peaceful. I don't know why you ever left here and came to Italy," she pronounced at last.

"Nor do I," he said. "Are you missing Palermo?"

She peered out at the brilliant green April landscape and shook her head. "Not yet."

After she and Dante had closed up the flat, Lea moved into Mario's place opposite the cathedral. Nick had joined her a few days later. She told him that Dante had taken it very well considering, but Nick felt the shreds of unhappiness still clinging to her. He didn't pursue it or ask any questions, just left Lea to her little pockets of sadness. A couple of weeks later she got a letter from Dante, saying he was in Rome and had found a small flat there. He wanted Lea to send on the things they had put by. He hoped all was well and that the book was selling.

"It isn't," Lea said drily. "And he knew very well it wouldn't be."

She got his stuff off by carrier, and that same evening broke down, saying she felt lost. They lay all night in each other's arms and he comforted her, and later she him. After that Dante faded away from their lives.

Paola had gone back to her job and had been talking of moving to a smaller flat in Palermo. According to Giulia (who gave Nick what news there was), her mother was spending a lot of time now down in the parish—helping to organize outings ("You know, to holy shrines, Padre Pio, that sort of thing"), visiting the poorer families with the priest, and so on. Apparently she got on well with him, said he understood her. She had also started going to her opera evenings again. By the way, had Nick heard about what had been happening there, about all those people in the audience being robbed? No? Well, pickpockets had somehow managed to get into the theater, probably using a forged membership card, which Paola was convinced was hers—the one that was never returned with the wallet. She flatly refused to go to the police about it anyway, saying they had shown themselves totally useless over the shooting and what was the use?

Bologna hadn't been mentioned at all, and when Giulia tentatively brought up Australia again, Paola had said that if that was what Giulia wanted then she should go. Her mother was "changed," she told Nick, and seemed much more at peace with herself now he had gone. "Oh, I didn't mean that," she said hastily. "Just that, well, maybe now the *strain's* gone, I don't know. She doesn't speak to me all that much, Dad. More to Sandro."

"Well, he hardly ever talks to me," Nick said, regretting it at once, for that was his own business. "He thinks it's all my fault, that I caused the accident, that if I hadn't gone off it would never have happened."

"That's ridiculous," Giulia said quietly.

After ten days Nick was ready to get back to Palermo, wanting to move into the flat they had found near the university and settle down with Lea. He wanted to wake up in the mornings with her beside him, gaze out of the window over the mauve-gray mountains, go to work and come back in the evenings to find her there. Make his life round her.

On the Friday before they left London he took Lea to his mother's. Contented with life and still very much with it at seventy-five, she seemed to like Lea, smiled, kissed her, and made tea for them. They sat looking out over the damp patch of back garden where a scattering of bluebells blew under the Sicilian sycamore.

"Are you going to get married again?" his mother asked while Lea wandered round outside. "I can tell you now, Nick, I never thought Paola was right for you."

He said nothing because it embarrassed and saddened him to think of his mother living with the knowledge so long and not feeling able to say anything. "Yes," he said. "I want to marry her, but I don't know when."

"Dad would have liked her."

"What do you do with yourself?" Nick wanted to know. "You don't get lonely, do you?"

"No, never. Life's far better now than it ever was. There are fewer worries, and I've so much more time for myself."

As it was a time for confessions, he asked her whether she missed his father.

"Yes, I do. But it's as though he's still here—around some-where—so it's not painful." Then she wanted to know how the children were taking the separation, and he told her they had grown used to the idea. Watching Lea out in the garden as she cupped her hand against the glass and peered into the little window of the shed, his mother said, "They used to like sheltering under the sycamore when it rained, do you remember?" She pressed her lips together in a little gesture of can't-be-helped and reached out and stroked his hair. "As long as you're happy to-gether, that's the main thing."

He nodded, unable to answer.

"Well, then, that's all right," his mother said and picked up the teapot.

"Somebody's always going to suffer," he said, meaning sep-aration. "But I think Paola's going to be happier on her own."

"Yes, I think she might well be."

Walking back to the tube station, Nick asked Lea if she had had enough of London and was ready to get back.

"I love it. I like seeing where you're from. I could quite easily stay here much longer. It's you who wants to go back to Italy."

"Work."

"Mm. I shall get them to send me over here again on an assignment."

They were met by a blast of hot air from the station entrance.

"Get who to send you over?"

"Whoever I'm working for. Say I know London well and speak perfect English."

And now, Dante thought to himself that same early April evening, I am on the loose again. To his surprise it was a pleasant sensation, as though a heavy ball and chain had been unfastened from his ankle. Rome was balmy and scented, the swallows or whatever they were darting low over the minuscule terrace of his tiny rented flat and the muffled sounds of traffic far enough off to be comforting but not to intrude. This is perhaps how things were always meant to be, he thought; entirely free of any kind of complications. He didn't envy Lea her new relationship, didn't envy *anybody* their relationships, because they entailed compromise, and one should never have to compromise or expect loyalty or love. It wasn't reasonable. And anyway, did one need a companion at all? At times maybe, but their absence didn't constitute a tragedy. You compensated. He still hadn't found his ideal partner—even if such a person existed—and at this late stage, probably never would.

Through no apparent logical association of ideas, Dante suddenly had a crystal-clear vision of the woman he had briefly met in the Milan airport, the one who had spilled coffee down his shirt. It had been back in January, right after Lea had told him about her guy—in fact, he had *gone* to Milan because of it, to give her (and him) time to reflect. A woman you couldn't call beautiful by any means but who had a kind of grace and serenity about her. Yes, he could happily have stayed in her company.

What attracted him to her? Sex? Yes, but of a different sort: a give-and-take, he decided, whatever that might mean. Well, it probably meant making love when both, not just one of you, wanted it, and finding a balance. He only remembered it being good once or twice with Lea, and the realization profoundly shocked him. One of the good times had been after she had told him about her new guy, for instance.

He laughed out loud at the absurdity of returning the wallet, and from there his thoughts pulled him back to Palermo. He honestly couldn't think now what had made him want to go back there. They had better cakes there than in Rome, Lea had joked at the time, and they did too. Superb and almost obscene in their oversweet creaminess. He swilled the whisky gently round and round in the bottom of his glass. They hadn't found those responsible for that shop owner's murder yet—the one who had refused to pay the protection money. Years would go by before they did, and even then the men would get suspended sentences. He had been down to Palermo a couple of times to interview the widow and the son. A woman of—well, what could you call it, exactly?—resigned and unwavering calm. Feared nobody and at the same time had faith in nobody. He had obtained her permission to include her story in his book on the lives of victims of the Mafia. Yes, finally a book! And so much easier to write away from Sicily. Could never have undertaken it down there.

Meanwhile, everything would go on as before. The Sicilians would stuff themselves with cakes, take buses, have their wallets stolen, meet, make love, leave each other, fall in love again, write books, kill one another, take buses . . . He threw back his head, swallowed down the last of the whisky, and went back indoors.

M3457paL

M3457paL

Marks, Gabrielle.

Palermo story

$$\frac{03}{1} \quad \frac{04}{1}$$